BEYOND THE BEYOND

Lee Goldberg

ST. MARTIN'S PRESS
NEW YORK

Design by Nancy Resnick

Library of Congress Cataloging-in-Publication Data

Goldberg, Lee,
    Beyond the beyond / Lee Goldberg.
        p.   cm.
    ISBN 0-312-15064-4
    I. Title.
    PS3557.03577B49   1997
    813'.54—dc20   96-34068
                                                        CIP

First Edition: March 1997

10 9 8 7 6 5 4 3 2 1

To my daughter, Madison, who isn't allowed to read this until she's twenty-one. And to my wife, Valerie, who probably won't let her even then.

Acknowledgments

I couldn't have written this book without William Rabkin, who read every draft and let me steal liberally from our personal and professional lives for this story.

And I *wouldn't* have written this book if not for the heroic efforts of Mel Berger and Jeremy Katz, and the enthusiastic support of booksellers like Audrey Moore, Kate Mattes, Barry Martin, Bill Farley, Sheldon McArthur, and the bright stars of the Mysterious Galaxy.

I'm also indebted to Arthur Sellers and Michael Lansbury, both of whom helped me see the potential of *Beyond the Beyond* years ago, and to Frank Cardea, George Schenck, Terence Winter, Patrick Hasburgh, Clifton Campbell, Dave McDonnell, Ernie Wallengren, and Michael Gleason for sharing all their hilarious anecdotes with me. I bet they're sorry now.

BEYOND
THE
BEYOND

Teaser

Conrad Stipe sat in the bar of the Spokane Marriott nursing his sixth Old Grand Dad, flashing his nicotine-stained teeth at the big-busted woman in the too-tight silver space suit. His dick was hard, which was a miracle, since the girdle cinched firmly around his flabby stomach had cut off all the circulation to his groin hours ago.

"I've seen the Crab Nebula up close and the Milky Way from a million miles," he slurred, staring into her blue contacts, "but I've never seen anything as beautiful as your eyes."

"Wow," the woman shrieked, her face-lift stretched taut. "When Captain Pierce said that, just before kissing the six-breasted nymph of Zontar, I had my first orgasm, right there in front of the TV set."

"I got a TV in my room," Stipe said, pinching his leg and feeling nothing. "Maybe you could show me how it happened." If he stood up now, using the bar for support, he figured the circulation to his legs might return. Then again, his hard-on might leave and not come back for weeks.

She smiled, her capped teeth catching the fluorescent light like the Formica tiles in the men's room. "I can't believe this is actually happening to me."

"Me, too." Stipe stifled a burp and marveled, for maybe the millionth time, at the sick, horrible unfairness of it all.

There were hundreds of people in the hotel tonight, and every one of them thought he was the single greatest man on earth. Unfortunately, most of them were on the wrong side of forty and dressed like space aliens, wishing they'd finally outgrow their bad skin and dreaming they could be one of the TV characters he created out of spite and greed.

Back in 1964, when he was a struggling TV writer, when his stomach was flat, his teeth were white, and his manhood was in constant tumescence, he signed a pilot deal for shit money to create a series for Pinnacle Pictures.

But before he got around to writing the script, he was hired on the Western series *Destiny's Journey*, where he quickly rose from staff writer to producer by writing the best damn episodic scripts on television. Those bastards who accused him of stealing credit, of simply sticking his name on other people's scripts, didn't understand the genius of his subtle rewriting. His little touches made all the difference. If you leave the yeast out of dough, the bread doesn't rise.

When the show ended five years later, naturally every studio in town was dangling big-money pilot deals in his face.

That's when those assholes at Pinnacle started nagging him to honor their insulting, shit-money contract. He tried to walk, telling them the statute of limitations had expired on the contract. But the lawyers told him a "statute of limitations" applied to crimes, not pilot contracts. The contract *was* a crime, he told them, but they couldn't see that. Lawyers. What the hell do they know?

So he took Pinnacle's money, spent it on a pair of shoes, and hacked out the silliest piece of shit he could think of. A story about a military spaceship, run by a blowhard captain who thinks with his pecker, a science officer with an elephant nose, and a lady doctor whose space tits were actually a set of high-tech computers. He called it *Beyond the Beyond.*

The network bought it. That's when Stipe realized how good *Beyond the Beyond* really was. He wrote it from his gut, from his anger, bypassing his intellect altogether. Instead of writing crap, like he thought he had, he created a work of pure creative passion. It was brilliant.

The pilot was unlike anything television had seen before. It blew the network away. They ordered twenty-five episodes. The ratings were lousy, but that was because the show was ahead of its time, it was smarter than the audience. The network picked it up for a second year, asking him to dumb it down, but he had integrity. He wasn't about to pander to the viewers. They would recognize quality programming.

Well, they didn't.

One day he woke up with an enormous hangover to discover he'd somehow married the actress with the computer boobs, the network had canceled the show, and his career was over. He was ostracized because he was too smart, too hip, for the medium.

Stipe fled to Europe, where he spent the next decade writing soft-core porno films—but with class. Once again, he was ahead of his time; his little-seen *Claudette's Boudoir* predated *Emmanuelle* by years.

He returned to the States just long enough to sign divorce papers, sell what little assets he had left, and see what was on TV. What he saw was Captain Pierce and Mr. Snork on the bridge of the starship *Endeavor*, shooting an aspirin beam at a cosmic space brain threatening to eat the universe.

Beyond the Beyond reruns were playing twice a day on stations nationwide. He was getting pocket change in royalties, but he found out his ex-wife had a tidy little mail-order business going selling old scripts, photos, and props to fans.

Finally, there were people out there who recognized that the show was about something and that he was a visionary. And he was. Among other things, he quickly envisioned turning that fervent devotion into cash.

The first *Beyond the Beyond* convention at the Fresno Hilton drew five thousand fans who inexplicably paid fifteen dollars each to dress in costumes, discuss minute details of each episode, and listen to him talk about all those courageous, artistic battles he never fought.

And that had been his life since. The conventions were still good for five or six grand in cash, a couple ardent but lousy blow jobs from obese women in polyester space suits, and a few free nights in an airport Hilton with a full minibar.

It was a slow death, but at least he wasn't enduring the ignominy alone. Kent Steed was stuffed into a booth in the coffee shop, wearing his decaying, rubber elephant nose and signing copies of his self-published memoirs, *Call Me Mister Snork*. And Nicole Huston, the yeoman who was reduced to a cube and crushed by an alien with donkey ears in episode 27, was selling pictures of herself in the lobby, one dollar plain, five dollars signed. Guy Goddard, who played Captain Pierce, was a recluse who never ventured out of his Van Nuys house without his uniform.

Stipe's long-stifled burp suddenly broke free, and if it hadn't, he might never have noticed the woman's hand on his thigh.

He had no idea how long her hand had been there, but it made him rethink the girdle issue. What was more important, hiding his flab or regaining circulation in his lower extremities? Of course, if women saw the flab, there might not be any action in the extremities to feel anyway.

Then again, who was he kidding? They weren't after his body, they wanted a piece of his soul, not that he had any to give. He worked in television. At least he had a long time ago, back when the hag with her hand on his thigh was young and found ecstasy in front of a nineteen-inch Magnavox.

"Why did the nymphs of Zontar have six breasts?" she asked.

He had absolutely no idea. "Because their young are very hungry." With one hand gripping the bar, he slowly rose to his feet. He could tell she wasn't happy with his answer.

"It was a metaphor for socialism in an idealized, yet decadent, democratic context," he added.

She trembled. "I'm the luckiest woman on earth."

Her illusions about Stipe ended the moment he peeled open his Velcro girdle, and his stomach flopped down over his crotch, hiding whatever might be there.

His illusions about her began the moment she unzipped her space suit, and her flesh burst out the seams like Poppin' Fresh dough. But they were too far along and far too desperate to stop now.

They had dream sex.

The wanna-be nymph of Zontar dreamed she was being colonized by Captain Pierce and the Confederation of Aligned Galaxies. Stipe dreamed he was young, successful, and frolicking with the buxom cowgirl from *Big Hooters* magazine's "Vixens of Double-D Ranch" spread.

Five minutes later it was over, leaving one of them unsatisfied and embittered, the other flatulent and fast asleep. She zipped herself back into her space suit and slipped out of his room, plotting to switch her precious sci-fi allegiance to *SeaQuest*.

Stipe woke up hung over early the next morning, had a good-morning vomit, then packed what was left in the minibar into his suitcase and hurried to the lobby before any Beyonders woke up to pester him. He'd be at the airport, heading back to Los Angeles, before they were even out of their *Beyond the Beyond* jammies. But he was only two steps out of the elevator when someone spoke behind him.

"Mr. Stipe?"

Stipe froze. So much for a clean getaway. He turned around expecting another pimply-faced goof in a Confederation uniform and a Snorkie nose. Instead, he saw a barrel-chested man in a chauffeur's tailored suit and dark, impenetrable sunglasses, reaching for his suitcase.

"I have a limousine waiting for you outside, sir."

If it was like the one that picked him up at the airport, it could mean a twenty-minute drive stuck in a Hyundai with three bald teenagers, each one wanting to show him the body parts they'd pierced with Confederation insignia pins.

"I'll pass." Stipe yanked the suitcase away from the man's grasp.

"You're keeping Milo Kinoy waiting, sir."

Stipe stared incredulously at the man. "Are you trying

to tell me Milo Kinoy, one of the richest sons of bitches on the planet, sent his limo to Spokane-fucking-Washington just to give me a lift to the airport?"

"That's what I'm saying."

"I'd love to, but Demi Moore is waiting for me in her limo, and she promised to blow me on the way."

"Mr. Stipe, it costs Mr. Kinoy one thousand dollars every minute his private jet sits on the runway. If he gets annoyed, he's liable to take it out of my Christmas bonus," the man said. "If that happens, I'll take it out of your face."

Stipe tried to stare into the guy's eyes but only saw his own pathetic reflection in his sunglasses. "You got a bar in your limo?"

"Yes, sir."

"I'm not talking about a Diet Coke in an armrest beverage holder."

"Will Dom Perignon satisfy you?"

Stipe handed him his suitcase. "Lead the way."

He didn't believe for a moment that Milo Kinoy, the international publishing magnate behind *Big Hooters, Big Butts,* and Big everything else, wanted to see him. But if this bruiser was so eager to give him a ride, why the hell was he arguing with him? Money saved on a taxi is money better spent on airplane cocktails.

He followed the big man out the lobby doors, where a Cadillac stretch limo was parked, gleaming in the early-morning sun. The man held open the door, and Stipe peered inside.

Sure enough, there was a bottle of champagne in a bucket on a carved teak countertop. And Milo Kinoy himself sitting in the rich leather seat, watching the opening titles of *Beyond the Beyond* on the tiny television set tucked into the sculpted marble entertainment center.

"Get in and close the door, Conrad. The glare is killing the picture."

Stunned, Stipe climbed inside, bumping his head on the roof and trying to look natural as he fell into the leather seat across from Kinoy. Stipe welcomed the pain, it cleared his head. Before Stipe could say anything, Guy Goddard's voice filled the limo in Dolby stereo.

"The darkest reaches of space. The farthest boundaries of adventure. One starship journeys into the unknown, exploring the mysteries that lie . . . beyond the beyond."

And as the limo pulled out and the *Beyond the Beyond* theme began, Stipe studied the deeply tanned, billionaire Brit across from him, a man on the downhill side of forty who always dressed for golf, a game the magnate never played. He was the black sheep son of a sir or a duke or something, who embarrassed his family by investing his trust fund in the girlie magazine all his Oxford chums were jerking off with.

But within ten years, he'd used his education to transform *Big Hooters* into a global porno publishing empire that grew so enormously powerful he was able to diversify into mainstream music, video, and software businesses with equal success.

"What do you know about the typical fan of your show?" Milo asked.

"If it's a guy, he's awkward, ugly, and his sex life is his subscription to one of your magazines," Stipe replied. "If it's a woman, she's fat, has a lot of unicorn jewelry and elf statuettes, and wishes she could find a man as affectionate as her cat."

Milo smiled, flashing obscenely perfect teeth. A poacher could probably sell them as jewelry. "Those are the fans you see, Conrad. The ones who don't live in suburban tract homes, drive midsize Japanese cars, and rank cable television as more important in their daily lives than God, sex, or nutrition."

Milo picked up the remote with one perfectly manicured hand and clicked off the TV, his cuff rising to reveal a solid gold, diamond-studded Schaffhausen da Vinci Perpetual Calendar Chronograph strapped on his tanned, hairless wrist. Stipe casually covered his plastic Swatch with one hand and waited.

"You flew all the way up here to tell me not all my fans have bad skin?" Stipe laughed nervously. He still had no idea what the hell he was doing here. Part of him couldn't help wondering if it had something to do with that little double-D fantasy he had last night. But how could Kinoy know about that?

"This morning, I bought Pinnacle Pictures from the Japanese, who lost their kimonos investing in American studios," Milo said. "Pinnacle owns the major independent stations in six of the top ten television markets. I'm going to use those stations to launch my own television network."

"The Big Network," Stipe said, trying to be funny.

"As a matter of fact, yes."

Milo Kinoy didn't laugh, and Stipe didn't care. He was beginning to connect the dots, and he liked the picture it was making. A big, fat dollar sign. Pinnacle also owned the negatives for *Beyond the Beyond.* But if Kinoy was here, they wanted something more. From him. And that would cost.

Stipe glanced at the champagne. "Is that bottle just for show, Milo, or were you planning on drinking it?"

The billionaire lifted the bottle out of the bucket and filled a Baccarat crystal glass for Stipe, who swallowed the bubbly like it was Perrier. Milo casually refilled it.

"*Beyond the Beyond* has a devoted audience of baby

boomers and their children," Milo explained, "all of whom fall comfortably into the eighteen-to-forty-nine demographic that advertisers covet. Just what I need to launch my network."

"I see." He saw dollar signs, and lots of them. "You want to revive *Beyond the Beyond,* and you need me to do it."

"I could go off and make it with someone else, but I think the fans would like to see you produce it."

"In other words, Milo, I got the remake rights and you can't do it without me."

Milo stared coldly at Stipe. "Nor can you without me, since I own the characters and the premise. Working together, we can make some money."

Stipe grabbed the Dom, poured himself some more, then took a big drink, swishing it around his mouth for a moment or two before swallowing it. He belched, long and loud. It felt good.

"I want a hundred grand an episode, a double-D girl in my sack every night, and your watch."

Milo unclasped the watch from his wrist and tossed it to Stipe. "Sounds reasonable to me."

Talent agents at The Company didn't start in the mailroom, they began their careers on the docks in San Pedro. They were there every morning at four A.M., standing in their suits and ties, reading *Daily Variety* while waiting for the fishing boats to arrive. Their jobs were to select the very best fish, still alive if possible, and bring them back to The Company's tall, circular building, a marble-and-glass straw sticking out of Beverly Hills and sucking it dry.

By six, the agent wanna-bes were riding up the service elevators with ice chests of salmon, tuna, squid, crab, and fish they didn't even recognize. They were met at the twenty-fifth floor by superagent Clive Odett's personal secretary, Zita, a crisp young woman of indeterminable nationality and race whose curves were as sharp as the shiny ginsu knife she wielded.

She'd randomly slice the fish with the practiced grace of a surgeon and, tasting the raw flesh, allow those that passed her inspection to be taken back to the walk-in freezers. The rest went to the homeless in Beverly Hills.

Legend had it that once, when an aspiring agent delivered too many fish she deemed unacceptable, she sliced off one of his earlobes and popped it into her mouth like a grape. Nowadays, the hapless fellow was supposedly living in a parking structure off Little Santa Monica Boulevard and munching on the free catch of the day.

Of course, the more exotic fish were flown in alive from whatever waters they came from in The Company's jet. The fish were killed only seconds before being served by Clive Odett himself, usually in front of his astonished lunch guest, who, on this particular day, was screenwriter Nick Alamogordo.

But Nick wasn't astonished. Not by the redwood bridge that arched over a dark pond full of colorful fish. Not by the gentle breezes wafting through the lush vegetation. Not even by the authentic pagoda he was sitting in, which had been shipped by boat, piece by piece, from Japan. He shrugged, as if he'd seen a thousand offices like this before.

The only thing that astonished the bushy-bearded, ponytailed scribe was the limitless boundaries of his own immense talent. After all, it was Nick Alamogordo who penned such blockbusters as *Carnalville* and *Full Frontal Force,* which made an international movie star out of Sabrina Bishop, TV's *Agatha's Niece.* When Bishop, as a government assassin, opened her shirt and nursed the injured cop she loved back to health with her breast milk, she earned a place in movie history. Siskel and Ebert accused Nick of stealing the idea from *Grapes of Wrath*. Didn't those two jerks know an *homage* when they saw one?

"I thought this was your office," Nick growled, "not a fucking Benihana."

If Odett was offended, he didn't show it. Odett stood across the table from him, swiftly cutting raw fish fillets into thin, translucent slices. He kept his eyes on his work, consciously ignoring the aromatic tufts of hair that fluffed out the open collar and short sleeves of Nick's loud Hawaiian shirt.

To Nick, Clive Odett resembled a Doberman who rose up on his hind legs one day and miraculously morphed into a man in Brooks Brothers slacks and a white sweater.

"This is my sanctuary," Odett whispered, as he always did, to make sure people listened. "This is where I feed my body and my soul." He carefully arranged the wafer-thin slices into the shape of a rose and slid the assorted sashimi platter in front of Nick.

"You're feeding both of them on my ten percent." Nick took a handful of fish in one of his hairy paws and shoved it into his mouth, dribbling rice into his beard. All this Zen and sushi shit didn't impress Nick one bit. Odett was a salesman, and lately, not a very good one.

Zita glided in from the garden with two hot sakes, a fish fin aflame in each.

"What the hell is that?" Nick asked.

"A fugu fin, Mr. Alamogordo," she replied. "In Japan, it is considered an aphrodisiac."

She was as pretentious as her boss. Nick decided to put them both in their place.

"Maybe your boss needs to toast a trout in his drink to get a boner." Nick sized her up. "I just got to look at you, Pita."

"Zita," she hissed, gently placing the sake in front of each man before disappearing again into the brush.

"Bring me a beer," Nick called after her, admiring her ass, his lips tingling.

Odett tenderly placed a slice of fish on his tongue and savored it. "I understand you had dinner at Drai's last night with Mitch Stein."

Nick turned back to Odett and popped some more sashimi into his mouth. He wasn't surprised Odett knew he'd met with another agent; every maître d' and waiter in town was spying for somebody, hoping to earn a favor he could exchange for an audition or a weekend read. The fact was, Nick *wanted* Odett to know.

"I fucked my wife last night, too," Nick said. "What's it to you?"

"You finished writing *Cop a Feel* over the weekend, and I haven't seen it," Odett said. "Mitch has."

"He liked it, too." Nick rubbed his tingling lips. Zita's ass must have made a strong impression, which wasn't unusual. What was weird was that *those* impressions were usually felt farther south. "Mitch thinks I can get two million for it."

"Does he?" Odett took a sip of sake.

"Of course, that was just his opinion of my rough draft." Nick popped another piece of sashimi into his mouth. "It'll take another month or two to polish it up before I can put it on the market."

"Two months. That would be when your contract with us expires." Odett took the knife and carefully cut along the grain of the fillet, making six fine tissue-thin slices. "You wouldn't be holding the script back until you sign with someone else?"

"I'm a slave to the creative process. It's finished when it's finished." Nick shrugged. "If that happens when I'm represented by you or someone else, well, that's just fate."

Nick believed that *Cop a Feel,* the harrowing story of a cop battling sexual addiction while working undercover as a male stripper, was not only his best script yet but could nab him an Oscar.

"Does this mean you won't be signing with us?" Odett inquired casually.

"You package my scripts only with *your* actors and *your* directors." Nick knocked back his sake. "That severely limits my playing field and diminishes my price. There are other actors and directors I'd like to work with. Mitch Stein can get me Scorsese."

Odett studied Nick for a moment. Ten years ago, Nick and a number of other high-profile screenwriters were represented by the Quill Group, a boutique agency for writers founded by Martha Dale. She doted on them like a loving grandmother. They were all fiercely loyal to Dale, resisting all attempts at wooing them away. That was, of course, until her freak accident, jogging into a tree shredder. Her agency crumbled after they buried her in sixty-eight individually wrapped pieces, and her roster of loyal clients were looking for representation. The Company was there for them in their time of need.

Back then, Nick was earning low six figures for originals and even less for rewrites. But under Odett's guidance, his spec scripts regularly sold for one million. And he didn't do rewrites for any price.

Now Nick was getting cocky. He thought he could leave. He was wrong. "You've done very well with The Company," Odett whispered.

"I could do even better," Nick whispered back, just to show him he was onto his stupid game. Fucking salesman.

Odett realized that Nick was operating under the old-fashioned notion that the agent worked for the artist. Apparently, Nick hadn't heard that Odett had changed all that. Odett didn't get clients work, he *allowed* them to work. All he asked was a small part of the immense reward. That, and lifetime servitude.

"I see." Odett motioned toward the pond. "You know what those fish are?"

"Piranha?"

"Puffers. *Tetraodontoidae*, to be exact. The Japanese call them *fugu*. I have them flown in live from Tsukiji every week."

"Nice to know the three hundred grand in commissions I gave you last year was well spent," Nick snorted, "even if it wasn't well earned."

"The *fugu* are very territorial, can enlarge to twice their size when threatened, and have teeth so sharp they can bite through coral." Odett touched the tip of his knife to the fillet. "It's a delicacy the Japanese have been enjoying for fifteen hundred years. A true connoisseur favors the delicate flesh beside the liver."

"That's real interesting, but I need an agent, not a sushi chef." Nick licked his lips, which reminded him again of Zita's ass. "Where's Zita with that beer?"

"The beer won't help. The tingling in your lips is from the *fugu*," Odett said, almost inaudibly. "It's caused by the poison."

Nick looked up slowly in disbelief. "Poison?"

"That's what gives the fish its flavor and its charm. Of course, we run the risk of dying suddenly of respiratory paralysis."

Nick stood up and backed away from the table, desperately rubbing his lips, realizing that Odett wasn't pretentious, he was crazy. "You *poisoned* me?"

"It's entirely natural, I assure you. The toxin is found in the organs. The trick is killing the fish and removing its organs before any of the poison gets into the bloodstream. Even then, a slip of the knife can contaminate the whole fish. That's why a *fugu* chef must be specially trained and licensed."

"Are you?" Nick squeaked, backing away until he bumped into the bridge.

"No, it's just a hobby." Odett took another piece of *fugu* and ate it slowly, savoring every morsel. "But I must admit, I've lost interest in eating anything else. Where's the excitement in pasta?"

Nick looked at his reflection in the pond and saw bits of rice clinging to his beard like maggots feeding on a corpse. "Call a paramedic."

"If you were going to die, you would have already." Odett turned to see Zita emerging from the trees with more hot sake, fins flaming like birthday candles. "Of course, anything can happen in two months."

"Are you threatening me?" Nick retreated over the bridge.

Odett blew out the flaming fin and sipped his sake. "I'm saying I don't eat pasta."

The mahogany display case in UBC president Don DeBono's office contained a pristine copy of every single issue of *TV Guide*. There was an identical display case, with another complete collection of *TV Guide*s, in the living room of his Hollywood Hills estate.

When he was a kid, there was no greater thrill than getting the new *TV Guide* each week. He would rush down to the mailbox, grab the issue, and hurry back to his room to read every listing. He'd sit on his bed, making notes on dozens of papers spread across his *Flipper* bedsheets.

While other kids followed professional sports, traded

baseball cards, and argued player stats, he studied a game that was much more exciting. There were only three teams in the major league, each vying for the domination of prime time television. Their players were weekly series, the penalty for failure was immediate death. How could hitting a ball with a stick compare to *that?*

TV Guide was his report from the front lines. Each time period was a battlefield. He tried to understand the strategies behind each scheduling move and predict the outcomes. Who would win the showdown between *Peyton Place* and *Gomer Pyle USMC?* Would *Daktari* and *The Girl from U.N.C.L.E.* finally break *Combat's* hold on Tuesday nights? Why did they move *Big Valley* against *Run for Your Life?* Which show would survive?

Then he'd go to his chalkboard, where he dutifully charted the network schedules, marking the week's winners and losers. He went to sleep each night staring at the chalkboard and woke up each morning to study it again.

Thirty years later, not much had changed, only now Don DeBono was getting paid tens of millions of dollars for it. His unmatched programming instincts had propelled UBC from a distant third to a decade as the number-one network. Even so, he still felt a thrill when the *TV Guide* arrived, and putting the latest issue into the mahogany case was a ritual he cherished.

He shifted his gaze away from the mahogany case and back to the executives who sat around the long conference table. All of them were staring at him, waiting for his reaction to the pilot they had just seen: Yasmine Bleeth in *Sexual Surrogate,* an hour-long drama about a dedicated psychotherapist who helps "people in crisis" by fucking them for $150 an hour.

In the pilot, she rescues a man from committing suicide, then saves his troubled marriage by helping him overcome his impotence and teaching his wife how to have an orgasm, thereby curing her alcoholism.

"You want me to buy a series about a hooker?" an incredulous DeBono asked Parnell Buckman, vice president of drama development.

"She's a licensed health-care professional." Buckman squirmed in his seat. "It's perfectly legal, a compelling side of the medical profession we've never seen on television before."

"Because it's about a goddamn hooker, that's why," DeBono snapped. "What were you thinking?"

"She's a thirty share, Don," replied Kimberly Woodrell, vice president of current programming, her eyes burning with razor-sharp, Trinitron clarity.

Her programming instincts were almost as good as DeBono's because he trained her himself. She started at the network as a reader in the TV movies department, summarizing scripts for executives too busy to read them themselves.

DeBono had noticed her when she was the lone voice arguing that the network should make *The Last Flight*, the harrowing story of a couple who survive a plane crash in the Rocky Mountains and are forced to eat the bodies of their dead children.

While everyone else was arguing that there wasn't enough story for a movie, that the ending was downbeat, and that the script was badly written, Kim's position was that none of that mattered. What was important was the promotional potential. She suggested retitling it *They Ate Their Own* and hyping the hell out of it. Even if people switched it off, revolted, midway through, she predicted they'd *still* get a twenty-eight share the first hour.

DeBono agreed with her and made the movie. It got

a thirty-five share. From then on, she became his protégée, moving quickly from low-level reader to top executive in two years.

Now she was widely regarded in the industry as DeBono's secret weapon. Kim developed *Valet Girls,* a hip sitcom about twentysomething girls eking out a living on the fringes of L.A. showbiz. The show was the season's biggest new hit. It was impossible to turn on the radio without hearing Alanis Morissette and Melissa Etheridge singing "Blow Me," *Valet Girls'* catchy theme.

She also had a body that could give the Pope a hard-on.

"*Sexual Surrogate* is perfect counterprogramming for *Adoption Agency,*" she said, referring to MBC's Saturday-night powerhouse, a weekly tearjerker in which adorable kids are hooked up with loving families by two gorgeous social workers who are actually angels.

"We can deliver family values *and* nipples," she added. "What more do you want?"

"Advertisers," he said. "Because if we put that show on the air, we won't be able to give away the spots. Even those crippled-kid charities would turn down the free air time."

"We've crunched the numbers, Don." Kim glanced at Alan Silver, vice president of research. "Show him the projections, Alan."

Silver slid a thick binder down the table to DeBono.

"*Adoption Agency* attracts a solid, female demographic, pulling in sixty percent of women eighteen to thirty-five and eighty-eight percent of women thirty-five to fifty-five. Their only male viewers are sixty-five years old or over, and they probably don't know what they're watching anyway," Silver explained. "The male audience eighteen to thirty-five is split between *Warmongers* on DBC and

Baywatch Nurses in first-run syndication, and the rest are renting videos. The two sitcoms we currently have in that period bring in our worst ratings and shares of the week."

That much was true. UBC's Saturday night was a disaster. Lyndon LaRouche campaign specials pulled in bigger numbers than *Fast Food* and *Trick's Question*. Maybe, DeBono thought, he should be developing a comedy for LaRouche.

He made a mental note to find out when LaRouche was getting out of prison.

"*Sexual Surrogate* will appeal to the female audience that watches *Adoption Agency* and bring in the men," Kim argued. "It's a show a college-educated, two-income married couple can watch together after putting their two-point-five babies to bed. It's also a great date show for horny kids making out on the couch. *Sexual Surrogate* actually delivers a dream demographic for advertisers."

Don DeBono shook his head. "All the women are going to see is a lady with terrific tits who can fuck their husbands better than they do. If we put *Sexual Surrogate* on the air, women will throw themselves in front of the TV to keep their husbands from watching it."

He slid the binder back to Silver, unopened. "We have to go after the male audience with a show they won't feel guilty watching," DeBono said. "*Warmongers* is going into its fourth year, it's tired and vulnerable to a direct attack. I think *Siamese Cops* is the show that can beat it."

"You can't be serious."

"It's true counterprogramming," DeBono replied, "a pure high-octane action-adventure."

"It's a cop with two heads."

"It's a cop with a difference," DeBono corrected.

"We're talking the ultimate buddy show," explained Buckman, eager to get back in DeBono's good graces.

"One head is an analytical, by-the-book cop, the other head is a gung-ho ass-kicker with a 'tude. There's built-in conflict every week."

"I can promote the hell out of it," shrieked Nancy Bardwil, vice president of promotion. "*Siamese Cops:* Two heads *are* better than one."

DeBono turned to Buckman. "Tell them they have thirteen episodes, on the condition that one of the heads is John Stamos. End of meeting."

Everyone got up from the table and filed out of the office. Everyone except for Kim, who remained in her seat, glaring across the table at DeBono.

"You're making a mistake," she said.

"And you still have a lot to learn about network programming." DeBono rose from his seat and walked up behind her. "But I admire your passion."

He slid his hands into her shirt and fondled her breasts, feeling her tiny nipples immediately hardening into stones. "God, do I admire it."

She twisted free of his hands and got up. "Not now, Don. We have some things to discuss."

If she had any doubts about what she was going to do, his decision to buy *Siamese Cops* over *Sexual Surrogate* erased them. His time in television was passing, and the Kim Woodrell era was just beginning.

"I did it, Kim," he said dramatically, as if it were a giant revelation Perry Mason had twisted out of him on the witness stand.

"Did what?"

"I left my wife. We don't have to hide anymore. I'm free and unencumbered. We can be the president and first lady of prime time."

She looked at him standing there, his erection poking against his slacks, and suddenly he seemed so ridiculous. What had she ever seen in this man?

"I don't think so," she said.

"Isn't that what you wanted?"

"What I *want* is to be the first woman to run a major network."

"You will be." DeBono reached out for her. "You're my hand-picked successor and love bunny."

She stepped out of reach. "This is my last day at UBC, Don."

"What?" He was still holding his hands out, as if waiting to catch something.

"I'm going to run The Big Network."

He stared at her in shock. It was like someone trading in a Mercedes for a used Yugo.

"It's not a network," he said. "It's a bunch of third-rate stations sharing bad syndicated programs."

"Maybe without me it is, but I've got the programming savvy to make them a player."

"You don't have any savvy," he said. "You have *my* savvy."

She ignored the comment. "I believe the revival of *Beyond the Beyond* is strong enough to get the network sampled. And once people see the programming I'm going to give them, they'll never change the channel again."

"But I left my wife for you. How can you do this to me?"

She shrugged. "Television is a brutal business."

Oh, did she have balls. He taught her everything she knew about television. And he didn't do it so she could use it against him. He'd given her everything—his trust, his knowledge, his love, even a 1962 *TV Guide* fall preview edition.

She wasn't going anywhere, except right back down to the script-reading department.

"You don't know brutal, baby," DeBono said. "You have two more years left on your contract, and you're going to spend the next seven hundred and thirty days washing cars in the parking lot and wishing you hadn't betrayed me."

She smiled at him. "You try and enforce that contract, and I'll sue you for sexual harassment."

"Bullshit. What we did was consensual. Besides, the only people who know about us are you and me."

"Not exactly. Remember last month, when you bent me over my desk after the affiliates meeting and fucked me? And I was saying, 'Oh God, no, no, no'?"

The memory of it made him even harder, despite his anger. "You were afraid you'd come too soon and miss out on all the fun."

"That's what you thought. But I'm not sure the people who heard it on my speakerphone thought the same thing."

His face flushed with anger. "You left your speakerphone on?"

"I also left it on that day you came into my office and pinched my nipples until I cried."

"You begged me to do that."

"That was *before* I turned the speaker on."

"You bitch." He swung his hand to slap her, but she caught him by the wrist and twisted his arm at such a painful angle it brought him whimpering to his knees.

"I'm going, and I'm taking *Sexual Surrogate* with me," she said. "You ought to retire while UBC is still on top, because it won't be for long."

Kim released his arm and walked out, pleased with herself. She'd brought Don DeBono to his knees already, and it wasn't even sweeps yet.

ACT ONE

One

When Barnaby Jones looked at Eleanor Roosevelt, he mentally undressed her with his eyes, but only so he could mentally dress himself in her discarded underwear. It helped him keep the energy up during the day's scenes, which was getting more difficult with each new each episode of *The Young Barnaby Jones Chronicles*.

It wasn't playing youthful Barnaby that bothered Spike Donovan, it was having to play the part in Vancouver, far away from warm, seasonless Los Angeles, his Brentwood condo, his Porsche convertible, and his walk-in closet of women's lingerie, collected slowly and methodically over the years.

Lately, the costume department had started locking the wardrobe trailer between shots in a futile attempt to prevent any more women's clothing from disappearing. But Spike wouldn't be stopped so easily. If he couldn't spend a few hours each evening in women's clothing, his performance would suffer, and not just in front of the camera, either. He was America's newest young heart-throb, but since he'd been up here, lingerieless, he'd hardly throbbed at all.

Which was why he put on a fake mustache and beard, slipped out of his Sutton Place Residence suite, and headed for the rental car he'd stashed in a garage off of bustling Robson Street. To get to his car, he had to pass by a mobbed Starbucks, which was in heated competition with the Starbucks directly across the street. The coffee war in Vancouver was *that* fierce.

He wanted a Mocha Frappuccino Swirl, but he decided to get it on the way back. Coffee always tasted so much better when he was wearing panties.

Once in his rented Contour, he drove over the bridge to the North Shore. The studio abutted a suburban shopping center and looked like just another office park. It had none of grandeur or sprawl of a real studio. No one would ever mistake Universal, Paramount, Pinnacle, or Fox for an office park. He simply didn't get a thrill passing through the gate, and even less of one deprived of his garters. But that was about to change.

He parked beside the White Spot, a vinyl-and-plastic restaurant he ate at only once. They served a house wine that tasted so bad he thought he'd accidentally drunk the salad dressing. But while he was gagging, he looked out the window and noticed that the building blocked the view from the street of a corner of the studio fence.

Certain that no one was looking, he now slipped a pair of bolt cutters under his jacket and sprinted to the fence. Unlike Hollywood, the fence was a simple cyclone job. No barbed wire. No electric charge. Not even a camera. There weren't a lot of people interested in stealing a peek at a Canadian star, if there even was such a thing.

Spike tossed the bolt cutters over, climbed the fence, then scrambled between the soundstages to the dressing rooms and trailers parked behind them.

A few minutes later, he was outside the wardrobe trailer, pinching off the cheapo padlock with the bolt cutters. He quietly opened the door, slipped inside, and closed it behind him.

The trailer was windowless and narrow but very tall. When he turned on the lights, he found himself standing in an aisle between two rows of clothes and accessories. The trailer was stacked so high with goodies that there were ladders on wheels and rails running the entire length.

It was as close as he could get to actually being in his own closet. Amid the tweed jackets, stacks of fedoras, Nazi regalia, and two-tone shoes, he found a wide selection of women's clothing from the thirties and forties: dresses, gowns, hats with scarves draped around them, high heels of every shape and size. He sorted through them all before finding the right outfit: a classic Victor Steibel evening gown, long, backless, slinky, seamless. Perfect. He quickly stripped naked, pulled the dress over his head, and turned to admire himself in the full-length mirror.

The dress clung to his skin and puddled seductively at his feet, the satin sheen reflecting the light of the single bulb. Goose bumps rose on his exposed shoulders and arms, but it wasn't from the cold night air. Spike turned and looked over his shoulder, marveling at the rippling muscles of his back, exposed in the wide, plunging V-cut.

There was a bright flash of light. For a moment, Spike thought it was a revelation, then saw in his reflection that it was a Nikon, held by a man in a Cerruti suit emerging from his hiding place in the Nazi regalia behind him.

"You don't have the body to carry off that gown," the man said, "but it will still look good in the *Enquirer.*"

Spike mustered up his voice and tried to strike a heroic young Barnaby Jones pose. "But that's not what you're after, is it? *Enquirer* reporters shop at Wal-Mart, not Cerruti."

"The Company would like to represent you." The man proffered a card, which introduced him as Chick Lansing. "If you decline, these pictures go to every newspaper and magazine in the country."

Spike studied the card. "I just signed with William Morris."

"That's your problem," the agent said. "I'd love to stick around, have a get-to-know-you meeting, discuss projects, possibilities, and potentials, but I've been locked in here for five hours without a toilet. Give me a call, we'll take a chopper to Victoria for lunch."

Chick smiled, opened the trailer door, and walked right into a fist. The agent fell straight back, his head clunking as it hit the floor, his nose a bloody splatter on his face. A puddle of urine spread underneath the unconscious agent, soiling his Cerruti.

Spike looked up, astonished, to see a figure framed in the doorway against the bright, full moon. As the big, broad-shouldered man stepped in, Spike wondered whether he was saved or trading up to something worse.

"Who are you?"

"Charlie Willis. I'm in charge of special security for Pinnacle Pictures. We were concerned something like this would happen."

Charlie snatched the camera off the floor. "You want these pictures for yourself, or would you like me to destroy them?"

"That depends." Spike thought about it for a moment. "How do I look?"

Charlie studied him. "Not bad for a guy in a dress."

"Do you know how to focus one of those?"

Charlie nodded.

"This will only take a sec." Spike hurried into the back of the trailer. "Stay right there, let me find a pair of heels."

Tourists hoping to see stars were wasting their money going to Los Angeles. They could take all the bus tours in town and buy every "map to the stars' homes" ever printed and still not see a single celebrity.

While the business was still based in L.A., and the stars still lived there, it's not where they worked. It was just too expensive to make TV shows and movies there. If you really wanted to see stars, you had to go to Canada, where an American buck magically transformed into a buck forty.

There were more stars per square block in Vancouver than anywhere else in the world, and most of them were in the lobby of the Sutton Place Hotel, formerly known as Le Meridien, still known as the Beverly Hills Hotel, BC.

You could bump into Robert De Niro at the chocolate lovers' buffet, run into Richard Grieco at the pay phones, or collide with Annette Bening coming out of the elevator. In the bar, you could fight over almonds with John Goodman, or sing a few show tunes with George Segal at the piano.

Or you could wander down a few blocks to the less swanky, more tacky Pacific Palisades and hobnob with the assistant directors, writers, producers, and this week's *X-Files* guest stars.

Charlie Willis spent a lot of his time between the two hotels, so much so that he kept rooms at both. He never knew when he'd have to hide someone's illicit lover from a visiting spouse, stash a drunken actor from public view, or hold someone against his will until he could solve his problem.

He had come to think of himself as less of a security man than a baby-sitter. Actors, writers, directors, the whole crazy bunch of them, were just children who looked like adults. Hollywood conspired to make them think they actually *were* adults. He saw it as his job to remind them they weren't and to provide order and discipline in their lives.

And the truth was, he enjoyed it. It fell somewhere between his two previous professions: being a real cop on the Beverly Hills police force and a make-believe one as the star of TV show *My Gun Has Bullets.* He still protected people, only now he didn't risk his life doing it.

The talent, as they were called, were spoiled, arrogant, self-destructive, egotistical, and entirely transparent. Most of the time, Charlie protected them from themselves.

"It's none of my business if you want to wear women's clothing," Charlie told Spike, who sat beside him at Starbucks, nursing his second Mocha Frappuccino Swirl. "But you're going to get into trouble if you aren't more discreet."

Everyone had little quirks, and in the whole scheme of things, wearing panties wasn't so bad. Charlie would rather deal with an actor with a ladies' undie fetish than one with a cocaine habit, gambling problem, or a taste for S&M.

"I was desperate," Spike said.

"Next time, come to me," Charlie said. "Give me a list,

and your sizes, and I'll be glad to get you whatever you need."

Spike smiled warmly at Charlie. "You'd do that for me?"

Charlie shrugged. Spike was a decent kid, quirks aside, and a lot nicer than a lot of actors he dealt with. "It's my job."

"You're a nice guy, Charlie. You don't find many in this business. My agent at William Morris is another one. We connected right away. As friends first, agent and client second. Our relationship isn't just about him making his ten percent off me. We talk about goals, feelings, art. That's why I don't want to leave."

"Then don't," Charlie said.

"You don't understand." Spike set aside his coffee. "The Company wants me."

"Forget about Chick Lansing. He's a sleazebag. He won't bother you again."

"There are other agents at The Company," Spike said. "They don't give up easily."

Charlie sighed wearily. "If you don't mind me saying so, you're falling into their trap. They're agents, Spike, that's all. Talent representatives who find you job opportunities and take ten percent of your income in return. They work *for* you. You're in charge."

"What if they come back? What if The Company doesn't take no for an answer?"

"Then they have to deal with me," Charlie replied. Spike didn't look convinced. "They aren't going to bother you again, and if they do, I'll handle it."

"The Company plays rough."

Rough. Charlie shook his head and took a sip of his coffee. The people in the entertainment business had no perspective. They attached such grave importance to trivial things just so they could believe that what they do—providing entertainment, a fleeting distraction from real life—wasn't trivial. If entertainment was important, then everything attached to it had to be, too.

"Relax," Charlie said. "It's just television. It's not life and death."

Spike nodded, unconvinced, and ordered another Mocha Frappuccino Swirl.

Charlie sat on an uncomfortable bench at the police station, putting a few more wrinkles in his wrinkled khakis, trading smiles with the officers he had come to know over the last few months. In general, he found Canadians to be among the friendliest people he had ever met. So much so that he feared for them.

It wasn't the massive influx of Chinese and Korean immigrants that worried him. Nor was it the threat of French Canadian succession, the rampant Americanization of the culture, or high cholesterol in black bacon.

With Hollywood invading their city, he figured it was only a matter of time before they all became either aspiring actors or aspiring writers. And those who didn't aspire to be part of the industry would want to feed off it, becoming as crass, greedy, and self-serving as the people they hoped to profit from.

But until that dark day came, Charlie resolved to enjoy the city, its people, its clean air, and its refreshingly delineated seasons for as long as he could.

"Eh, Charlie." Detective Scott MacPherson ambled up, a steaming Starbucks cup in one hand and an appreciative smile on his face. He reminded Charlie of Don Knotts on the old *Andy Griffith Show.* But it would be a mistake to take the resemblance too seriously. It was common knowledge that MacPherson, while off duty and shopping for a six-pack and some smokes, single-handedly disarmed two drunken lumberjacks holding up a convenience store—without drawing his weapon or dropping his bag of groceries.

"When you apprehend a felon," MacPherson said, "it isn't necessary to bring us all Starbucks."

"I know how bad your coffee is," Charlie explained.

"That's a cliché." MacPherson sipped his Starbucks. "The idea that police precinct coffee is always awful, it's been done a million times. They did it every week on *Barney Miller*. Fact is, our coffee here is great. I grind the beans myself."

"In your bare hands, seeing as how you're so tough."

"That's what gives it that masculine flavor."

"You've never seen *Barney Miller*."

"So?"

"You've been taking screenwriting classes, haven't you?" Charlie was disappointed. "Didn't I warn you about that?"

MacPherson shrugged. "It's not a crime."

"It should be."

Charlie stood up, stretched, and checked his watch. "I guess we'd better go if we're going to make the L.A. flight."

MacPherson motioned to two officers, who disappeared into the back where the holding cells were. The detective knew what Charlie's job was but never once asked, or seemed to care, who or what Charlie was protecting. He simply trusted that Charlie was doing the right thing.

"We're shooting *The Young Barnaby Jones Chronicles* in Gastown for a couple nights next week," Charlie said.

"We could use some crowd control, if you're interested in a little honest moonlighting."

"Hey, that'd be great," MacPherson said. "Thanks a lot."

Chick Lansing emerged from the holding cell, escorted by the officers, a big stain on his crotch, his nose taped under a fat wad of gauze. His wrists were handcuffed in front of him.

"This is an outrage," Chick snortled through the gauze. "I demand to see a lawyer."

One of the officers tossed Charlie a set of cuff keys. He caught them and shoved them in his pocket. "No time, Chick. You have a plane to catch."

"I'm not going anywhere."

"You have a choice, Chick. You can sit in jail in your soiled pants until someone from The Company flies up to bail you out. Or you can come with me."

The officer handed Charlie a manila envelope containing Chick's personal items. Charlie waited for a moment, looking at Chick. "What's it going to be?"

Chick sagged, defeated, and nodded. Charlie headed outside. Chick followed him to a Ford Taurus parked at the curb.

"Take me back to my hotel," Chick said. "The Sutton Place Residence suites."

"You've checked out. Your bags are packed and in the trunk." Charlie opened the passenger door and pushed Chick in, slamming the door behind him.

Charlie got in, rolled down the window so the car wouldn't smell like a urinal, and headed down Granville Street, which would take him straight to the airport. During the half-hour drive, Charlie kept his face turned to the window and told Chick how it was going to be. He'd been charged with burglary, lewd conduct, and resisting arrest. The police were releasing him into Charlie's custody on the condition that Chick leave the country immediately and never return.

"If you come back," Charlie said, "they'll prosecute you for your crimes."

"This is a travesty of justice," Chick whined as they pulled up outside the terminal. "I'm going to sue you, the studio, the hotel, and the Canadian government. You will rue this day."

Charlie popped the trunk, got out, and handed the luggage over to the skycap, then came around and opened the door for Chick.

Chick jerked his head towards the skycap. "Stop them, they're taking my luggage!"

"You tip them a couple bucks and they put it on the plane for you."

"But I have to change my clothes."

"Sorry, we don't have time."

"I pissed my pants," Chick protested. "You can't let me go on the plane in pissed pants."

Charlie looked at him. "I think you're missing the point."

"I'm a Company agent, goddamn it. Do you know what that means?" Chick sat defiantly in the car, staring straight ahead. His thighs stung, his nose pulsated with pain, and it was time this studio tinshield realized who he was dealing with. "I have drive-on privileges at every lot. I have my own table at Planet Hollywood. And Clive Odett returns my calls."

Charlie sighed. "The plane leaves in five minutes. Either you get out of the car now, or you go back to jail. Your decision."

"Fine." Chick got up and held out his wrists to Charlie. "I'm an Executive Club member, they'll give me the pilot's pants if I ask for them."

Charlie unlocked the cuffs and handed Chick his tickets. Chick stared at the tickets in horror.

He could live with soiled pants, even make it a badge of honor. He had major clients who got onto planes dead drunk, covered in their own vomit, and it only added to their renegade allure. It might even help his image with the Johnny Depp, Drew Barrymore, Keanu Reeves set. But *this,* this he would never live down.

"Coach?" Chick's eyes swelled with tears. "Please, no. I can't fly coach."

Charlie handed him the manila envelope that contained his valuables. Chick took the envelope and began sobbing.

"I'm finished," Chick said.

Charlie offered him a Kleenex and led him into the terminal. As soon as Chick's plane was gone, Charlie booked himself on the next flight back to L.A.

Two

Beyond the Beyond to Launch
Big Net Slate

A revival of the sixties cult favorite *Beyond the Beyond* will be the cornerstone of The Big Network, Pinnacle Studios' ambitious bid to launch a fourth broadcast network.

"We're aiming our programming squarely at the 18-to-49 demographic," said Kimberly Woodrell, Big's president of prime-time programming. "The future of broadcast television is in niche programming, and we're on the cutting edge."

Pinnacle is committed to spend $1 million plus per episode and has hired Conrad Stipe, the series' original creator and executive producer, to helm the new effort, which is currently in pre-production.

"It's the old show, updated for the nineties," promised Jackson Burley, Pinnacle's prexy of TV. "We'll lure back the old fans and attract a hip, young audience of new ones. This will be the TV event of the century—and beyond."

Industry wags, while skeptical of the net's long-term chances for survival, were quick to praise the move. The series has a devoted cult following that could rub off on the web, slated to bow on a strong lineup of indies nationwide this fall.

Six months ago, Woodrell ankled UBC, where she was vp of current programming, with two years still left on her contract. Woodrell, widely credited for developing *Valet Girls*, was personally recruited for the Big post by Milo Kinoy, chairman and CEO.

Kinoy's Big Communications bought Pinnacle Studios early last year and immediately announced plans to build a network on the studio's television station group. Since then, The Big Network has signed affiliates in 28 of the top 30 TV markets.

"The three networks have become stodgy and stale, out of touch with the new generation," said Woodrell, who apprenticed under UBC's legendary prexy Don DeBono. "We're going to become the network for today. The network that takes risks, that isn't afraid to fail."

Her slate, still in the development stage, also includes *Caine & Able*, the hilarious misadventures of two gay bouncers at a strip club frequented by "zany ethnics, Generation X'ers, and Estelle Getty"; *The Two of Me*, described as a "gritty drama" about a teen hermaphrodite struggling through his first year in the police academy; *Con Artist*, a "magical anthology with a social conscience" about a young convict whose jailhouse tattoos come alive and help people in need; and *Sexual Surrogate,* a UBC reject starring Yasmine Bleeth as a therapist who "uses her body and soul" to help "families in crisis."

Although the Big schedule is still in the early stages, insiders report that *Sexual Surrogate* is slated to go up against MBC's hit *Adoption Agency* and UBC's new high-concept actioner *Siamese Cops,* starring John Stamos and Matthew Lawrence.

"Spacedate 980122. Captain's personal log. Two decades ago, the starship Endeavor *was nearly destroyed in a sneak attack in deepest, darkest space, cut off from the Confederation. We crashed on a class-M planet, most of the crew was lost. But I held on. I never gave up command . . . or hope."*

Captain Pierce's uniform was a little faded, and very tight, but it still fit, and Guy Goddard wore it, and the mission it stood for, with pride. He sat in the captain's chair on the circular bridge, staring ahead at the main viewscreen as he made his report. But instead of deep space stretching out in front of him, he saw the his weed-infested backyard and the rotting fence that surrounded his downed starship.

"I hid the wreckage, salvaging what I could and initiating repairs."

The studio scrapped the set within a week of cancellation and stacked it under a tarp on the back lot. He stole it, piece by piece, and reconstructed it in his living room.

"But without nitrozine energizers and Chief Engineer Glerp's guidance, there was little I could do."

He looked at what was left of his bridge. The lights on the consoles were dark. The sophisticated armrest control panels on his chair were retrofitted with a cassette recorder, a portable phone, and a remote control, which activated the VCR and TV at what once was Mr. Snork's science station.

"I did what I had to do to survive, against incredible adversity."

Captain Pierce was more than a role to him, it was the perfect meld of actor and character. So much so, that soon after taking the job, it stopped being one. It was a calling. But no one else saw it that way. To the industry, *Beyond the Beyond* was a flop. He was consigned to ten years of sporadic guest shots as stiff politicians and rigid newscasters in bad cop shows, returning each night to his starship to relive his greatest role.

Pretty soon, the casting directors stopped calling and he stopped caring, scratching out a living doing mall openings and Beyonder conventions, but always in uniform.

Then he got the word.

"But in the end, my faith was rewarded. Yesterday, I received a transmission from Confederation high command."

He glanced once again at the *Daily Variety* open on the helm and the glorious headline: BEYOND THE BEYOND TO LAUNCH BIG NET SLATE.

"The Endeavor *has been discovered. She'll be rebuilt, and I'll once again embark on a daring mission to that distant, unknown corner of space that lies . . . beyond the beyond."*

He clicked off the recorder with a dramatic flourish and noticed the red "battery low" light glowing. Alkaline batteries were no substitute for nitrozine power cells.

Guy Goddard rose from his command chair, forced open the maglev tube doors, and walked through the kitchen to the carport outside, where his '71 Buick Riviera was parked. He backed *Shuttle Craft One* out of the launch bay, eased into the interstellar traffic of Victory

Boulevard, and headed for Pinnacle Pictures.

He made terrific time, getting to the main gate well within four light-years.

"I'm here to see Conrad Stipe," Guy said to the astonished guard.

"Guy Goddard," the guard said, turning to his colleague in the booth. "I thought he died."

"He did." The other guard stole a glance at Guy. "And he was buried in his uniform."

Guy took his pass and drove onto the lot, giving the guards a chance to see the words *Shuttle Craft One* emblazoned on the Buick's side.

He emerged from his car and breathed the sweet studio air. This was definitely his home planet. His communicator trilled. Guy opened his flip phone with practiced grace and held it close to his mouth.

"Yes?"

"This is *Shuttle Craft Two*," said the squeaky voice on the other end. "We're in orbit."

"Maintain position. Pierce out." He flipped the phone shut, clipped it onto his space belt, and strode fearlessly toward Stipe's small Spanish-style bungalow.

He opened the door and found himself facing a secretary with enormous breasts sitting at her desk, which was cluttered with recent issues of *Variety, Hollywood Reporter, National Enquirer,* and other required reading of the trade.

"Nice computers." Guy admired her breasts. "I haven't seen mainframes like that in light-years."

"Yeah, they should be in the Smithsonian." She glanced at the IBM PC on her desk and shrugged, mistaking his galactic compliment for sarcasm. "I have an electric razor with more RAM."

She looked back at Guy. "Mr. Stipe told me to send you down to see him on stage fourteen."

Guy gave her a curt nod and left, walking around the bungalow to the soundstage directly behind, opening the heavy soundproof door and letting it close behind him with a dull thud.

The cavernous soundstage was dominated by a giant structure made up of plywood flats braced with long two-by-fours. To anyone else, it was the bland exterior of another set. But to Guy Goddard, it was the riatanium hull of the magnificent starship *Endeavor*. He walked along the edge of a set, where a row of portholes looked out on a giant backdrop of stars and planets.

Guy studied the stars and recognized it immediately as the Gamma Sector, where he once battled an entire fleet of Umgluck warstars. He peered through the porthole and saw the med-bay. Gleaming white brain reenergizers hung above every space bed. At the main med console, he spotted the data-cords that plugged into Dr. Kelvin's computer breasts and remembered the time he strangled a globulan mebocite with one of them.

Those were the days.

He walked around the edge of one flat and suddenly found himself at the end of the long silver corridor that led to the bridge. Taking a deep, proud breath, he marched down the corridor, admiring his ship. When he looked at the walls, he didn't see spray-painted egg cartons, colanders, and lawn genies. He saw interstellar baffles and high-tech energy conduits. When he studied the data screens, he didn't see transparencies on light boards. He saw plasmatron readouts from the bio-net computers. His ship was ready for action, and he was ready to take her to meet it.

Guy reached the end of the hall, forcing open the sliding space doors to reveal the *Endeavor* bridge. The command consoles were aglow with blinking lights, probably running a full diagnostic of the ship's sensor array. At Mr. Snork's science station, dazzling geometric shapes gyrated on the video screens. Although they were still in space port, the irascible Mr. Snork was already running some experiments. He'd have to toss a few extra space peanuts his way.

Guy settled into his command chair and gently stroked his armrest control panels. All the major switches were there, even a few new ones. There would be plenty of time to learn what they were for. The important thing was to get back out *there*, to the very edge of the unknown, to the worlds that exist only . . . beyond the beyond.

"Don't get too comfortable, Goddard." Stipe's voice rudely broke into his reverie. "This won't take long."

Guy rose to see Stipe entering the bridge with a young man in what appeared to be a Confederation uniform. Stipe's eyes swam in the three screwdrivers he washed down his Egg McMuffins with that morning. Guy started the day with a glass of delicious Tang and five of the space food sticks from the cases hidden in his garage. It's how Guy stayed so sharp.

Stipe turned to the man next to him. "I want you to meet Chad Shaw."

Guy studied the kid. He appeared to be a humanoid in his late twenties, good build, surgically altered nose, and hair at least an inch longer than regulation length. His uniform was similar to his own but a different cut. What disturbed Guy was the blue stripe across the chest, a *captain's* stripe.

"Aren't you a little young to be in a command position?" Guy asked Chad.

"Who is he?" Chad asked Stipe.

"Guy Goddard. He played Captain Pierce in the original series," Stipe replied, then faced Guy. "Chad was the star of *Teen PI* for five years. He can command any series he wants. We were lucky to get him."

"I've never watched *Beyond the Beyond*," Chad told Guy. "I don't want it to color my performance. Nothing personal."

Chad clapped him on the shoulder and turned to Stipe. "Maybe we can screen our first episode at the motion picture home for the entire original cast."

"That's a great idea, Chad," Stipe replied.

"Nice meeting you, Guy." Chad smiled and walked off the set. As soon as he was gone, Guy confronted Stipe.

"What's he doing on my ship?" Guy demanded.

"It's not your ship," he replied wearily. "It's a set. It's not real."

"He shouldn't be wearing a blue stripe." Guy narrowed his eyes at the airlock Chad disappeared through. "I'll bet my asteroids he hasn't even graduated from Star Academy. Security Chief Zorgog will be taking a close look at him with every one of his six beady eyes."

Stipe stared at Guy for a long moment. "Chad is our new Captain Pierce."

Guy jerked. "What did you say?"

"We're bringing the show back with an all-new, young cast."

Guy's lower lip began to tremble. "You can't do that. *I* am Captain Pierce."

"Not anymore, Goddard. Nobody will watch a fat, crazy old fart as an action hero. In fact, I don't want to see you in public wearing this uniform again." Stipe ripped the Confederation insignia from Guy's chest. "That means no more conventions, no more mall openings, no more nothing as Captain Pierce. You got that?"

"I won't let you do this."

"You don't have a choice," Stipe said. "My show. My characters. My fucking ship. Now get out."

Guy pushed past Stipe and stormed out of the bridge. There was a rip in the time-space continuum. Duplicates were taking over the Confederation. If he didn't do something, reality as he knew it would be shattered.

Outside, he ducked out of sight and flipped open his communicator.

"Pierce to *Shuttle Craft Two*, red alert."

A voice responded from somewhere deep in space. "The caller you are trying to reach is unavailable or has traveled outside our coverage area. Please try your call again later."

The temporal rift in the continuum was worse than he thought. Guy snapped his communicator shut and hurried back to his shuttle craft, his mind already searching for ways to save the Confederation from this dire threat.

Eddie Planet, from his vantage point inside the dumpster behind Conrad Stipe's bungalow, did a double take when he saw Guy Goddard storm out of the soundstage in his decaying *Beyond the Beyond* uniform.

He hadn't seen him in years. No one had. Eddie had heard that Guy Goddard actually thought he *was* Captain Pierce, and even had some groupies who believed it, too.

What a loser.

Not like Eddie Planet. The creative force behind such TV classics as *Saddlesore, Hollywood and Vine,* and the infamous *Frankencop* finished stuffing his trash bag with discarded drafts of *Beyond the Beyond* scripts, half-written scenes, and various memos. That idiot Stipe had been out of television too long. He was throwing out cash.

It didn't look like cash now. But once it was all

cleaned up, Xeroxed, and shrink-wrapped by his third wife, Shari, this trash would fetch him a cool couple grand at the next SF convention. Turning trash into money; that was a producer's job. And no one did it better, or with more class, than Eddie Planet, pronounced *Plan-A*, which, as everybody knew, was French for *"to soar,"* or at least sounded like it.

Either way, it was a classy name, like the guy who possessed it.

Eddie took a good look around, then tossed the bulging bag into the back of his golf cart, one of the perks of his three-year overall writing-producing deal at the studio.

The deal came off of *Frankencop* ("The best pieces of a dozen dead cops sewn together to make one incredible crime fighter"), a hit series that would still be on the air if it hadn't been financed by the mob. And if the hitman turned co–executive producer hadn't tried to murder the stars of every series it was up against. And if Charlie Willis hadn't stumbled into the whole mess just to clear himself of a trumped-up murder charge.

But that wasn't Eddie Planet's fault. Creatively, the show was *way* ahead of its time. Groundbreaking television. Just like his new show, *Peter Pan*, a highly promotable killer franchise, sold on a simple pitch: *He's a fairy with an attitude . . . and a badge.* The only reason its ratings were lousy was because MBC put it in the death slot opposite UBC's *Valet Girls* and *He's My Wife,* the wildly successful sitcom starring Scott Baio as a gay ad exec who passes his cross-dressing lover off as his wife to fool his conservative family.

Eddie pulled off his galoshes and his rain pants and shoved them under the seats, stopping for a moment to appreciate the smell of the cart's leather upholstery. Every producer on the lot had a golf cart, whether he or she needed one or not. The important thing was making sure yours was better than everyone else's. His even had a burled walnut dash. But Eddie was in danger of losing his if *Peter Pan* didn't get picked up for a back nine.

Eddie knew the only way to keep the show alive was to get the studio, and Pinnacle Television president Jackson Burley, solidly behind it. To get them to call in every marker they had with the network, use every strong-arm tactic they could, to keep his show on the air. And the only way to do that was to make Jackson Burley one of the stars.

Acting had long since eclipsed the personal trainer, the European secretary, the golf cart, the restaurant table, and the Aspen home as symbols of status within the television industry. If you were somebody in the business, it wasn't enough to write or produce the shows. You had to be a recurring character in them as well.

So when the ratings for *Peter Pan* started to fall faster than Tinker Bell strapped to a lead weight, Eddie Planet quickly created Dixon Drew, bounty hunter, and told Burley he was born to play the part. It didn't take much convincing, since Burley was a former writer-producer himself and therefore believed he could play any part as well as the high-paid monkeys who ruined his scripts.

Eddie weaved between the soundstages in his golf cart, purposely cutting off ordinary carts and sideswiping any that dared come alongside, until he arrived outside Stage 23. Burley's Pinafarina golf cart was parked outside, its V8 engine still warm under the hood. Eddie checked out his reflection in the tinted glass and, satisfied that no trash was hanging from his black T-shirt, white jacket, and tan slacks, went into the soundstage.

He came in just as the AD rang the bell and the director yelled "Action!"

Peter Pan and Dixon Drew were standing in a warehouse, confronting two thugs who held sawed-off shotguns at their sides. Peter Pan glared at the thugs from underneath his pointy hat. Drew stood beside him in leather pants and a tight, black shirt and stroked his goatee.

"I'm looking for the scumbucket, bat load of pizza trash who high-handled my goatee," Drew said, speaking dialogue that only Burley could have written for himself, since he was the only one who understood it.

"I don't know what you're talking about," the thug grunted.

Truth was, neither did Eddie. But neither he nor anyone else at the studio had the guts to tell Jackson Burley that.

"Run that line on someone else's knuckles," Drew said, "because that sticker-jive doesn't sing the song with me."

The thug whipped up his shotgun, and Peter Pan threw fairy dust in his eyes, blinding him. Drew decked the thug. The other thug turned to shoot Peter, but the fairy cop flew into the air, did a somersault, and kicked the thug in the back, sending him flying.

"These two are going to never-never land," Peter said, "for fifteen years to life."

Dixon Drew nodded. "You can take that to the bank and smoke it, but not on my Astroturf, pal."

And after a significant moment, and a couple of macho nods and grimaces, the director yelled, "Cut, print. Moving on, folks. Scene forty-two."

A bell rang, and Burley strode off the set to see Eddie, who stood to one side in the darkness behind the cameras.

"What did you think, Eddie?"

Eddie shook his head, feigning amazement. "Powerful stuff, incendiary performance. Pacino could take some pointers from you. You've got so much presence, you're almost two people."

"You're out there with your ass in the wind if you don't have the words," Burley said.

"Damn straight, Jack." Eddie was only half certain he understood what Jackson Burley said, but he had a safe comeback in mind. "It's a good thing you took a pass at the material, because you really understand the language of the mean streets. You're plugged in to the dark underbelly of society the way no one else in this town is."

"Yeah." Burley nodded in agreement. "It's a shame I couldn't rewrite this show from the start."

"There's always the back nine." Eddie was referring to the number of episodes the network would order if it picked up the series for the rest of the season.

"No, there isn't." Burley headed for the door. Eddie scurried after him.

"Of course there is, Jack. This show is on a roll."

"Straight off a cliff." Burley opened the stage door, pulled out his keys, and hit a button on his key chain. His golf cart alarm beeped off. "If I didn't have seven dramas on the networks, I'd write this show myself and save it. But I'm a studio executive now. I've got eight series to oversee, and we're launching our own network. I just don't have the time."

"This show could be a major hit," Eddie said. "As a studio executive, you have to see the potential."

"It was canceled this morning, Eddie. Morrie Lustig called me at the periodontist." Burley got into his cart and plucked a mineral water out of the fridge in the back. "Two more episodes and it's off MBC."

Eddie couldn't let it go at that. There had to be a way to make this a good thing, to somehow turn a death sentence into a plus. Suddenly, it hit him.

"Which frees *Peter Pan* up for The Big Network," Eddie shot back. "Brilliant move, Jack. You're a visionary. By not putting up a fight, you got them to release the show so you could program it against them. Those jerks at MBC don't even realize they walked right into your trap."

"*Peter Pan* doesn't fit into The Big Network picture, it's old-style television."

"I see," Eddie said. "So what do you call a rehash of *Beyond the Beyond*?"

"Progressive television," Burley snapped back, his face tight.

"Me too," Eddie quickly replied, forcing a smile. "I was just searching for the right words, and those would be the ones."

So *Peter Pan* was dead. It wasn't good news, but the blow was softened by the knowledge he still had three months left in his overall deal.

Jackson Burley started up the cart and backed out of his spot with a screech. Before shifting into drive, he glanced back at Eddie, who slouched sadly toward his cart.

"You've been working awfully hard, Eddie. If I were you, I'd take the next few weeks and relax. Regroup. Center yourself."

Burley smiled and sped off. Eddie stared after him, shocked. Take the next few weeks *off? Regroup?* There it was, flat out. Pinnacle wasn't going to renew his deal. Eddie's bowels seized up.

He staggered to the nearest guest-star trailer, opened the door, and commandeered the toilet for what was sure to be forty-five minutes at least. If Greg Evigan came back and had a problem with it, fuck him. He was still Eddie Planet, at least for three more months, and he needed to think.

Three

Before she became an actress, Patty Lok was an international swimsuit model. Jeans and a T-shirt did little to diminish her astonishing beauty.

Actor Vaughn Bryant's boyish, classic handsomeness first got him noticed as the young Robert Redford in *The Way We Were Before We Were.*

Together, they looked like the perfect couple. In fact, all it took was a poster featuring the two of them to pre-sell Pinnacle's $25 million romance *Love's Lustful Drumbeat* internationally. Before a frame of film was even shot, the movie had already broken even.

They looked so good together, rumors were already flying that they were a couple offscreen as well. *People* magazine called them "Barbie and Ken," and they were dubbed "Hollywood's new royal couple" by the swishy gossips at *Movieline.*

The studio flacks didn't go out of their way to discourage the rumors, because they were actually the ones spreading them.

So it was with considerable concern that Alison Sweeney sped down to Stage 11 in her golf cart. Word had already spread from the stage to the tower that Vaughn Bryant was refusing to do a party scene and that Patty Lok had run crying to her trailer.

It was a major crisis. If the slightest hint of disharmony between the two actors leaked off the lot, it could kill the movie.

Alison pulled up outside the stage. She looked very little like the typical studio exec, casually dressed in jeans and an oversized, untucked denim shirt and a suit vest, her ponytail sticking out the back of her Pinnacle Studios baseball cap. It was one reason everyone felt comfortable with her right away. She was nonthreatening.

She took a quick sip of flat Sprite, set the can back in the beverage holder, and hurried over to the production office trailer.

The director, Anson Costo, was waiting for her, a sheepish smile on his face, the same one he'd been trading on his entire career. Fifteen years, two face-lifts, and a head of hair ago, he was one of the kid stars of the sitcom *The Wacky Wackersons*. When the series ended, all his sheepish smile could get him were gigs as the celebrity contestant on bad game shows. So he became a director.

"I appreciate you coming down, Ms. Sweeney," Costo said, shaking her hand. "I've got eight pages to shoot today."

"What's the problem?"

"Fucking actors, that's the problem. If they were any good, they'd be directors."

Costo walked with her around the soundstage to the

actors' trailers, large mobile homes that doubled as dressing rooms.

"Vaughn Bryant was supposed to bump into Patty at the party and say, 'Hey, you look terrific.' Only he wouldn't. I ask him why not, and he goes, 'Cause she looks like a moose.' So now Patty Lok is sobbing in her trailer, I'm an hour behind, and some idiot extra in the party scene nearly chokes to death trying to eat one of the prop shrimp."

Alison chewed on her ponytail, a nervous habit she'd been trying to kick since high school. She didn't know what to say. Patty Lok was one of the most beautiful women in the world and, therefore, one of the most insecure. Patty probably believed Vaughn and was no doubt jamming her fingers down her throat right now in a desperate bid to lose the offending pounds.

"Our line producer told me to give you a call," Costo said. "Don't take this personally, but what do you do?"

"I'm talent liaison for Pinnacle Pictures," she said. "I interface with the talent on behalf of the studio."

He looked at her. She looked back at him.

"It means I do whatever is necessary to keep the actors, writers, directors, and producers happy so there won't be trouble."

Costo nodded. "And what happens when there's trouble?"

I call Charlie Willis, she thought, then felt a pang of loneliness. She missed him.

"There won't be. I'll take care of it. You just get Patty Lok on the set." Alison spun on her heels, inadvertently swatting Costo with her wet ponytail, marched over to Vaughn's trailer, and knocked on the door.

Vaughn opened on the first knock. "Is the prima donna ready yet?"

"I'm afraid not, Vaughn. Could I talk to you for a sec?"

He motioned her inside. "I hope you're going to do something about her, Alison. She's holding the entire company up. Espresso?"

"No thanks." Alison sat down on the couch and watched Vaughn futz with the espresso machine, a hissing, burping, five-thousand-dollar contraption that was flown in from Italy, as specified in his contract. "I understand you have a problem with the script."

"There's one line I can't get behind."

" 'Hey, you look terrific,' " she said.

"I'm sure when the writers wrote it, they didn't have that cow in mind." Vaughn held his cup under the machine, which sprayed out the most expensive espresso per cup in Los Angeles.

"She's looks pretty good to me," Alison replied.

"Get real," Vaughn said. "She's a hag."

"But not to your character, a country boy in the big city. To him, she's stunning."

"To him, she's a pig."

Alison had seen this happen with actors before. He was afraid he was no longer the prettiest face on the set. This was his way of asserting his attractiveness.

"Surely there's something nice your character can say," Alison said.

He sipped his espresso and shrugged.

"How about her eyes?" she offered, but he shook his head. "Her smile? Her hair? Her skin?"

He stared at her blankly. In desperation, Alison suggested, "What about her clothes?"

Ten minutes later, Vaughn and Patty were back on the set and ready to do the party scene. Anson Costo yelled, "Action!"

Willie wandered through the party, a country boy lost and self-conscious among the crème of high society.

"Hello, Willie."

Willie whirled around and awkwardly faced Savannah, a woman he loved fiercely but who was engaged to marry a rich lawyer. What could he possibly say to convince a debutante like her to fall for a simple Nebraska farmer like him? He smiled awkwardly and said:

"Hey, nice pants."

Alison had no way of knowing, as she slipped quietly out of the soundstage, that those three words would become famous, studied for generations by film historians who would marvel at their economy, subtlety, and profound emotional impact.

She was barely out the door when a production assistant ran up to her. "The tower is looking all over for you. They need you right away. There's a major crisis."

Alison shook her head wearily. They were all major crises.

"The story of my life," she said.

The weeds in front of Guy Goddard's deteriorating ranch-style house were at least three feet high, and since Eddie Planet hadn't brought along a machete, he didn't bother trying the front door.

Instead, he parked his Lexus behind *Shuttle Craft One* under the carport and knocked on the screen door, which hung onto the house by one rusty hinge.

The door behind the screen opened enough to let out the barrel of a gun. Eddie took a big step back.

"Identify yourself," Guy said from behind the door.

"I'm Eddie *Planet*," he said, pronouncing his name the way it looked for the first time. "Named for my deep, abiding love of the cosmos."

The door opened a little farther, enough for Eddie to see Guy's suspicious eyes. "State your business."

Getting Conrad Stipe booted from the show so Eddie could move in. It had occurred to Eddie, as he sat on Greg Evigan's toilet, that the only reason Stipe was running the show was that the studio thought the fans wouldn't accept anyone else. But if he had Guy Goddard and the fans on his side, *that* could change.

"I'm an acclaimed writer-producer with a deal at Pinnacle. And when I, your biggest fan in the universe, came across this"—Eddie held up a shrink-wrapped piece of paper, collected from Stipe's trash, for Goddard to see—"I was just sickened to the very core of my being. It's a memo from Conrad Stipe to Jackson Burley, president of Pinnacle Television, outlining his plan for *Beyond the Beyond.*"

Eddie turned the memo back toward him so he could read from it. " 'The appeal of *Beyond the Beyond* is the characters, *not* the actors who play them. The biggest mistake we can make is bringing back the original cast. Time has not been kind to any of them, particularly bovine Guy Goddard, a flatulent, incontinent has-been who—' "

Before he could get out another word, Guy burst out of the house and jammed the gun against Eddie's forehead, cocking the trigger.

"I'm on your side," Eddie stammered, looking cross-eyed at the gun. "As far as I'm concerned, you're Captain Pierce. Anyone else is just a bad imitation."

The captain narrowed his eyes at Eddie. "So you know about the evil doubles."

Guy Goddard was further gone than Eddie even imagined. Eddie took a deep breath. "Oh, yes."

Guy was relieved to know there was at least one other person besides himself left in the Confederation who saw what was happening. He lowered the gun.

"How many others in the Confederation high command know what's going on?"

Eddie assumed Guy meant the studio.

"No one," Eddie said as gravely as he could. "But it's not too late to save the show. You have to convince the fans to rise up against Stipe and what he's doing. If you don't, the show will be ruined *forever.*"

"You're suggesting that I lead a rebellion against the Confederation."

"No, Captain, I'm asking you to save it."

Eddie knew that if he kept talking, he ran the danger of saying the wrong thing and getting himself shot. He also knew he couldn't top that line. It was the perfect act ending. So he abruptly turned on his heels and marched back to his car, feeling Guy Goddard's insane eyes on him the whole way.

Charlie Willis didn't know much about Southern California history, but he figured when Canoga Park was founded it at least resembled its name. At one time, it must have been a community of grassy slopes and gentle streams, not the cement and asphalt wasteland of bleak warehouses it was now.

Canoga Park was smack on the industrial, western boundary of the San Fernando Valley, in the flat, smoggy pocket between the hillside, gated estates of Encino and Tarzana, and the housing developments spreading over the San Gabriel Mountains.

He steered his rented Ford Contour down a boulevard lined with junkyards, lumberyards, masonry yards, everything but *green* yards. The only people who lived here, in the run-down apartment buildings tucked between the warehouses, were poor, predominantly Hispanic workers who milled around on the street corners, hoping to be hired as day laborers.

And Charlie Willis.

He took a left onto the side street beside Home Depot hardware and parked at the curb in front of Canoga Stor-All, a prison camp for memories and life's unwanted clutter.

A tall wrought-iron fence surrounded six long, gray cinder-block buildings containing about thirty storage units with orange-painted, corrugated metal, roll-up garage doors. Each storage unit was secured by one or more padlocks and an occasional chain. At the front of the complex, beside the code-key gate, was the main office, a cinder-block building with miniblinds on the windows and a flat tarpaper roof. A golf cart was parked out front.

It wasn't an establishment that would be on the cover of *Architectural Digest*. But it was home, ever since the Northridge quake flattened his house in Reseda. His *uninsured* house.

Hours after the quake, Charlie rented a U-Haul and took what was left of his belongings and put them in storage at Canoga Stor-All. He arrived just as the resident managers, terrified by the aftershocks, were leaving to catch the next plane back to Israel.

So he, and his belongings, stayed. Canoga Stor-All became his home, and his job, until Pinnacle Studios offered him a job as their "troubleshooter."

Charlie popped the trunk, unloaded his suitcase, and trudged toward the front office, pausing on his way to watch two guys lug a garden statuary version of Michelangelo's *David* from their Toyota into one of the units. In the next row, a weary-looking fellow was trying to cram a crib into his Volvo, while his two kids threw french fries at each other in the backseat.

The place was hopping.

He threw open the screen door and stepped up to the scratched wood-grain Formica counter. There was nobody at the old IBM PC, which had been left on so long the image of the Stor-All lease was burned into the amber computer screen.

"If you're a vicious gang member with an automatic weapon, help yourself to the computer 'cause we got no casn," called out Lou LeDoux through the half-open door that separated the office from Charlie's apartment. "You can also have the half-eaten sugar cookie on the counter."

Charlie squeezed around the counter and nudged open the door to his apartment with the toe of his shoe.

"Glad to see you're watching out for the place," Charlie said to his brother-in-law. "I feel so secure knowing it's safe in your hands while I'm gone."

Lou sat in Charlie's recliner in a yellow tank top and purple sweats, the latest issue of *Big Hooters* open on his lap, a beer in his hand, and a football game on the television. He didn't look much like an LAPD detective.

"What you got here, Charlie, is a slice of heaven."

"Is that so?"

Charlie stole a beer from the six-pack beside Lou, pushed his dog, McGarrett, over on the couch, and sat down, dropping the suitcase at his feet and using it as an ottoman.

"After a long night of crime fighting, I can relax with a cool beverage, interesting literature, and cable TV," Lou said. "Sometimes I got to fill out a lease and show somebody a unit, but I don't mind that. It's not like, say, your sister coming at me, her hair in curlers, nagging me to fix that, clean this, every five fucking minutes."

"So you could say I'm doing you a favor, letting you moonlight as my manager, read my magazines, drink my beer, and enjoy the company of my dog." McGarrett put his head on Charlie's lap and licked the beer can in his hand.

"If you're thinking about not paying me, think again. I ain't doing this out of kindness." Lou burped loudly, enjoying it. "Speaking of which, why are you doing this?"

"Doing what?"

Lou shook his head. "Living in this dump."

"This slice of heaven," Charlie corrected, pointing at him with a tip of his beer can.

"You got a job that pays pretty good, you travel, what's the point of keeping this gig? I know you aren't doing it to make my life better."

Charlie thought about it as he got up and poured some beer in McGarrett's plastic dish. The dog rolled off the couch and lapped up the beer, finishing with a belch to rival Lou's.

He was a cop once, and that didn't work out. Then he became an actor *playing* a cop, and that didn't work out, either. Now he was something in between the two and wasn't sure how it was going to end up.

"You can't trust Hollywood, Lou," Charlie said. "Nothing about it is real."

"If the check clears, it's real."

"Let's just say I feel better knowing I have something real to fall back on."

Lou looked at him for a minute, then held up *Big Hooters* and waved it to make a point. "There's a guy rents a unit here, thin, eyes dart around like a squirrel. He has every single issue in storage."

"Gharlane."

"Yeah, Gharlane. You can show him any tit and he

can identify the woman." Lou shook his head, impressed. "I couldn't do that, could you?"

"Nope."

"That's real."

Charlie held his hand out to Lou. "Let me see that magazine." He took the magazine from Lou and looked at the cover. There was a subscription sticker on the front, addressed to Charlie.

"How long have I been getting this?"

"A couple weeks. One of the perks of my job. Yours too, I guess."

"I guess," Charlie handed the magazine back to him. "I'm taking a shower." He shuffled off toward the bedroom.

"I know what you mean." Lou opened the magazine to the centerfold. "The magazine has the same effect on me."

Before he got to the bathroom door, the phone rang. He was going to let the machine take it, but then he heard Alison's voice.

"Don't unpack yet, Charlie," she said. "We've got trouble."

Four

*L*ooking out from the thirty-third floor of the Pinnacle Studios office tower, Charlie could actually see the hills that ringed the valley and the snow-topped peaks to the east.

It was a clear, crisp day in the San Fernando Valley. A rainstorm had flushed all the gunk out of the air and onto the streets, where it washed into the drains and poured into Santa Monica Bay, poisoning the water and prompting the closing of ten miles of prime beachfront.

Days in L.A. didn't come any nicer than this.

But the view had its price. Until recently, the building was known as Litigation Center, after its original reflective surface blinded drivers on the freeway below, causing a bloody forty-car pileup. The tragedy had a happy ending. Pinnacle remodeled the exterior, bought the film rights to the victims' stories, and made a very successful miniseries starring Stevie Wonder and José Feliciano.

"Is this an office, or what?"

At the sound of Alison Sweeney's voice, Charlie turned and once again was assaulted by Milo Kinoy's distinctive decor. His desk was a glass tabletop with only a sheet of white paper on a black tablet, a black pen, and a slim black telephone. His chair was black leather and faced the matching black leather sofa. At the center of the room, right between Charlie and Alison, was a large, gold bust of a woman's enormous bust.

"I'm dizzy," Charlie said, looking at Alison. She had the smooth, even tan of a native Californian and a swimmer's lean body, which she unsuccessfully hid beneath a baggy man's shirt. She managed to be sexy and adorable at the same time.

"Is it the office or the jet lag?" Just seeing him made Alison smile, yet they rarely saw each other face-to-face. She often felt like the guy who left those tape recordings for Mr. Phelps and the Impossible Mission Force.

"The office doesn't thrill me," he replied. "And there's no time difference between Canada and Los Angeles."

"Then it must be me." She stepped into the office, a *Daily Variety* under her arm.

"I can't see you," Charlie said. "The breasts are blocking my view."

"There's more to me than my bosom, Charlie."

"I'm sure there is." He stepped around the statue and motioned to it with a tilt of his head. "But I was talking about hers."

She stood beside him, crossed her arms under her chest, and studied the well-endowed statue.

"She doesn't have a head," Alison noted. "What do you think that means?"

Before Charlie could answer, someone else did. "With breasts like that, she doesn't need one."

They turned to see Milo Kinoy striding into the room, a jacket slung over his arm. "How was your trip to Vancouver?"

"The usual," Charlie replied.

Milo's agenda was as clear as his desk and as straightforward as the titles of his magazines. It wasn't about pornography, it was all about making money. And he wanted to make more of it. Charlie understood Milo and was pretty certain Milo understood him.

Milo hung his jacket on one of the statue's erect nipples and settled into the leather chair behind his transparent, empty desk. "I'm very impressed with you, Charlie. You get things done, I appreciate that."

"Then I suppose I have you to thank for the subscription to *Big Hooters*."

"Just a small token of my appreciation." Milo smiled. "Have you seen *Daily Variety*?"

"Not since I started getting your magazine."

Alison swatted Charlie in the chest with the paper, a little too hard, in his opinion. "Page three," she said, holding it out to him.

He snatched the paper and opened it to a full-page advertisement, a blowup of a letter typewritten on Nick Alamogordo's personal stationery, X'ed out corrections and all.

It was a long, rambling, single-spaced misspelled diatribe about tortured creativity, about the threats and intimidation writers have faced over the centuries, about being willing to risk your life for your vision and your art.

"So he's a tortured artist," Charlie said, "making two million a script."

"Go to the bottom." Alison tapped the page. "Where he says he'll never eat fish again."

Charlie read the last paragraph and looked up, surprised. "He says Clive Odett threatened to kill him if he left The Company."

"He left Odett a few months ago and signed with Mitch Stein," Alison explained.

"So why wait until today to take out this ad?" Charlie asked.

"Because today we started filming *Cop a Feel* in Hawaii," Milo said. "Nick thinks Odett may try something."

" 'I don't eat pasta' doesn't sound like much of a threat to me."

"What can I tell you, Charlie?" Milo's fingers tapped the table. "The man is terrified. This ad is his cry for help."

"And you want me to help him."

"Obviously he's in no danger at all. But it will make him feel better if you're there for a while. Think of it as a paid vacation."

He speared the *Daily Variety* on a golden nipple.

"Aloha," Charlie said.

The darkened theater at The Company had several hundred seats, the latest digital, Dolby, and THX sound systems, and a cellular phone recharger in the armrest of every leather-upholstered seat.

Sitting in those seats were Odett's 122 agents, each sitting ramrod straight, cell phones and beepers switched off, all eyes on their imperious leader, who stood in front of the theater, a single light from the floor shining up into his face. Behind Odett, on the giant curtain that covered the screen, was The Company's ubiquitous logo, a giant *C*, its upper and lower cusps so sharp that the letter resembled a snarling, fanged mouth of a particularly vicious creature.

As mesmerizing as the sight was, a few eyes couldn't help but stray to Chick Lansing, who sat in the far corner of the theater, hunched low in his seat, a ball of gauze on his face where his nose should be.

"The prevailing wisdom the last few years is that the future of television is in cable," Odett said, "and that the days when the three broadcast networks dominated viewership are nearing an end.

"While I believe that cable television is an exciting frontier, the dollars aren't there yet. Broadcast television still reaches more homes, and more viewers, than basic or pay cable. Therefore, I view the emergence of a new television network, the first in forty years, as a significant and important event."

Odett was still upset that he hadn't brokered the sale of Pinnacle Studios to Milo Kinoy. But that didn't mean he couldn't control the network anyway, or there would be no network at all.

"I think The Big Network, by aiming solely at the young demographic, could radically transform the network landscape," Odett said, gradually lowering his voice as he spoke. "We want to be a part of that. Starting with *Beyond the Beyond.*"

He paused. There was an audible swish as 122 bodies leaned forward to hear more.

"The talent behind thirty-five percent of the programming on network television today is represented by The Company. I don't see why we can't represent *all* of the programming on The Big Network. Any and all talent not already represented by The Company should be pursued aggressively."

A collective murmur swept through the room and, in Chick's case, one snortle, as agents immediately began devising scenarios and hatching plots, checking their pockets for brass knuckles and thumbscrews, silencers and stilettos.

"I expect results immediately," Odett said. "This kind of opportunity doesn't come around twice."

The light beneath Odett switched off, and he took one step back into the darkness, completely disappearing. Instantly, the sound of a hundred flip phones being whipped open reverberated in the darkness like a horde of bats taking flight.

Chick Lansing slid out of his seat, hoping to slink quietly out of the theater before the lights came up. He turned toward the aisle and was shocked to see Zita, Odett's Eurobitch assistant, standing there, staring right at him.

Fifteen minutes later, Chick was standing in Clive Odett's pagoda, trying to act nonchalant, resisting the urge to scratch at the big gob of gauze on his face.

He was fairly certain that Odett had no idea what happened to him. When Chick got off the plane, he went straight to the terminal bathroom to hide from The Company's driver. After two hours in the stall, he paid a custodian two hundred dollars to claim his luggage and bring it back. Now, somewhere there was a big black man in a too-tight Cerruti suit having a good laugh at Chick's expense.

Chick waited angrily until dark, so his soiled, stinging crotch wouldn't be so noticeable, hailed a taxi, and went back to his apartment on Doheny to shower for a couple of hours and work on the clever story he'd tell Odett.

He told him he was mugged by a gang of vicious Canadians thugs, and after he left them broken and whimpering, he went to see Spike, their blood still on his hands. His intimidating presence was all it took to get Spike to see the wisdom of leaving William Morris.

"I think he got my message," Chick said.

Odett circled him, the ginsu knife in his hand. Chick kept his eyes on Zita and, to stay calm, concentrated on imagining her writhing in his bed.

"And what message would that be, Chick?" Odett whispered into his ear.

"You don't fuck with The Company." Chick threw a smile Zita's way. She didn't lob one back. Euro*bitch*. A night in his sackaroo of delight and she'd never stop smiling.

"Why do you think people don't fuck with us, Chick?" Odett whispered into his other ear.

"Because we're the agency that makes things happen," he replied. "Or they don't happen at all."

Odett stopped in front of Chick. "Do you think we got that reputation by wetting our pants every time we faced a studio security guard?"

Chick nearly wet his pants again. How the hell did he find out? "No," he sputtered, looking past Odett to see a thin smile on Zita's face.

"I'll tell you how we got it." Odett began to circle Chick once more. "I started in the mailroom and worked my way up from assistant to agent to vice president until finally the agency was mine. You know how I did that?"

Chick shook his head and willed his knees to stop shaking.

"I lied, cheated, and stole," Odett whispered into his ear, "and if there was someone between me and what I wanted, I stabbed him in the back."

To Chick's horror, he felt something warm and wet

running down his legs. Humiliated, he looked down, relieved to see it wasn't urine. It was blood. Before the implications of that discovery could sink in, Chick Lansing was already dead.

Odett put his foot on Chick's back, pulled out the knife, wiped the blood off on Chick's jacket, and set it on the counter next to Zita. "Are we resolving the Nick Alamogordo situation?"

She nodded. "Everything is in place."

"Good. Where do we stand with *Beyond the Beyond*?"

"They're all clients, except Conrad Stipe and Chad Shaw."

"They'll sign. And if they don't . . ." He let the thought dangle, but Zita took it as a hint to get her knives sharpened.

Odett walked over the bridge and out to the waiting room, where a big black man in a too-tight Cerruti suit waited stoically.

Odett smiled. "Sorry to keep you waiting, Luther."

"No problem, Mr. Odett." Luther had never seen the man before, but he knew his name from all the *Hollywood Reporter*s and *Variety*s people left in the airport shitters. When Luther found the business cards in the sucker's suitcase, he got an idea how he could take a big step up.

"You did the right thing calling me last night," Odett said. "It showed initiative and a natural instinct for the profession."

Luther twitched his shoulders, which for him passed as a shrug. He had that laid-back, half-asleep attitude that said "I don't give a fuck" in every language. His hair was cut so short, it could be mistaken for a shadow that died on his head.

"You're going to make a fine agent, Luther. I hope you'll consider joining us."

Odett held out his hand. Luther shook it firmly. "When do I start?"

"As it happens, an office just opened up."

ACT TWO

Five

A couple hundred miles southeast, in the Barstow Holiday Inn convention center, amid several hundred science fiction fans and memorabilia dealers, where it was possible to buy a *Babylon 5* tea coaster, learn to speak Klingon, and convert from Catholicism to The Force, Melvah Blenis sat behind her table of *Beyond the Beyond* fanzines and educated a few young people about the difference between literature and crap.

"You want to become a name in literature, start small, do a Chief Engineer Glerp story, set in the universe of the original series," Melvah advised the half-dozen aspiring fanfic writers standing before her in their homemade *Beyond the Beyond* uniforms, Snorkie noses, and stuffed Dr. Kelvin bras. "Whatever you do, don't try a Captain Pierce story, and don't even *think* about a crossover."

She held up a copy of her self-Xeroxed *Beyondzine,* issue number 22, August 1991, selling for only $24.95, which featured her classic crossover fanfic "Captain Pierce and the Daleks," where characters from *Beyond the Beyond* met *Dr. Who.*

"Those are the major leagues," she said, "and it takes years of experience to even attempt something that complex. Study Confederation history, know your Beyonder universe, then let your imagination run wild with the secondary characters."

She knew the wanna-be writers were listening and would heed her warnings. But there was no way to reach the "writers" working on the new TV series. She'd bet her collection of Confederation commemorative plates that they knew *nothing* about the universe, had never even read one piece of authentic fanfic.

They wouldn't know anything about how the universe had changed since the series ended. Their scripts wouldn't be at all consistent with established fanfic, where the only true *Beyond the Beyond* writing was being done. They were writing stories for pay, not for love. She couldn't understand why writers weren't being recruited from the fanfic community that supported the series, creatively, for years.

"Writing for secondary characters is where the literary giants of tomorrow get their experience," she told the fans, who listened with rapt attention. "If you make a mistake with them, it's a lot easier to fix in later fanfic. But blow it with Snork and your reputation as a serious writer is ruined. You might as well start writing *Starman* fanfic."

The wanna-be writers nodded in agreement and forked over their allowances for her zines to take home and read, reread, and study. They knew they were getting sage advice from an acknowledged master, one of the fanfic titans who kept the *Beyond the Beyond* universe alive after the series was canceled. She was the first person to even speculate that Mr. Snork's regular use of Dr. Kelvin's computer bosom was not entirely scientific.

But while *that* theory was acceptable to contemplate, a valid line of reasoning based on *facts* slash fanfic was not. The first time Melvah saw one of those Captain Pierce–Mr. Snork zines, she was livid. What those stories had Mr. Snork sucking for Captain Pierce with his wondrous nose was totally outside the universe. It was blasphemy.

She found the greasy little man who wrote it living in the detached garage of his parents' house in Orlando, Florida, and beat him to death with a rake.

That act was a revelation for her. Ever since then, she'd committed her entire being, which was currently clothed in a Urgonian sloth princess's golden halter top and skirt, to protecting the *Beyond* universe from all who would destroy it. To prove that devotion, she'd pierced her pale, gaunt body with Confederation insignia pins in her eyebrow, nose, tongue, ears, nipples, and a special one in what her lover, Thrack of Oberon, affectionately called her "intergalactic space port."

Thrack's own "superwarp plasma pleasure warhead" was tattooed with the starship *Endeavor*'s call letters and, when engorged, also displayed two of its five serial numbers. Only a few lucky space gals knew that, and they would never forget the experience.

It was an experience Thrack was hoping to share with Shari Covina, the one and only Dr. Kelvin, who sat behind a table selling *Beyond the Beyond* memorabilia. She was everything she'd once been and more. Her original, 1960s breasts were rebuilt and reinforced for the 1990s. Her full red lips were even fuller, the suckers puffed up with collagen. And her blond hair was even blonder, thanks to massive doses of bleach. Thrack could feel his warhead fueling for launch.

She smiled at him. "What can I do for you?"

He could think of a thousand things. "I want to show you my tattoo."

"I want to show you something, too." She picked up a coffee-stained, shrink-wrapped script from the table and handed it to him. "An authentic, discarded scene from the first episode of the new *Beyond the Beyond*. Autographed by me."

It was a steal at fifty bucks. Thrack took out his wallet and opened it for her, so she could see the huge condom inside. Actually, it was a balloon with "XLG" scrawled on it with a ballpoint pen, but it usually did the trick with the babes.

"Now do you want to see my tattoo?" He winked.

She snatched the money out of his wallet and, before he could say another word, turned to talk to a woman dressed like a killer carrot from episode twenty-three, "Roots of Evil."

Still, it was a moment he would never forget. Their flesh had actually touched, if even for a second. Besides, now he had a genuine *Beyond the Beyond* script. He decided to give it to Melvah.

She deserved it. Her fanfic was what enabled him to get through those difficult years until he turned eighteen, became a legal adult, and no longer could be imprisoned for the justifiable murder of his parents. He'd cut them in half with a chain saw after they threw out his Confederation uniform and took away his TV. The judge ordered him held in a juvenile detention facility for three years and, in a stroke of cruelty, deprived of television for the duration. His only contact with the universe was through Melvah's inspirational stories.

When he was released, he went from convention to convention, searching her out. And when they finally met, she lost herself in the lunar landscape of his acne-cratored face, just as he always knew she would.

Together, they were a formidable force for the Confederation. All they needed was a little direction.

Thrack's communicator chirped. He flipped it open and got the direction he so desperately needed. A voice boomed out: "Captain Pierce to *Shuttle Craft Two*, come in."

"Thrack here, Captain," replied Thrack sharply in his squeaky, uneven voice. This was a great time in the *Beyond* universe. The series was coming back, and Melvah and Thrack were poised for greatness alongside their captain. Their years of devoted service in his command was about to pay off.

"Where the hell are you?" Pierce yelled. "I've been trying to reach you all day."

Thrack hadn't heard Captain Pierce sound this angry in a long time, not since Melvah and Thrack accidentally burned down his mother's house instead of his ex-wife's.

"We're at Intergalacticon twenty-two in Barstow," Thrack said. "Everyone's talking about your new commission."

"Well, get your ass back to the ship," Pierce barked. "We're on red alert."

"R-red alert?" Thrack stammered. Never, ever, had they been on red alert, not even when the mailman lost the captain's residual check and they had to break his legs with a crowbar.

"You heard me," Pierce snapped. "If you aren't on the

bridge in four hours, I'll bust you both down a rank. Pierce out."

Thrack flipped the communicator shut and pushed, shoved, and elbowed his way across the ballroom to Melvah's table.

She only had to look at the fear and desperation on his pitted face to know the unthinkable had happened.

Red alert.

Whatever the crisis was, she already knew it would take a lot more than a rake, a chain saw, a match, or a crowbar to set the universe right this time.

The elevators of the Grand Royal Kona were paneled in smooth koa wood, each with its own cut-crystal chandelier and Persian rug. It made Charlie Willis feel very uncomfortable. He didn't like riding in an elevator better furnished than his own home.

He was tempted to scratch his initials in the wood with his special key, the one that, when inserted into the control console, allowed the elevator to go past the seven floors of regular accommodations to the two floors of deluxe suites above. But that would have been petty and childish.

He was about to do it anyway when the elevator stopped on the eighth floor, the doors opening to reveal a magnificent eighteenth-century oil painting of a tall-masted sailing ship, mounted on a koa-paneled wall. Charlie stepped out into a short hallway serving two $2,500-a-day suites, one on each end. Charlie heard Nick Alamogordo's voice even before he reached his door.

". . . I'll be glad to spell it for you," Alamogordo yelled at someone behind the door. "It's *A* as in *asshole. L* as in *lick me. A* as in *you asshole*—"

Charlie knocked on the door. Nick opened it, barely acknowledging Charlie before turning his back on him and continuing to talk on his portable phone.

Charlie walked in, closing the door behind him and taking in the suite, which was essentially furnished in the same old English style as the elevator, with a spectacular 180-degree view. Straight ahead, the Pacific Ocean stretched into the clear, blue horizon as far as he could see. To his left, the tropical garden, swimming pool, and a white-sand lagoon ringed by swaying palms. To his right, a bright, green golf course rolled out atop a desolate lava desert, black and craggy, which flowed from the hills into the sea.

". . . M as in *motherfucker.* O as in . . ." Nick, at a loss, snapped his fingers rapidly at Charlie for help.

"Osteoporosis," Charlie shot back.

". . . *osteoporosis.* G-O as in *Go fuck yourself, you miserable shithead. R* as in—" Nick held the phone away, glaring at it as if it just spit at him. "The son of a bitch hung up, can you believe that?"

"Maybe he figured out how to spell the rest." Charlie shifted his gaze from the view to Nick in his pleated tan shorts and untucked Hawaiian shirt. Enormous tufts of hair fluffed out of every opening, making Nick look like a Don Ho chia pet.

"Fucking studio jerks," Nick grumbled, then turned to Charlie. "Where's my lunch?"

"I don't know, Mr. Alamogordo, but if you're ordering something, I'd appreciate it if you could get me a sandwich. It was a long flight."

Nick studied Charlie for a moment. "You're not from room service."

"I'm a studio jerk." Charlie held out his hand. "Charlie Willis, Pinnacle Studios. I just got in from L.A."

"Well, it's about time." Nick ignored Charlie's hand and used the antenna on the portable phone to point at the ceiling. "I want him thrown out of this hotel and escorted off the island."

"Who?"

Nick threw the phone at the ceiling in fury. *"Him.* Javier Grillo, the hack, credit jumping, ratfucker the studio is paying a hundred thousand a week to do a production polish on my script."

Nick advanced on Charlie, jabbing his finger at the narrowing space between them. "No one touches my script but me. Understand? If it needed a polish, and it *doesn't,* I would have done it myself."

"I don't know anything about that," Charlie said. "I'm here to protect you."

"You can start by protecting my script."

"I'm talking about your life. I'm here to stop The Company from killing you."

Nick stopped, still pointing at Charlie. "You are?"

Charlie nodded.

Nick lowered his arm. "Clive Odett may be a crazy, vicious prick, but he wouldn't actually kill anyone, would he?"

"Not if I can help it." Charlie took off his jacket and tossed it on the couch. "I'm staying here until I'm satisfied you're out of danger."

"Right here?"

Charlie nodded. Nick played nervously with his wedding ring. "Well, the thing is, I've got an actress friend coming over tonight to go over her lines."

"That's your business, Mr. Alamogordo. I'm here to protect your privacy as well as your life."

"Call me Nick." Nick smiled, relieved, then clapped Charlie on the shoulder and headed for the deck, his thongs clicking on the souls of his bare feet. Something occurred to him when he reached the sliding glass door. He stopped and looked back at Charlie. "Osteoporosis. That's a bad thing, right?"

"Very bad."

Nick gave Charlie the thumbs-up. "We're gonna get along just fine."

Six

Melvah sat at the helm of the starship *Endeavor*, studying her fellow crewmates while waiting for Captain Pierce to show up on the bridge. Because of the seriousness of the situation, Captain Pierce had assembled the major forces in fandom.

Bev Huncke rested her considerable astrogirth on a barstool at Ops, balancing uneasily, her butt nearly swallowing her seat. As usual, she was wearing her Snorkie nose and her "I ❤ Snork" T-shirt. She once offered to make Melvah a Snorkie-nose vibrator like the one she used each night, but Melvah politely declined. The idea of a vibrating elephant nose in her crotch, even if it was Mr. Snork's, didn't excite her. But Melvah appreciated the gesture.

Artie Saputo was helping himself to some potato chips from the replicator, which appeared to Melvah to be a bread box taped to the wall with masking tape. He studied the box with the keen eye of an engineer. He had blown his other eye out with one of his pipe bombs. But he didn't miss it much, he just popped a plastic eyeball from the Security Chief Zorgog Halloween mask into the socket, which gave him a really cool look. Every time he turned his head, the yellow pupil rolled around in his plastic eye like a marble, which it was. The trick, though, was doing something about all that goop that oozed out around his homemade prosthetic eyeball.

Thrack sat in a folding chair beside Melvah, fiddling with the useless switches on the dead console in front of him and making interstellar "whoosh" noises.

There was a loud flush from the captain's quarters, and Pierce stepped onto the bridge, hiking up his space zipper and clearing his throat.

"The entire Confederation is in peril," he said, letting his gaze pass over each and every one of them, "and we are the only ones who can save it."

When Melvah looked at him, she didn't see the sagging, droopy-eyed actor in a faded costume. She saw Captain Pierce as he was on the show, the rugged hero who powered her imagination and fired her libido, almost as much as Dr. Kelvin's heaving computers, though that was a little secret she kept to herself.

"An alien force has invaded the highest echelons of Confederation command to carry out an insidious conspiracy." Captain Pierce circled the bridge, his hands balled into fists. "Their poisonous tendrils have even reached Conrad Stipe."

"They have tendrils?" Thrack squeaked. "Cool."

Melvah suddenly saw it all very clearly. Now she understood why fanfic writers weren't hired or even consulted for the new series. Conrad Stipe had sold out. He didn't care about the show. He was willing to let them destroy the *Beyond the Beyond* universe, as long as he got his precious money. All the hard work she, and every other fanfic author, devoted to keeping the universe alive all these years was going to be trashed by the very man who created it.

Captain Pierce drilled Thrack with an intense glare. "They are plotting to launch the *Endeavor* with evil doubles pretending to be our crew. Me, Snork, Dr. Kelvin— we've all been replaced with aliens."

Bev Huncke's plump lip quivered like slug glued to her face and desperate to escape. "They can't do that. There's only one Mr. Snork."

Pierce put his hand on Bev's shoulder. "There's only one of each of us. We are unique. We are . . . *human beings.*" He stared off into some distant place. "That's why we must fight them. With every fiber of our being."

"They can have *all* my fiber," Thrack whispered to Melvah. "Makes me shit like a cannon anyway."

But she didn't hear him. She was still reeling from the implications of the captain's words.

Melvah knew Guy Goddard wasn't *really* Captain Pierce, but like her, he understood the sanctity of the *Beyond* universe, of the need to preserve and protect it. He embodied the character of Captain Pierce the same way she embodied the universe. The way Conrad Stipe no longer did. He would have to answer for that.

They had to be stopped.

"Captain, what are your orders?" Melvah asked.

"I took a vow when I put on this uniform, to protect the Confederation of Aligned Galaxies and everything it stands for. I can't let the *Endeavor* launch with a crew of evil doubles." Captain Pierce settled into his command chair. "Kill them. Kill every one of those miserable fuckers."

The Queen Kaahumanu Highway cut through a desolate plain of pahoehoe lava, its smooth, swirly, surface making Charlie feel like he was driving a Mustang convertible across a giant brownie. The bleak, lifeless expanse was a vivid, lasting testament to the violent forces that were still shaping the island paradise.

It was also a massive blackboard for environmentally conscious graffiti artists, who carried piles of white coral from the coastline to fashion messages within view of the road. Someone had written "Hollywood" in coral against the side of a decades-old lava bubble. Soon, everyplace to be anyplace would have to have a Hollywood sign. Or at least a Planet Hollywood within a twenty-mile radius.

"I noticed you used my bathroom this morning." Nick picked his nose in the passenger seat. "Did you take a dump?"

Charlie gave him a look.

Nick said, "That's the problem with the world today."

"I don't follow." Charlie sped up to pass a slow-moving white van, a satellite dish on its roof. Against the craggy terrain, it looked like a moon buggy.

"I bet you didn't think twice about it. You ate a meal in North America and shit in the South Pacific." Nick twisted in his seat to face Charlie. "Go one step farther. With modern air travel, it's possible for someone in Africa to eat a yak and, the same day, take a dump in Paris."

"They don't have yaks in Africa."

"My point is, you then have digested yak flesh, which is not, in any way, indigenous to France, entering the ecosystem," Nick said, looking grim. "You always hear people complain about nuclear waste, global warming, carbon monoxide, but no one ever talks about travel shit. Why? Because they can't face the enormity of the problem. It's bigger than all of us."

"Shit, you mean."

"Exactly." Nick turned his gaze back to the road. "I think there's a movie in it."

As far as Charlie was concerned, Nick had already written shit movies.

Suddenly, Charlie regretted not buying Advil while they were at the market in Waikoloa village. Then again, with Hawaii's inflated prices for everything, the Advil would probably have blown his entire expense account. He was still stinging from the forty-three-cent-per-gallon gasoline tax.

He turned off the highway onto the road leading to Grand Royal Kona Resort. The lush green grass and vibrant pink bougainvillea that lined both sides of the road blazed like neon against the black lava on which they inexplicably survived.

"You didn't have to come with me," Nick said. "I could've bought my own condoms."

"I'm not about to let you go out alone," Charlie replied, "or leave you by yourself while I run your errands."

"Are you planning on being in the bedroom while we fuck?"

"No. But I'll be right outside the door."

As Charlie pulled up under the grand portico of the Grand Royal Kona Resort, Nick had the grand realization that the *Variety* ad was a mistake.

The message light was blinking on the telephone when Nick and Charlie came into the suite. Nick called the operator, listened to his messages, then called Susie Glot's room and invited her up to "go over the script."

Nick hung up and dug the condoms out of his pocket. He examined the packets. "Which do you think she'll like, Charlie, macadamia nut or pineapple?"

"Since you aren't doing the production polish," Charlie said, "shouldn't she be giving her notes to Javier Grillo?"

"Forget it. I'm gonna need them *both.*" Nick shoved the condoms back in his pocket and marched out of the living room.

Charlie shrugged and went out on the lanai to look at the view. The sun was setting on the water. Lovers strolled on the beach and cuddled in hammocks, watching the embers of the day burn out. And out on the road, Charlie could see the white van with its satellite dish raised into the air on a telescoping base. It was probably a TV station catching a live beauty shot for the weather report.

Nick stomped out onto the lanai, wearing a silk bathrobe and nothing else. There was so much chest hair fluffing out, it looked like an enormous squirrel dove into Nick's robe and got stuck. Something was on Nick's mind.

"Grillo isn't a writer, he's a thief. He comes in, adds a stupid joke or idiotic car chase, then tries to fuck you out of your screen credit. Everyone knows that," Nick said. "The reason actresses come to me is because I'm the star maker. I'm the guy with the vision."

"I didn't mean to offend you," Charlie said. "I'm sorry."

"Hey, Nick Alamogordo isn't offended. I'm just telling you this to educate you about how movies are made so you won't offend somebody else."

Someone knocked at the door. Charlie went to the door and peered through the peephole. Susie Glot stood outside in a short red sundress, cut low to reveal her standard-issue synthetic bust. A script was tucked under one arm, and she held a tiny evening bag.

So far, she'd made a career out of doing slasher movies, typecast as the first girl to take off her shirt and the first one to die. She still was, only this time it was for top billing as the stripper who befriends sex-addict undercover cop David Caruso, right before she takes off her shirt and dies.

Charlie opened the door. "Good evening, ma'am."

Susie sashayed into the room past Charlie, fanning herself with the script. "This script is so hot I get blisters on my fingers every time I pick it up."

Nick smiled. "That's a good note."

Charlie sat on the arm of a chair and watched the show.

"All it needs is a stronger, final moment for Electra," she said.

Nick folded his arms across his chest. Charlie expected to see the fur start to squirm. "What kind of moment?"

Susie opened the script and leaned in close to Nick, so her breast brushed his arm. "In her final scene, Electra's doing the striptease at the club and accidentally steps into the assassin's line of fire, taking a bullet meant for Trent Zane."

"She falls off the stage into the cop's arms," Nick said. "Naked, dead, blood-soaked, a powerful metaphor for his addiction and his guilt."

"I think before she dies," Susie said, "she should say something."

" 'Ouch'?" Charlie suggested.

Susie turned, noticing Charlie for the first time. "Who's he?"

"The butler." Nick took the script and, pretending to study it, walked away from Charlie toward the bedroom. "You might be on to something, Susie. What sort of beat did you have in mind?"

Susie rushed up behind him, pressing herself against his back on the pretense of peering at the script in his hands. "Before I die, I tell him that I'm carrying his baby."

Nick shook his head. "Too melodramatic. But I know what you're going for."

A close-up and one last chance to steal a scene, Charlie thought.

"You want an emotional moment that resonates." Nick paced. "What if . . ." He tossed the script on the floor and whirled around to face Susie, as if spun by the sheer force of his mighty inspiration.

"I got it. She takes the bullet while doing a lap dance for him. Intimate. Close. Grinding. They're both writhing in ecstasy, the tempo of the music going faster and faster. Jungle drums. Electric guitars. They're both about to climax and, *blammo*, she's shot."

"Yes," she panted.

"Then, in a tight close-up, with her dying breath she says, 'I came.' And she dies. We intertwine the intimacy of life and death in one remarkable, cinematic moment."

"Wow," she said. "That resonates."

Nick's face suddenly soured. "I just don't see it yet. I think we need to work on the scene, act it out a few times, see if it really plays."

She smiled coyly and glanced in Charlie's direction. "Here?"

Nick motioned toward the bedroom. "Make yourself comfortable, find the soul of the scene. I'll be right with you."

As she went into the bedroom, something occurred to Nick.

"You like pineapples, don't you?" Nick called after her.

"Sure," she replied.

Nick turned to Charlie. "You better turn up the TV, it's going to be noisy." Nick winked and disappeared into the bedroom.

The conversation Charlie just overheard was already too much to bear. He reached for the remote, turned on the television, and searched the airwaves for a good *Adam-12* or *Police Story* rerun but settled on the only show that wasn't an infomercial, something cheesy from the 1960s.

The starship Endeavor *left the orbit of the big green planet and headed for deepest, darkest space.*

On the bridge, Mr. Snork and Dr. Kelvin stood on either side of Captain Pierce's command chair.

"I'd like to come back here in a few light-years and see how everything turned out," Captain Pierce said.

Dr. Kelvin stared at the main viewscreen as the planet receded from view. "Imagine, an entire planet modeling its society on an ancient Playboy *magazine."*

"Fascinating, indeed," Mr. Snork agreed, scratching his elephant nose. "The females even evolved with staples across their waists. Think what might have happened if the merchant ship had crash-landed with a cargo of those ancient Three Stooges movies instead."

"One discarded cultural artifact can reshape a species, a planet, an entire galaxy." Dr. Kelvin's breasts heaved, computing the possibilities.

"Oh, no." Captain Pierce slowly rose from his seat.

"What is it, sir?" Mr. Snork snortled.

"I left a pair of bikini briefs in the queen's boudoir."

"Your herculite briefs?" Dr. Kelvin asked, suddenly very concerned. The captain nodded gravely. "Herculite is the basic material from which argulon is formulated—"

"And argulon is the basic component of our totonian warp drive," Captain Pierce said.

Dr. Snork stared at his captain. "Are you saying because you left your underwear on the planet, the aliens could develop warp drive and colonize the cosmos?"

Captain Pierce looked grim. "I'm saying in a hundred light-years, they may be wearing the pants in this universe."

And on Captain Pierce's laughter, Mr. Snork's consternation, and Dr. Kelvin's puzzlement . . .

The scene abruptly freeze-framed. The music swelled, and the words "Executive Producer Conrad Stipe" flashed across the screen.

Charlie groaned and switched to an infomercial. Tom Bosley sat on a couch, listening intently to three men extolling the virtues of R-788, a cream that cured impotence.

"Now I have the zest and vigor of a sixteen-year-old," one man proclaimed.

Tom turned to the camera. "And that's not all—it's great for dandruff and those pesky insect bites, too!"

Seven

*T*here were no customers for R-788 in Nick Alamogordo's bedroom. Nick sat on the edge of the bed, while Susie Glot took an enthusiastic spin on his lucky barstool. Nick was pretty certain the scene would work. It worked for him.

He thought it worked for her, too, but if he was a better student of her *oeuvre*, he would have recognized her shrieking, writhing, grab-your-chest-hair-with-both-fists-and-hold-on-for-dear-life orgasm from her performance in the erotic thriller *Cheek to Cheek.*

He was still catching his breath from his own simpering, whimpering, huffing orgasm, and only beginning to notice the stinging sensation from his yanked-out chest hair, when the phone rang. Nick instinctively reached for it, forgetting for the moment that a vital part of his anatomy was still wearing an actress.

"Was it as good for you as it was for us?" Clive Odett asked him.

"What the fuck are you talking about?"

"You're much better at writing sex scenes than performing them. You grunt like a pig. Not very erotic."

"You don't know shit, Odett," Nick said.

"You're holding the phone in your right hand," Odett said, "and clutching Susie's ass with the other."

Nick immediately let go of Susie's buttock.

"Now you've let go of her ass, and your jaw is hanging open."

Nick closed his mouth, his eyes darting around the room.

"There's a camera in Susie's evening bag, which is transmitting to a truck outside the hotel, which is beaming it via satellite into my office, where we recorded your little Method acting session."

Nick looked at Susie, who climbed off his collapsing barstool with an apologetic shrug. "He's my agent."

She smiled and waved at the evening bag on the dresser. "Hi, Mr. Odett. How's the weather in L.A.?"

"You can tell her it's a bit windy," Odett said.

"Fuck you." Nick pulled his bathrobe self-consciously over his lap and glared at the evening bag. "What's the matter, the burning fish drink not getting it up for you?"

"A copy of this tape will be messengered to your wife within the hour."

Nick glanced at Susie, who was examining her rock-solid breasts in the mirror.

"Go ahead." Nick tried to sound casual, or at least as casual as someone can sound sitting naked on his bed talking to an evening bag.

"Your wife will divorce you and get fifty percent of

everything, and we'll help her find all the money she's en-titled to," Odett said. "Then there's the alimony. Balance that loss against future earnings with another agency and ask yourself, Is it really worth it not to be a Company client?"

"I thought you wanted to kill me."

"I don't want to kill you, I want to own you," Odett replied. "You're worth a lot more to us alive. I have an agent in the building with the papers. All you have to do is sign."

Nick glanced again at Susie, bending over to pick up her dress, and came to a decision.

"You want me back, you have to do something for me."

"I thought we just did."

Nick told him what he wanted, hung up the phone, then got up and tossed the evening bag into the trash can. He turned to Susie and smiled lasciviously.

"Do you like macadamia nuts, Susie?"

Kimberly Woodrell drove her jet-black Jaguar convertible, which was leased to director Marcus Dolen until *Gun Point* tanked on opening weekend, up the Pacific Coast High-way that night to her Malibu beach house, which had be-longed to producer Scott Devereaux before his wife caught him in bed with two of his development execs.

It didn't bother Kim that everything she had once be-longed to someone else. The business was just a bunch of hermit crabs scurrying around for cast-off shells to inhabit, and she was fine with that. Moreover, she was *good* at it.

Long ago she realized it was impossible to take a step in this town without going where someone else had been before, whether you were moving into a new office or a lover's pants. So she went after what other people had without remorse; it was how business was done. And it was why her new job, as president of The Big Network, was so important to her. It was the one thing in her life that had never belonged to anyone but her.

She was the first person to run The Big Network, no one had warmed the seat before she put her perfect ass in it. She wasn't stuck with a schedule of rotten shows, wrongheaded series commitments, or a staff of idiots who would have to be broomed out.

But more important than all of that, she was the *first woman* to run a major network. That would *always* be hers and hers alone.

Kim Woodrell lived in a strip of "custom homes" tucked snugly between the Pacific Coast Highway and the beach. The private street was a design gallery for architecture students. There was a hacienda, a villa, an English Tudor, and then her place, which looked like an origami flamingo dropped onto the sand by a benevolent Japanese giant.

She parked the car in her garage, got out, and was surprised to see that the alarm panel was deactivated. It had either been disconnected or she forgot to set it before she left. Either way, there was nothing she could do about it now.

Not that she cared. She bought the place furnished, so the decor reflected the previous inhabitant's fascination with chrome. If someone wanted to steal it all, he was welcome to it.

The first thing she noticed when she stepped into the cavernous living room wasn't something missing but something new. Empty Evian bottles were scattered everywhere, on the chrome-and-glass coffee table, on the chrome-and-leather chair, on the winding chrome-and-metal staircase leading upstairs.

At the same instant, she recoiled from a heavy, acrid stench that was at once repulsive and familiar.

Piss.

She took a few more steps into the room and saw that the walls were streaked with urine, as if someone had sprayed them down with a hose. There wasn't a single wall that hadn't been pissed on.

Kim shivered, feeling the intruder's presence as strongly as the odor, even though he was probably long gone.

Some guy spent an entire day here, just pissing on everything, filling up on Evian whenever his bladder ran dry. And she had a pretty good idea who it was.

He was marking his territory, the way a dog would.

The message was clear: *You're mine.*

Charlie woke up early the next morning, stiff and sore, and took a jog on the beach to loosen the jet lag from his joints, returning to Nick's suite forty-five minutes later, drenched with sweat, his heart pounding like a small beast trying to break out of his chest.

He was spending way too much time sitting in airplanes having cocktails and not enough time sweating them off. He mopped up the sweat with a thick Grand Royal Kona towel, dug his exercise gloves out of his suitcase, and ambled into the suite's small gym.

The gym was basically a converted bedroom with a weight set, treadmill, and a fully stocked wet bar, just in case a guest was worried too much time might pass between losing the pounds and putting them back on. Nothing like a handful of cashews and a frothy mug of imported beer after rigorous exercise.

Charlie picked up a couple of sixty-pound barbells, sat down on the edge of a padded bench, and did some curls while admiring the spectacular ocean view. He took a moment to rest between his first and second set of twenty reps, and that's when he heard the scuffling upstairs.

Several sets of feet stumbled around, bumping into things. Then he heard breaking glass, a heavy thud, and a scream of agony, followed by another thud.

That's when he remembered *who* was staying upstairs. Javier Grillo, a Pinnacle Studios employee, which made his safety Charlie's responsibility.

Charlie dropped the barbells and rushed out of the suite, taking the stairwell up two flights to the next floor. He opened the door slowly, stepping into a hallway identical to the one leading to Nick's suite, only with a different maritime painting on the wall.

One of the double doors to Grillo's suite was ajar, and Charlie could hear someone groaning inside. Charlie crept cautiously toward the suite, pushed the door open, and saw a man in Bermuda shorts and a T-shirt slumped over a laptop on the dining room table. It had to be Javier Grillo.

As Charlie got closer, he saw that Grillo's hands were smashed to bloody pulp, probably with the hammer that was now lying at the screenwriter's feet. And it must have just happened, because the blood was only now beginning to spread across that tabletop. Grillo was hurting, but at least he was alive.

A flicker of movement on the computer screen caught Charlie's eye. A reflection.

He shot up his hands just as the attacker wrapped the garrote around his neck and pulled it taut. The two men staggered backward, the wire cutting into the rubber palms of Charlie's gym gloves and pinning his arms against his chest.

Charlie hurled himself backward, slamming his attacker against the wall again and again and again, until he heard a moist smack and felt the man sag behind him.

He ducked under the wire and let the attacker slide to the floor, painting a swath of blood on the wall with his head.

The experts were right, Charlie thought, examining his sliced gloves while he caught his breath. Lifting weights can prolong your life.

He looked down at his attacker. The guy was dressed like a bellman, his white uniform spattered with blood, probably from smashing Grillo's hands. Charlie crouched beside him and patted him down for weapons. He felt a bulge under his jacket and reached inside to find a folded set of papers. He stood up and sorted through them.

It was a Company contract made out for Nick Alamogordo. Charlie glanced at Grillo, then back at the contract. The connection was obvious.

"Fuck, fuck, fuck," the attacker grumbled drowsily, rivulets of blood running down his cheeks like red tears. "I didn't work my way up from the mailroom to die like this."

"You'll live." Charlie shoved the papers into the waistband of his shorts, went to the phone and dialed the hotel operator to get the police and paramedics up there. "And if you're a half-decent agent, you'll negotiate your prison sentence down by testifying against Clive Odett and The Company."

"That will never happen," the assassin said. "Clive Odett would get to me first and eat me alive."

"He's just an agent."

The man laughed. "You have no idea who you're dealing with." And with that, he gritted his teeth.

Suddenly the assassin started jerking wildly, his whole body undulating, a strange gurgling sound coming from his throat. Before Charlie could do anything except drop the telephone receiver, it was over. The man was dead, eyes and mouth wide open.

Charlie stared at the man in shock. He couldn't figure out what had just happened. One minute the man was lucid, talking, and the next, it was like . . . it was like something he saw in a bad war movie, only it couldn't possibly be . . .

Could it?

He peered into the man's mouth and saw the broken tooth that had once contained the cyanide capsule.

Eight

Charlie marched into Nick Alamogordo's suite and found him out on the lanai, holding a tropical drink and sucking a pineapple wedge.

"Where have you been?" Nick asked.

"Getting some exercise," Charlie said, removing his sliced weight-lifting gloves.

Nick picked some pineapple strands from between his teeth and flicked them over the rail. "Listen, I've been giving this whole situation some thought."

"What situation?"

"This thing with me and The Company. It's been blown way out of proportion, and I got to take the blame for that. I'm a volatile personality, you know? The point is, I shouldn't have left The Company. They're like family to me, and you don't walk away from your family."

"I see. And this revelation just came to you during the night?"

"Yeah, I get some of my best ideas in my sleep or sitting on the can. What's it to you?"

Then something occurred to the screenwriter. He got it now. "Hey, you want to stay in Hawaii a couple more days, that's fine with me." Nick winked.

"A Company agent smashed Javier Grillo's fingers with a hammer." Charlie pulled the contract from under his shirt and tossed it to Nick. "I found this on the agent."

Nick looked the contract over and dropped it on the chaise lounge. "So?"

"The Company did it for you."

"The agent tell you that?"

"The agent is dead."

Nick shrugged and took a sip of his drink. "Have a nice flight back to L.A."

"You told Clive Odett if he got Javier Grillo off the movie, you'd go back to the agency."

"Says who? You?" Nick laughed. "You're a studio security officer. What are you gonna do, revoke my drive-on pass?"

"I could do that," Charlie said. "Or I could tell the police what I know."

"But there's no proof, the publicity would embarrass the studio, and the movie would be ruined before it even opened." Nick was cocky and self-confident, as if acting out a scene he intended to write. "So you'll do the smart thing, forget about it, work on your tan for a couple days, maybe let me arrange for a couple of hula girls to lick your sugarcane."

"That's one way to go," Charlie said. "Another would be for me to call your wife."

"No, you will *not* do that." Nick shook his finger at him, as if Charlie were a misbehaving actor daring to ad-lib a couple lines in the scene.

Charlie looked him in the eyes. "I *did* that."

"Bullshit." Nick's hand, the one holding the drink, was beginning to shake.

"I told her I sat outside your bedroom door while you had sex with Susie Glot and that I would gladly testify to that fact in any court proceeding."

Nick's whole arm was shaking now, the drink sloshing all over his hand, but the screenwriter didn't seem to notice. "Do you have any idea how much your little prank will cost me?"

"Not nearly as much as Javier Grillo paid." Charlie turned and walked away.

The new twentysomething cast of *Beyond the Beyond* assembled on the bridge of the starship *Endeavor* for the first time in full makeup and uniforms. There were no lines to learn, no complicated shots to set up. All they had to do was stand together for a couple of quick publicity photos for the fall preview edition of *TV Guide*.

Alison knew it should be easy. Alison also knew it wouldn't be. Nothing concerned an actor more than their PR, so the photo session would be a sneak preview of tantrums and fights to come all season long.

And they'd all come complaining to her, and she'd try to solve their problems before they went crying to their agents, managers, lawyers, publicists, shrinks, psychics, nutritionists, astrologers, stylists, herbalists, aromatherapists, colorists, meteorologists, colonic irrigators, and significant others of whatever sex or species they might be.

Chad Shaw just came off a single-lead action show. Alison figured the new Captain Pierce wasn't going to share the camera, or anything else, with anyone. Leigh Dickson was a recent grad of the Royal Shakespeare Company who flaunted his British accent and felt superior to everyone in the room, even if he was the only person wearing an elephant nose. And Spring Dano, totally obsessed with her body, was a natural for Dr. Kelvin, even if her qualifications for the role weren't.

This ensemble promised to be living hell. And that was just the forecast for today.

Chad stood in the center of the bridge, flanked by his costars. The photographer had taken only one shot when the trouble started.

"This isn't working." Chad glared at Leigh. "His nose is casting a shadow on my face."

Alison's irritation was briefly deflected by a feeling of pride that her assessment of the situation was right on the mark.

"And this is not the best angle for my boobs," Spring whined, adjusting her breasts in her low-cut uniform, the heavy, electronic ports on her chest drawing the neckline even lower. "They'd look much better if I was standing on Chad's right."

The cast's behavior, although annoying, did reaffirm for Alison that she was indeed a professional, that she really understood her business, and that she was damn good at it.

"Your breasts look delightful from any vantage point, darling," Leigh said condescendingly. "But I really must stay here because, as I've learned from my years on the stage, this is my good side."

"It won't be anymore if you don't do something about your fucking nose," Chad said.

Leigh swung around sharply to face Chad, inadvertently slapping himself in the cheek with his floppy nose. "You'd appreciate the emotive advantages of a physical prop for an actor if you had any formal training. Obviously, you've never played Cyrano de Bergerac on the West End, as I have."

"No," Chad replied, "I was busy pulling thirty-seven grand an episode on my own TV series, dick nose."

Now Alison was irritated. She clapped her hands together and spoke up in her most upbeat, nonconfrontational voice. "I have an idea. Let's take a break and do some individual shots while we rethink the group picture. Why don't we start with Chad in the captain's chair."

Chad immediately settled into the chair and struck a heroic pose, his anger forgotten now that he was the center of attention once again, the photographer moving around the chair, snapping pictures.

Leigh went back to his canvas director's chair, making a big show out of taking a dog-eared copy of *Ulysses* out of his script pouch and pretending to read it.

Alison found Spring at the craft services table, her paper plate overflowing with cheddar cheese, M&Ms, pretzels, and guacamole.

Spring caught Alison staring at her plate. "You're asking yourself how I keep this to-die-for body if I eat like this. I'm not anorexic, if that's what you're worried about, though I used to be."

"Really? I had no idea." Alison didn't have to. Anorexia was such a popular disorder it was nearly a requirement. Most actresses put it on their résumé under "related skills" just to be safe.

"Usually I eat only yogurt and tofu, but I'm having my period," Spring explained. "You know how that is."

No, Alison thought, *I left my uterus in the car today.* She quickly changed the subject. "This photo session is so exciting for me. Seeing you together on the bridge, you can

108

just feel the chemistry. I think you're all going to bring a thrilling, new energy to the show."

Spring smiled, obviously flattered. "It's my new look." She set down her plate and puffed up her chest. "These are new."

To Alison, it looked like someone had surgically implanted a couple of basketballs in her chest. "They look natural to me."

"They're my third set," Spring said. "I was born with A cups, like yours, but they didn't stand out and say *woman* to me."

Or NBA. The thought kept Alison smiling.

"I tried some large Bs. They worked for me on *The Cheerleader Gang* for three seasons. But I knew if I kept them I'd be typecast as a teenager. I had to grow up. I needed adult breasts. So this summer I went back to my surgeon and traded up to C cups."

Alison searched her brain for something positive to say. "And you became the perfect combination of talent and beauty we needed to bring Dr. Kelvin into the nineties."

"I grew up watching the show." Spring tossed a couple M&Ms into her mouth. "A generation of women were empowered by Dr. Kelvin. She was one of the first true feminist characters on television."

Certainly the first with computer breasts, Alison thought, then realized, from the quizzical look on Spring's face, that she'd actually *said* what she was thinking.

"It was a wonderful, ironic statement against the sexual objectification of woman," Alison covered quickly, then hurried away before she could embarrass herself any further.

Leigh Dickson was peering over the top of his book

at Spring, thinking how much he looked forward to downloading from her computers, when Alison came up to him.

"I hope you don't take Chad's comments personally," Alison said. "He's under a lot of pressure."

"It's good for the show. We can play that tension in our performance," Leigh said. "I like to incorporate my personal reality into the broader, theatrical experience. It's something I learned doing *Equus.* I get along well with horses and most other farm animals, and I think that came across."

"That's great." Alison's suddenly felt as if the walls of the soundstage were closing in on her. "Excuse me."

She bolted for the door, feeling a desperate need for air, not that it was any fresher outside. Even so, once outdoors, she took deep, satisfying breaths of smog. Even the pollution she was drawing into her lungs was a relief from being around those actors. Another few minutes out here, collecting herself, and she could go back in, restage the group shot, and move on to the next crisis.

Alison was chewing nervously on her ponytail when she happened to glance at the studio gate and saw the fat woman with the elephant nose and the "I ❤ Snork" T-shirt peering through the bars, her eyes burning with hatred. A tour bus rolled past Alison, blocking her view of the gate for a moment, tourists snapping pictures of her in case she was someone famous. When the bus passed, the elephant woman was gone, and Alison seriously wondered if she was ever there at all.

After three screwdrivers, six bags of peanuts, and forty excruciating minutes of *Waiting to Exhale,* Charlie finally had the nerve to call Alison from the airplane using the "airfone" in the seat back in front of him.

His trip to Hawaii had been a disaster, and the bad publicity would no doubt embarrass Alison, maybe even cost her job. He wouldn't blame her if she fired him. In fact, he was expecting it.

Canoga Stor-All, here I come.

She picked up on the first ring.

"It's me," Charlie said, struck by what a stupid, obvious thing that was to say, yet that's how everyone everywhere who knew each other well introduced themselves over the phone.

"The connection is terrible," she said, sitting in her office at Pinnacle. "Are you on location?"

"I'm on a Delta jet, two hours outside of L.A."

"That was quick. You must be a pretty smooth talker to make Nick Alamogordo feel safe enough to let you go in just one day."

He sat up in his seat. "Haven't you heard about Javier Grillo?"

"Who's he?"

That explained why she was being so pleasant. She didn't know. This was even worse. Now he'd have to tell her, endure her shock and fury, and *then* get fired.

"He was the guy doing the production rewrite on *Cop a Feel*, at least until a Company agent broke his hands with a hammer."

"What?"

"You haven't heard the worst of it. The agent is dead."

Charlie told her what happened and that he was certain it was all part of a deal Clive Odett struck with Nick Alamogordo.

But Charlie, being a loyal studio employee, didn't implicate Nick Alamogordo in his statement to the police or tell them about the contract he swiped.

What he didn't tell Alison was if he had had the ev-

III

idence to back up his theory, he would have told the police, regardless of who signed his paycheck. Not that he would be getting any more of those after this conversation.

There was a long silence on the phone. For a moment, Charlie thought he'd lost the connection, then realized Alison must be searching for the right words to fire him. He decided to save her the trouble.

"If you want my resignation, I can have it on your desk in the morning."

"Why would I want that?" Alison was surprised that her heart was racing, that the idea of losing Charlie Willis frightened her.

"Because my job is to protect your people and keep negative publicity out of the papers. I failed on both counts."

Alison covered the mouthpiece and took a deep breath. They'd never had anything but a strictly professional relationship. What did she care if he left? She'd just hire another "troubleshooter" and be done with it.

But she knew that wasn't true. At some point, and maybe it was right now, it became important to her not to lose him.

"You had no way of knowing this was going to happen. On the contrary, we should be giving you a bonus. You could have been killed. Besides, we need you."

And so do I, she thought, then realized she'd actually said aloud what she was thinking. Again. If this continued, she'd have to stop thinking altogether.

"Because we have another problem, and I don't think I can find anyone else on such short notice." She spoke in a rush, before he could give her slip of the tongue too much thought.

"What's up?" Charlie asked.

"Someone broke into Kimberly Woodrell's house and urinated on the walls."

It clearly wasn't a random act of vandalism. This was personal. Charlie couldn't help wondering if The Company was involved in this, too, perhaps trying to intimidate some concessions of some kind from the new network.

"Do the police have any leads?"

"They weren't called. We want to keep this quiet, and so does she. She's asked for round-the-clock protection, and you're it."

If Clive Odett wanted The Big Network, he'd have to go through Charlie Willis to do it. "I'll go straight there from the airport."

After they said their good-byes, Alison stared at the phone. What she told Charlie was true, that she was afraid to lose him because there was no one else she could trust to protect Kimberly Woodrell.

Yeah, that was it. There wasn't anything more to it than that.

But she chewed on her ponytail and replayed the conversation in her mind for another hour anyway.

Nine

*E*ddie Planet was tooling across the Pinnacle Studios lot in his golf cart, in a hurry to go nowhere.

Ever since Jackson Burley made it clear his production deal wasn't going to be renewed, Eddie spent his days cruising around the lot, trying to look very busy, hoping to run into someone he could pitch, schmooze, or suck up to.

So far that day, he'd chatted up Deborah Harkin, the cute, perky producer of *Horse Sense*, a dramatic updating of *Mr. Ed* for DBC (a talking horse, with Patrick Stewart's voice, and a defrocked nun, played by Lindsay Wagner, wander rural America, helping people with their problems). It was Harkin's first show-running job, and he warned her if she screwed up, her career in the biz was finito.

What she needed was an "executive consultant," someone with Eddie's experience to make sure she didn't blow her big chance. Turned out she already had one. Schyler Dart ran into her in the commissary a couple weeks back, right after his series *.357 Vigilante* got shit-canned on DBC. The parasite.

Eddie was on his fourth go-round of the studio that morning, when he nearly collided with superagent Clive Odett's Hummer, a huge military vehicle designed for charging up 60 percent grades, plowing through rivers, three-foot snowdrifts, and scores of enemy bodies.

Odett parked his Hummer outside Chad Shaw's trailer, nearly crushing Shaw's Porsche under its massive wheels.

Eddie pulled up beside it and saw that Odett, from the comfort of his plush leather seat, was watching CNN and *Oprah* on the two in-dash video screens while taking a meeting on his scrambled digital cellular phone system. Eddie wondered how many cars Odett had plowed over on his way to the studio. With an agent like that, Eddie could pick and choose his next gig. He'd lucked into the ultimate drive-by schmooze.

Eddie was standing outside the Hummer, offering a handshake, when Odett finished his call, switched off his TVs, and climbed down from the vehicle.

"I don't have time for a detailing today." Odett peeled a couple bills from his thick money clip and palmed them into Eddie's outstretched hand. "But keep an eye on it for me, I don't want it dinged."

Eddie was about to inform him that he wasn't the studio car-wash guy but realized there was fifty bucks in his hand. "You got it," he replied and shoved the cash into his pocket.

He watched Odett knock on the door of Shaw's trailer. Shaw opened the door in his Confederation uniform and beckoned Odett inside.

Since when was Chad Shaw so important that Clive Odett came *to him*? *Teen PI* was a hit, but it probably didn't even register on Odett's radar, and that was a couple seasons back. So it had to be *Beyond the Beyond*, and since the show wasn't even on the air yet, the superagent must think it had some real potential.

And Eddie Planet wanted a bigger piece of it than just Conrad Stipe's trash.

If Guy Goddard was going to do something, Eddie wished he'd do it quick.

Chad Shaw's trailer was a standard-issue Winnebago that had been gutted and redecorated by Ralph Lauren. There was even a moose head mounted on the wall.

It spoke volumes about Shaw's status in the industry and his lackluster representation at Glueck, Schleffle, and Hobbs. If he was represented by Clive Odett and The Company, Philippe Stark would have been flown in from Paris at the studio's expense to personally oversee a postmodern overhaul of the motor home.

Odett sat on the leather couch and faced Chad, who leaned against a totem pole, sipping a mineral water.

"I've taken an interest in your career," Odett said, bestowing upon Chad an honor all actors coveted and few received. "I think you're ready to make the jump to superstardom."

"No thanks to you," Chad said.

That was not the reaction Odett was expecting. Nor was it one he would accept.

"Although I run The Company, I represent only a chosen few personally," Odett said. "Arnold. Meryl. Clint. Sly. Sharon. Marty. I rarely take on someone new, but I'm making an exception for you. I see in you a tremendous talent that I can mold into superstardom."

"Pardon me if I don't genuflect," Chad sneered, "but I just had the uniform pressed."

It was a good thing they weren't having this meeting in Odett's office, or Chad would be sneering with a ginsu knife in his chest.

"I've *always* had tremendous talent, Clive," Chad said, "but when I came to The Company looking for representation six years ago, no one saw it. Christine Foster at Gleuck, Schleffle, and Hobbs did. She devoted herself to my career, she even paid my rent when I couldn't find a job. Now you want me to toss her so you can have ten percent of a career I wouldn't have without her."

Odett thought about grabbing a set of spurs off the wall and raking them over Chad's smug face.

"Your loyalty is admirable, and I respect that," Odett lied. "But at a certain point you have to start thinking about your future. I can get you in an A-list picture with Brad Pitt and Mira Sorvino for the series hiatus right *now.*"

Odett snapped his fingers for emphasis. "Can Christine Foster do that?"

"This second? Probably not. But after *Beyond the Beyond* hits, even a chimp could get me an A-list movie during the hiatus. I don't need you any more now than you needed me six years ago."

"Let me put it a different way." Odett stood up and took a step toward Chad. "I can make someone a superstar overnight. I can destroy a career with a phone call."

Chad held a quarter out to Odett. "Be my guest."

Odett left without taking the quarter. Chad would need it for his medical bills.

All the windows in Kimberly Woodrell's house were open that night, the cool ocean air blowing the smell of wet paint out of the house and onto the street, where Charlie Willis stood on the curb, having just been dropped off by the studio limo.

The scent of polluted ocean spray, mixed with the exhaust of a hundred cars on Pacific Coast Highway and paint fumes from the house, made Charlie long for the comparative freshness of the recirculated air in the plane.

Even so, he hefted his suitcase and trudged up to Kim's front door, which doubled as some blowtorched work of art, a thick metal sculpture with a dead bolt and a handle. He was looking for a place to knock that wouldn't slash his knuckles when Kim opened the door wearing only an untucked oversized man's shirt and cut-offs.

Her shirt was open just enough for Charlie's eyes to fall into the deep crevasse between her breasts. While his eyeballs were climbing out of her shirt, her gaze was on his suitcase.

"I hope you're the security guy," Kim said, "because if you're not, you're awfully presumptuous."

"I'm Charlie Willis, Ms. Woodrell. I apologize for how I look. I just got off a plane."

She stepped aside to let him in. "You're the first man who's ever come into my house with a change of clothes. Usually I have them out of here by sunrise. This will take some getting used to."

He followed her in, and when he saw the stark white walls and chrome furniture, he half expected to hear the theme from *2001* and a greeting from HAL: *Welcome aboard, Charlie, but please refrain from looking down Kim's shirt.*

"Urine is impossible to clean off," she said. "So I had a crew come in and entirely repaint the place."

"What did you do with all your artwork?" Charlie

asked. There was enough wall space to hang half the Getty collection.

"It's all in here." She led him into the stainless-steel kitchen and pointed to the door of the Sub-Zero refrigerator. There was a *Valet Girls* calendar stuck to the door with a plastic hotdog magnet.

"There it is," she said.

"I get the impression you're not a lady who likes to be tied down."

"Depends. You got any handcuffs on you?"

First the clothes, or lack thereof, then the come-on. Maybe it was the jet lag, or the paint fumes, but Charlie felt like he missed a step somewhere. He decided to press on.

"Do you have any enemies, Ms. Woodrell?"

"Of course I do. When you cancel a show, you're also canceling careers, marriages, and mortgages," she said. "I've canceled a lot of shows."

"Old boyfriends, maybe? Disgruntled help?"

"My old boyfriends *are* the disgruntled help. But that's not who did this."

"Who did?"

"I think it was Don DeBono."

Charlie knew DeBono from his thirteen weeks as the star of *My Gun Has Bullets* and found him to be pretty direct in his dealings. DeBono certainly didn't mince words when he fired Charlie and canceled his show. Of course, Charlie had just accidentally killed his guest star with a prop gun that somebody loaded with *real* bullets.

"I have a hard time seeing the president of UBC breaking into your house and pissing his day away."

"Cute." She smiled at Charlie and took a step toward him. "Can you see him squeezing my breasts, Charlie?"

She started fondling her own breasts as she walked up to him. Charlie wanted to take a step back but over-ruled his instincts and didn't move.

"Can you see him bending me over my desk and fucking me up the ass?"

No, but he could see what was happening here, what began the moment she opened the front door.

"Are you going to demonstrate that too?" Charlie asked. "Because if you are, Ms. Woodrell, I think I'd appreciate it more if I was sitting down."

She was a power freak, someone who had to be in charge on every level. By asking Charlie for protection, she was exposing her vulnerability, which probably made her need to establish her power even more. If he let her intimidate him now, she'd wipe her butt with him every day this job lasted.

"Use your imagination." She let go of her breasts but remained well within Charlie's personal space, almost close enough to feel the erection he wished he didn't have.

"Were you willing or unwilling?" he asked.

She met his gaze. "I liked it, for a while. But our relationship wasn't just the office quickies. I was his protégée. He was Henry Higgins and I was Eliza Doolittle."

Now Charlie was stuck trying to shake the image of Audrey Hepburn draped over a table, Rex Harrison giving it to her from behind, while both of them gleefully sang "The Rain in Spain."

"He taught me everything he knew about network television and I . . ." She let her voice trail off. "Let's just say I was there for him. But he became obsessed with me, and I had nothing more to learn. When Milo Kinoy offered me The Big Network, I was ready to leave."

"So now you're going to use everything you learned from Don DeBono against him."

"*Now* can you see why he would do this?" She walked past him into the living room.

Charlie followed her, still holding his suitcase, only now it was strategically placed in front of his groin.

She was facing the window, watching the waves crash against the shore, washing up the Santa Monica Bay's rich bounty of used syringes, motor oil, and Styrofoam.

"What about Clive Odett?" Charlie asked. "What does he have against you?"

She started to laugh. "That I made him too rich. *Valet Girls* is a Company package. He gets a cut of everything from that show, even the merchandising. Maybe he's upset I got the calendar for free and gypped him out of his dime."

Kim turned to Charlie. "The opportunity to run my own network is very important to me, Charlie. It's the culmination of everything I've worked for. Someone wants to take it away from me."

For a moment, Charlie saw something approaching fear in her eyes, even neediness, but then it quickly disappeared, replaced by cold resolve.

"I expect you to make sure that doesn't happen," she said.

"I will," Charlie said. "From now on, if someone wants to hurt you, he will have to hurt me first."

Kim looked at him and knew he meant it. No man had ever said anything like that to her before, and if any of them had, they certainly would have been lying.

"Would you mind showing me to my room?" Charlie asked. "I'm so tired I can barely stand. I've had a killer day."

She led him to a room just off the kitchen, with its own door to the beach. It was no doubt designed to be a maid's quarters. The room was as stark as the rest of the house, with only a bed, a nightstand, and a reading light that resembled a dental drill.

"I'm just upstairs if you need me," she said.

"I think it works the other way around."

"We'll see." She smiled and walked out, leaving Charlie to his dreams.

Ten

*A*t five-thirty in the morning, Charlie awoke to voices in the kitchen. He pulled on sweats and a T-shirt and went to check it out.

Kim was leaning against the counter, munching on a croissant with one hand and talking on the cordless phone with the other, her loosely sashed bathrobe revealing that she wore only panties underneath. She acknowledged him with a smile and a slight nod and kept talking on the phone.

"I don't care what contracts we have, Phil. You made those deals before I got here. We're not going to build a network on UHF stations. Go back to every one of those cities and get me a two through thirteen or I will find someone who can."

Charlie went to the refrigerator, mainly to turn his back to her and give her a chance to close her robe. He found a carton of orange juice.

She hung up the phone but seemed unconcerned about her nakedness. If she wasn't, Charlie wasn't going to be.

"You get an early start, Ms. Woodrell."

"If I didn't, New York would be three hours ahead of me. I don't like anyone to be ahead of me."

Kim let her eyes roam over Charlie, who felt stupid just standing there in his rumpled sweats and T-shirt, holding an orange juice carton. But she didn't seem to mind.

"You're the first man who's ever spent the night," she said. "I think that earns you the right to call me Kim."

"Where can I find a glass, Kim?"

She tilted her head toward the cabinet directly behind her, but she made no effort to move or to get the glass for him.

"Or you can just drink out of the carton like I do."

Charlie popped open the carton and drank from it. He decided to start the day the easy way.

He insisted on driving her to the studio himself, keeping a close eye on the rearview mirror, but he didn't see anyone tailing them.

Kim spent the entire drive on the cell phone and somehow managed to talk to thirty-five people in the forty-five minutes it took to get to the studio. Her conversations were short, but he admired their efficiency. She got right to the point and made it clearly. This was a woman who knew exactly what she wanted out of every person she dealt with and didn't waste time with any unproductive conversation.

It made Charlie rethink everything that was said between them since they met. He came away with the same conclusion he made last night. She needed him but didn't want to appear weak and was desperate to assert control over the situation.

Once on the lot, he walked her to her office in the Pinnacle Tower and made her promise to beep him if she intended to leave the studio. She agreed and marched into her office, closing the door behind her.

Now that Charlie was stuck at the studio for the day, he realized he had nowhere to go, not even an office to call his own. The closest thing he had to an office was Alison's, so he headed there.

When he got there, her door was open but she wasn't around. He decided to hang out there anyway. Besides, her office practically invited him inside.

Alison made a point of rarely closing her door, and she always had a couple of jars of candy on her paper-cluttered desk and her coffee table. She never touched the sweets herself—they were lures.

You'd be surprised, she once told him, how many executives will pop in as they are passing by just to get a handful of jelly beans or steal a mint. Inevitably, they would sit down and chat for a few minutes, so it wouldn't look like they were there just to steal candy, and she'd get to know them. It was an easy way to develop relationships with executives who, ordinarily, wouldn't have much interaction with her.

But that was the only premeditated aspect of her office decor. Otherwise, it seemed an extension of her own warm personality. The shelves were overstuffed with props and mementos from the TV shows and movies she'd worked on. A collection of baseball caps from various productions hung on pegs on the back of the door. And her walls were cluttered with photographs of her laughing and smiling with family and friends, not one of them a famous celebrity.

He asked her once how she got in the business. She told him she was born into it. Alison was raised by her mom, who worked as a unit publicist on movie sets. So that meant Alison spent most of her childhood on the road, spending two or three months at a time on location, being tutored on the set along with movie star brats while her mom hyped lousy movies and covered up scandals. Alison figured what she was doing now was sort of the family business.

Alison barreled into the office and slammed the door behind her.

"Goddamn son of a bitch asshole shitbag!" she yelled, surprising Charlie, who had never seen her be anything but perky and enthusiastic.

"I guess I should have waited outside," Charlie said quietly.

Alison jerked, startled, noticing Charlie for the first time. She was mortified. "Oh my God, Charlie, I didn't see you there. Forgive me."

"It's *your* office. I'm the one who should be apologizing."

"I've had a horrible morning, and it's not even ten A.M. yet."

"What happened?"

She went to the window and pointed down at a soundstage. "You see the Cadillac down there?"

Charlie glanced down and saw a red Coupe De Ville. "Nice car."

"It says in Toby Lober's contract that he gets a new Cadillac every season. There's a whole list of options he's got to have on the car. It was my job to pick up his car at Casa de Cadillac and bring it to him at the studio."

Toby Lober was once a movie star, but after a decade of movies that were DOA at the box office, he took refuge in TV as the $100,000-an-episode star of *Space Case*, about an interstellar private eye. Charlie met him on his last picture, *Borderline Psycho*, in which Lober portrayed a Border Patrol officer pursuing a serial killer along the California-Mexico border.

"So he comes out of his trailer to see the car and stops, this horrified look on his face. I ask, 'What's the matter?' He says 'It's blue.' I go, 'Is that a problem, Mr. Lober?' He says, 'It certainly is. My psychic colorist told me blue is bad color for me this year. I can't have a blue car. I can't have blue in my life at all. Take it away.'"

"It's not the first time you've had to deal with crazy actors."

"Wait, it gets better. I couldn't return the car, because it was a special order, it had all those options he wanted. So I took it to a body shop and had it painted red. I brought the car back to him this morning and he says, 'What did you do?' I tell him I had it painted. He says, 'I can't take this car.' I ask him, 'Why not?' And he says, 'Because it's *still* a blue car underneath, you stupid bitch.'"

She stared out the window, angry all over again. Charlie started to laugh.

She glared at him and snapped, "What?"

Which only made him laugh more.

"I don't see what's so funny," she said but was smiling despite herself. "Charlie!"

But it was too late. She couldn't hold on to her anger in the face of Charlie's hearty laughter. She started laughing, too, and once she started, she couldn't stop.

Charlie took her in a big, warm hug, and she rested her cheek against his broad chest, soothed by his laughter and his strong embrace.

"Are we the only sane people in this business?" Alison asked, when she could finally catch her breath.

"I'm afraid so," he replied, his laughter ebbing, gently stroking her hair. "You can't let them get to you, Alison, or one day you'll quit and I'll be out here all alone."

Alison closed her eyes and pressed her hands against his strong back. She felt as long as he was here, nothing would ever bother her again.

Charlie was looking out the window and was just becoming aware of how nice, how comfortable, it felt having Alison in his arms, when he saw a black Hummer come through the front gate.

Conrad Stipe had dreamed of this moment hundreds of times over the last twenty years. Just six months ago he couldn't get a meeting with a custodian at The Company, much less the superagent himself. Now he had an office at a studio, and Clive Odett was sitting on the other side of his desk, practically begging to represent him.

Stipe adjusted his girdle, leaned back in his chair, and made a show of glancing at his diamond-studded Schaffhausen da Vinci Perpetual Calendar Chronograph. "Make it quick, Clive. I'm a very busy man."

"I think, with the considerable resources of The Company behind you, we can take your career to the next level."

Finally, after twenty-five years, he was getting the success and recognition that he deserved, that were *owed* to him. Clive Odett coming down to see him confirmed that he was a major industry player once again.

"That's real nice, Clive. But I got agents falling all over themselves to sign me. What can you do for me the others can't?"

Clive Odett knew there were no others. Once the series was a success, he was going to force Stipe out and put one of his younger, more talented, clients into place. Stipe could stay on as an executive consultant. Or die.

"I think a multiple-series deal and a feature film commitment are well within reach," Odett said. "If I'm doing the reaching."

Stipe wanted to sign that instant, but major players in the industry aren't desperate. They make *other* people desperate.

"I'll consider it, Clive." Stipe stifled a smile. It was fun watching Odett squirm. He had the power, and he was going to use it.

Odett casually took a folded paper out from inside his jacket and laid it gently on the desk. "This is a one-time offer that expires in ninety seconds."

Stipe sat still for a moment, shocked. Just like that, his power was taken from him. If he signed that paper, Odett was in control, and Stipe was forever a notch below him. He was tempted not to sign, just to show Odett who was boss. But Stipe knew who was boss.

He snatched the paper before Odett could change his mind and signed it. Odett smiled thinly and tucked the paper into his jacket pocket.

"You've made the right decision." With eighty-nine seconds to spare, by Odett's calculations. "Now that we've got that out of the way, let's talk about the show."

"It's going to be the biggest hit of the season," Stipe said.

"Not with Chad Shaw," Odett replied. "Consider Dustin Woods instead."

Stipe was wondering if maybe he was too hasty signing with Odett. How could Odett be a superagent and recommend Dustin Woods over the hot star of a sensational hit series? Woods's only series role was as the angst-ridden boyfriend of the angst-ridden girl in the short-lived drama *Miserable Me.*

"Chad Shaw is the wet dream of every woman under thirty in America," Stipe said. "And we've got him on a five-year contract."

"He's also a very unlucky young man. He's prone to all kinds of disfiguring accidents." Odett stood up and shook Stipe's hand. "My advice, think about Dustin."

"Maybe we could have lunch at the club sometime." Stipe didn't belong to a club, but he figured Odett did. "If I can get away."

"Getting away is impossible now, Conrad." Odett smiled and walked out.

Something about the way he said that made Conrad Stipe, a major player in the industry, wish for one insane moment that it all really was a dream.

Odett emerged from Stipe's bungalow and was shocked to discover that his Hummer was gone. He hadn't bothered to set his alarm because nobody on the Pinnacle Studios lot would dare *touch* his car. That his Hummer was gone was unthinkable.

"You shouldn't have parked in Barry Van Dyke's spot," somebody said.

The superagent turned and saw Charlie Willis leaning against the bungalow.

"He's very sensitive about that," Charlie said. "And believe me, you wouldn't want to get on his bad side."

"You had my car towed?" Odett asked in disbelief.

"It wasn't easy. I had to get a special truck and everything. But we have rules around here, and the spot is clearly marked." Charlie pointed to a sign mounted on the wall of the bungalow: VISITOR PARKING IS ACROSS THE LOT.

"Do you know who I am?" Odett hissed.

"Oh, yeah." Charlie got up and ambled over to Odett. "You're the greedy, power-mad asshole who tried to blackmail Spike Donovan and had Javier Grillo's fingers smashed. And I'm the guy who's going to stop you."

So this was Charlie Willis. Hard to believe that this mouth-breather in off-the-rack clothes could have been such a nuisance.

"I wondered when I would meet you." Odett smiled. "How's your sore throat?"

"I feel fine, which is more than I can say for your man in Hawaii."

"Everyone has a lucky day, Charlie," Odett said, knowing full well that Charlie wouldn't be having any more of them. "You should quit while you're ahead."

"I won't quit until you're in jail."

"The only power you have in this town is to get cars towed off the lot. Now that you've done it, you've already shot your load. You have no surprises left."

Charlie nodded, started to turn, then whirled back around, hammering Odett with a right hook that knocked the superagent off his feet. It didn't change a thing, but it sure felt good.

"Surprise." Charlie winked and walked away.

Eleven

*T*he first thing Chad Shaw did with his first million dollars was buy a condo in the tallest building on the Wilshire corridor.

As a struggling actor, he used to park on Mulholland at night, stare down at the glittering lights of the city, and promise himself that some day that would be his view, high above everyone else. Now his dream had come true.

He was in the enviable position of having to come up with some new dreams. He decided to head up to Mulholland that night to work on them.

When Chad Shaw emerged from the elevator into the underground parking garage, all he had on his mind was getting into his beautiful new Porsche and breaking a few speed limits.

He had no idea that Melvah Blenis was hiding behind the Allante to his left, a baseball bat in her hand.

And Melvah Blenis had no idea that Zita was

crouched behind the Suburban to his right, ready to wield her ginsu knife.

Melvah swung her bat as Chad passed, striking him behind the knees. He dropped with a surprised, agonized shriek, and she clubbed him over the head. That's when Melvah looked up and found herself facing Zita across Chad's twitching body. Zita wore a black leather outfit and a curious expression on her face. She also held a knife.

Melvah had never seen a more beautiful woman in her life. She didn't want to kill her. There was a tense silence, broken only by Chad's whimpering. She wasn't quite sure what to say.

"Does this bother you?" Melvah asked.

Zita regarded the scene in front of her and, within a moment, saw it for the incredible opportunity that it was. She leaned over Chad, lifted his head up by the hair, and slit his throat. "Not particularly."

She released his dead head, letting it thunk against the cement.

Melvah sighed with relief. It was so nice to be dealing with a reasonable woman. She rested the bat on her shoulder and relaxed against the Allante. "Was this something personal?"

Zita slipped the knife into the sheath on her belt and closed her jacket over it. "Strictly business."

The woman's accent was strange, vaguely European, not unlike the slave princess of Naren-3. Melvah nodded. "Me, too."

Zita admired the rings in Melvah's nose, lip, and ears and the self-assured way she carried her bat. This was the first time since she got into this business that she'd met a woman with similar interests.

"Can I buy you a latte?" Zita asked, her bizarre accent giving way to a true Texas twang.

"Sure," Melvah said. "I'd like that."

Zita bent down, took Chad's wallet from his back pocket, and pulled out a couple hundred bucks in stiff, fresh twenties. "Chad's treat."

"I could get to like having a driver," Kim said, following Charlie into her kitchen. "Gives me an extra half hour or so to think."

"Did you think of anyone else who might have broken in the other night?"

She gave him a look. "I have a few other things on my mind."

"I don't." Charlie walked past her and checked out the living room.

"You're not running a television network." She followed him out.

"Tell you what. I'll think about the network for a while if you think about who could be trying to intimidate you."

Charlie went up the stairs and stuck his head into each room. She stayed in the living room, watching him search the house.

"Okay, where do you think I should schedule *Beyond the Beyond,* keeping in mind that the entire network is riding on its success?"

"What makes *Beyond the Beyond* so important?" He stood on the landing that stretched across the entry hall.

"It's the draw, Charlie. It's what's going to get all those eighteen- to thirty-five-year-olds to sample us. They'll switch from their favorite series on UBC because Captain Pierce, Mr. Snork, and Dr. Kelvin were in their homes every day when they were growing up. They *want* to see them again. We will have a massive tune-in that first night. During that hour, we'll hit them with a barrage of promos for our other shows and hope they stick around to watch them. Once they do, we have them hooked."

Satisfied that everything was okay, Charlie came down the spiral staircase. "And if you didn't have *Beyond the Beyond*?"

"It might take us months to get the same sampling, if ever."

"Then it doesn't matter what night you schedule it. Flip a coin."

"Now you know why I'm the president of The Big Network and you are a . . ." She paused, looking at him. "What *are* you, Charlie?"

"The help."

Kim smiled. "How would the help like a glass of wine?"

"I'd feel a lot less disgruntled."

She went into the kitchen to get the wine. Charlie settled into one of the chrome seats. It was even more uncomfortable than it looked. This wasn't a house, it was a movie set. It was made to be looked at, not lived in.

Kim screamed, a deep, shrieking wail of terror so primal, so instinctive, there wasn't a creature on earth that could mistake its meaning.

Charlie bolted out of his seat and ran into the kitchen. Kim staggered back from the open refrigerator and into his arms.

He held her tight and looked in the refrigerator. The shelves were crammed with dismembered arms and legs, severed ears, and plucked-out eyeballs.

His first reaction was revulsion, but instead of looking away, he couldn't take his eyes off of the grotesque sight.

Something wasn't right about it. Not a drop of blood, no jagged strips of flesh. It was too clean.

He took a step closer and saw the refrigerator light re-flecting off the shiny plastic surfaces of the severed limbs.

Mannequins.

"It's okay," Charlie said. "They aren't real."

She was shaking. He stroked her hair and rocked her gently, her face nuzzled against his chest, soothing her while he thought about the mystery intruder.

First the guy pees all over the house. What does that say?

I own you and I can get you.

Then the guy fills the fridge with fake body parts. Put the two incidents together, and it gets more ominous.

I own you, and I'll chop you into little pieces if you don't do what I want.

Now the question was, What was it the guy wanted? Kim knew, Charlie was certain of that, and she wasn't telling.

What she was doing instead was moving herself against him, her hands caressing his back.

"Protect me," she murmured.

"I will," he said, trying to ignore the quickening of his pulse, "but I can't if you aren't honest with me."

She let her hands drift down his back to his ass and grabbed hold, forcing him even closer. He felt himself begin to harden and knew she could feel it, too.

"Who is doing this to you, Kim?" Charlie put his hands on her waist and tried gently to push her away, even as he ached for more.

"You are." She lifted her face to his and kissed him, her tongue slipping between his lips, her pelvis grinding against him more deliberately now, making him need her, too.

Even as his hands slid up under her shirt, kneading the smooth skin of her back, he knew he couldn't let this happen, no matter how good it felt, no matter how many *months* it had been since he'd made love.

He broke away from her, breathing hard. "Kim, we have to talk."

"Later." She reached for his zipper, but he grabbed her wrist, stopping her.

Kim flashed a devilish grin. "Tell me you don't want me, Charlie, and I'll stop."

"I don't want you," said Charlie with as much conviction as he could muster, which wasn't much.

She wrenched her wrist free and backhanded him across the face. "You bastard."

And with that, she stormed out of the kitchen, leaving him with a hard-on and a refrigerator full of fake body parts.

"My daddy was a butcher. He ran the family slaughterhouse business in Texas. I spent my childhood knee-deep in cow guts," Zita said. "But he taught me to respect knives and a clean cut of meat."

Melvah leaned across the tiny Starbuck's table and lit Zita's cigarette with her miniature photon gun lighter, an authentic replica of the weapon the muck gerbils of Antaire Prime carried in their scrotums.

"But I knew the slaughterhouse was going to my brothers, and that I was expected to marry, do laundry, and have kids." She blew out a stream of smoke. "I wanted something more. I had two things going for me—good looks and butchery. So I decided the entertainment industry was my calling."

She went on to tell Melvah that she knew it wouldn't be easy breaking in. She started out working in a temp agency and soon learned that all the best jobs went to women with European accents. So she changed her name (from Etta Mae Pettigrew) and adopted an indecipherable accent, an improv mix of French and Italian. Overnight, she found herself temping at The Company.

She turned a temp job at The Company into a permanent position by catching Clive Odett's attention with her accent and her skintight clothes. She also found the woman she was subbing for and stabbed her to death. Through this kind of hard work and initiative, she became Clive Odett's personal assistant.

Melvah thought it was an inspirational story, something all women could learn from, and told her so.

"Ultimately, what I want," Zita said, snubbing out her cigarette, "is to run The Company. What do you want?"

Melvah studied her photon lighter. "No one understands *Beyond the Beyond* like I do. My life has been those characters, that universe. My fanfic has kept it all alive. I'm the only one qualified to tell their story. *All* the fans know that."

Zita reached out and wiped a tear from Melvah's cheek.

Melvah didn't even realize she was crying. She was laying herself open for this woman. Even though they'd known each other only a few hours, they had shared so much. She took Zita's hand and held it in her own.

"I'm sorry, it's just that *Beyond the Beyond* means so much to me." Melvah looked Zita in the eye. "It makes me sick to see what they're doing to it. They're greedy hacks, pretenders, frauds. They've never read the fanfic, they know *nothing* about how the universe has grown since the series ended."

"You want to produce, don't you?"

Melvah squeezed Zita's hand and nodded. "I'd like to see Guy Goddard back in the captain's chair, but the really important thing is to have the right person in command *behind* the camera. That person is me."

"I'll be honest with you, Melvah. I've never seen the show, but I respect what it means to you. And I know you could run it better than anyone else in the business, because you *care*."

Melvah stroked Zita's hand, lingering on her long fingers and sharp nails. "Maybe we can help each other get what we want."

Zita brought Melvah's hand to her lips and kissed it tenderly. "I'm sure we can."

Twelve

*C*onrad Stipe was very impressed with Clive Odett's pagoda, the little stream that ran through the office, and the lush foliage. It meant that Clive Odett made money, which meant that his clients made even *more* money.

Zita brought sake to Stipe and Odett, who stood in his kimono at the grill, wielding knives in both hands.

"We're so glad you're going to be part of The Company family," Odett said, knives spinning over sizzling meat, slicing and flipping succulent chunks onto their plates. "We believe strongly in you and the *Beyond the Beyond* franchise."

"I appreciate that, Clive. I've had my eye on you for a long time. I've watched you grow from a mere agent to an industry leader." Stipe pinched a chunk of meat between two chopsticks. "Like me, you've become a trendsetter. Your business acumen, paired with my vision and creativity, could reshape television for the twenty-first century."

Stipe popped the meat into his mouth. It tasted strange, flavorful but gamy at the same time.

"How do you like it?" Clive asked.

"Delicious. I've never tasted anything like it before," Stipe said. "What is it?"

"Chick," Clive replied, sharing a glance with Zita. She smiled thinly.

Stipe picked up another piece with his chopsticks and examined the moist morsel. He'd never seen brown chicken meat before. It was also the first time he heard it called chick. Obviously it was the cool new lingo. Fortunately, Stipe was a quick study when it came to being hip.

"You've given it an entirely original flavor." Stipe dipped the meat in a little soy sauce and ate it. "Put this chick on a pizza and you'll ruin Wolfgang Puck."

"I'm glad you like it." Odett speared a chunk of chick and bit it off the knife.

"You have to give me the recipe," Stipe enthused, stuffing more into his mouth.

"Certainly," Odett replied. "But first, I'd like to hear what's happening with *Beyond the Beyond.*"

"We're right on track." Stipe spoke between chews. Once he got used to the taste, it was hard to stop stuffing himself with chick. "The first draft of the pilot is done, and we start casting the guest roles and staffing up tomorrow."

"No need," Zita said.

"Huh?" Stipe would have said more, but his mouth was full.

Zita handed him a list of names. "These are your guest stars for the premiere."

"We like Carleton Eastlake for the alien." Odett took a sip of sake.

"I'm not a fan." Stipe wiped his greasy lips with a napkin.

"You are now," Odett said firmly.

Zita slipped another piece of paper in front of him. "This is your writing staff."

Stipe glanced at the names. "Melvah Blenis? I've never heard of her."

"She's a Company client," Zita said. "That's all you need to know."

Stipe pushed his plate aside. "I'll take notes from the network, I'll even entertain suggestions from the studio, but it will be a cold day in hell before I take orders from my agent."

Odett leaned close to Conrad and whispered, "Then you better buy a parka."

Stipe involuntarily shivered, then a voice deep inside him spoke up. *What's the matter with you? He's an agent. You're Conrad Stipe, creator of* Beyond the Beyond, *a major talent in this business. Crush him under your Florsheims.* He looked Odett in the eye.

"You work for me, don't you *ever* forget that." Stipe rose slowly from his seat and tossed his napkin on the lists. "Don't insult me again, or I'll take my business to CAA."

"Don't go without the recipe." Odett handed him a card.

Stipe glanced down it. He was holding a California driver's license. "I don't get it."

"It's the main ingredient," Odett said.

Stipe looked at it again. The license belonged to Chick Lansing. Realization hit him in the stomach.

Chick?

No, it couldn't be.

"Carleton Eastlake is your guest star, and Melvah

142

Blenis heads the writing staff," Odett whispered, "or to-morrow we're having you for lunch."

Odett picked up a chunk of chick in his fingers and tossed it in his mouth.

Zita smiled to herself. Odett had no idea who Melvah Blenis was and no idea that putting her on staff of *Beyond the Beyond* would close the deal that sealed Odett's fate.

Stipe's stomach started to convulse, but he wasn't sure whether it was revulsion or terror. Either way, he didn't want to puke in this cannibal's pagoda. Who knew what Odett would do?

He told himself the important thing was that this ruthless monster was on *his side*. Ultimately Odett wanted the show to succeed as much as Stipe did. If Stipe was smart, he'd do whatever Odett asked and be happy about it.

After all, Stipe figured he couldn't end up any worse off than he had been for the last twenty years. He gripped his stomach with one hand and reached for the list from Zita with the other.

"Melvah can start tomorrow," Stipe said, forcing a smile. "I'll get a script to Carleton as soon as it's locked."

Odett smiled. "Good to hear. Oh, think about Dustin Woods as Captain Pierce. I have a strong feeling Chad Shaw won't be coming through for you."

Stipe staggered out of the office. Odett looked after him, then offered Zita some meat.

"I'm so glad we worked that out," Odett said. "I would hate to have to eat someone who disagreed with me."

Usually, the thing with the arms and legs in the fridge got an immediate response. It didn't work as fast as, say, chopping up someone's cat or stapling the cockatoo to a wall. And although animals were often unreliable and messy, using them encouraged creativity. The time he tied a guy's pet snake in a knot and left it on his pillow was a particular favorite.

But Kim Woodrell didn't have any pets, so Doyle Klemm had to go with the mannequin bit. It was no problem, really, because Klemm kept his van stocked with mannequin limbs "just in case."

In his business, it paid to be prepared. He kept his van loaded with everything he needed to instill fear and, when necessary, severe bodily harm. The nice thing was, from an inventory point of view, that a lot of the items could be used for either purpose. Take his power drill. Klemm could use it to terrify, like screwing a dog to somebody's door, or he could use it for torture, like giving somebody an extra nostril.

Each job was unique, though he often used the same tried-and-true techniques. Pissing on the walls wasn't one of his favorites, because he liked to be tidy, and it meant staying in a stinking house for quite a while. But most people usually responded to that simple message right away. It was the real hard cases who needed more convincing.

Apparently, Kim Woodrell was one of them. So tonight the call came down to deliver the message on her body. Nothing fatal, though, because she was no good to Klemm's boss dead. Disfigured was okay.

He selected a gun-shaped cordless drill and a 13/64 high-speed steel bit, recommended by Black & Decker for metal, wood, and plastic, and recommended by Doyle Klemm for kneecaps, wrists, and skulls.

Klemm parked a couple of blocks from Woodrell's place and approached her house from the beach, where he was virtually invisible in the darkness in his black out-fit. Deactivating her alarm was no biggie, he used to be a SafeSec installer. SafeSec was a wonderful place to learn your trade and case homes at the same time.

He picked the lock on the door to the maid's quarters and slipped inside.

After Charlie Willis cleaned out the refrigerator of fake body parts, he asked himself how the intruder kept getting into the house and bypassing the alarm.

Charlie went outside to check the alarm box and wasn't surprised to see indentations where clips had been placed on the wires. He then studied the house for the intruder's likely entrance, the one best shielded from view from either the street or neighboring houses.

It was the door to his room.

So Charlie wasn't surprised when the door opened and a man crept in, holding a power drill. He let him get a few steps into the room, then punched him in the solar plexus, knocking the wind out of his lungs.

Charlie shoved him facedown on the floor, jammed a knee into his back, and wrapped a towel around his lower jaw, preventing Klemm from closing his mouth. He picked up the power drill with his free hand and put it against the back of his Klemm's head.

"Don't even think of biting that cyanide capsule," Charlie said.

"Hyandhide?" Klemm gurgled. It wasn't easy to talk with a towel in his mouth.

"The only way you're dying tonight is if I kill you. Now, you can either tell me what I want to know, or I'll go looking in your head for the answers myself."

Charlie squeezed the trigger of the drill, letting the bit spin in Klemm's hair, so the guy would get the point.

"Do we understand each other?" Charlie asked.

"Yeff," Klemm said.

"What does Clive Odett want from Kim?"

"Who ig Qwife Oehhh?"

Charlie squeezed the trigger and touched the point of the whirring bit to Klemm's scalp, drawing blood.

"I woof for woher hinglehein," Klemm spit out in a terrified rush, drool sloshing out of his mouth.

Charlie loosened his grip on the towel. "Dr. Himmelstein? The plastic surgeon?"

Klemm nodded, but it was more of a rhetorical question. Dr. Himmelstein was the most popular plastic surgeon in Beverly Hills, so sought after by celebrities that he accepted a wide range of payment, from cash to stock to securities and property, as well as flexible credit terms. There were several A-list actors who simply had him on commission, along with their agents, managers, and lawyers.

"Okay," Charlie said. "What does he want from Kim?"

"His two hundred and fifty thousand dollars," Klemm said.

"What did she have done that could possibly cost that much?"

"Everything, Charlie," said Kimberly Woodrell.

She stood in the doorway in her loosely tied bathrobe, tears rolling down her cheeks, her arms crossed under her surgically enhanced breasts, the bosom she dreamed of having all those years ago when she was a man.

Thirteen

*T*he bomb wired to Conrad Stipe's front door was strong enough to blow it, and most of Conrad Stipe, clear across the street—or something like that. Artie Saputo wasn't entirely sure. That was part of the thrill of working with explosives.

That morning, Artie broke into the ranch-style house "south of the boulevard" in Encino by tossing a brick through the sliding glass door. After eating all the sweets in the house and jerking off a couple times with Stipe's collection of *Big Hooters* magazines, he set to work on the bomb, using material he found in Stipe's house.

He could improvise like that because Artie was an inventive, can-do guy, with the tools and the know-how to create the right gadget for the job, just like the *Endeavor's* wily Chief Engineer Glerp. Of course, he had no formal training in engineering and explosives. He learned by trial and error. Mostly by error.

He leaned back to admire his work, the yellow pupil rolling around in his hollow Zorgog plastic eye. The explosive device was spread across the entire wall on either side of the door. It was a complex tangle of Christmas lights, Styrofoam cups, extension cords, lighter fluid, fertilizer, paint thinner, thumbtacks, model glue, and a propane tank. The finishing touch was a *Beyond the Beyond* wet 'n' stick decal. Not very sleek, but the device was state-of-the-art in the Confederation.

Artie reached for a pair of wire cutters from his plastic Chief Engineer Glerp action belt and made the final adjustments, ensuring the device would explode the instant Stipe came through the door, which, unfortunately, was at that exact moment.

Stipe and the door were blown to smithereens, just as Artie had predicted, along with the entire front wall of the house, which he hadn't. Artie found himself lying on the warm hood of Stipe's Acura, covered in debris and Stipe flesh. He was also missing his left ear, which wasn't so bad, since he was pretty sure they were still selling Security Chief Zorgog masks at Toys "Я" Us.

But it wasn't Conrad Stipe who opened the door. It wasn't even Conrad Stipe's house.

The house belonged to Dermot Elroy, thirty-seven, a rising star in the answering machine message voiceover field. And while bits of poor Dermot and his house were falling all over 190 South Ardwyn Street, Conrad Stipe was coming home to his apartment at 190 *North* Ardwyn in his '77 Eldorado.

The Sunset Vista Palms, where Stipe lived, was a half block of stucco and window air conditioners and laundry hung on tiny balconies to dry. The two sickly palm trees that gave the building its name were on either side of the only entrance and were pissing posts for every dog within a three-mile radius. Stipe had to leap a puddle of pee just to get in and out of his home.

But his days of crossing the piss moat would soon be over. A man of his stature in the industry belonged south of the boulevard, in a massive house with a front gate, stone lions, and a long flagstone driveway. A team of real estate agents were already scouring the valley for a suitable abode.

So when Stipe came in and heard the shower running, he wasn't concerned. He was relieved. It meant another one of Milo's double-D girls was waiting for him. She would be a welcome distraction from the gloom of his past life and an exhilarating reaffirmation of his newfound power.

Stipe strode into his bedroom. Steam from the running shower spilled out of the open bathroom door and gave the bedroom a humid, tropical heat. Behind the frosted glass of the shower, he could make out the top-heavy figure of a woman.

He turned off the lights and hurriedly undressed, peeling off his girdle and letting his stomach flop free. A man of his power and influence didn't have to bother with the niceties of romance and seduction anymore. It was straight to the main event.

Stipe kicked the girdle under a chair and sprawled on the bed, lying on his back and letting gravity flatten his stomach. What gravity didn't hide, the darkness would.

The woman emerged from the bathroom in a burst of steam, backlit by fluorescent light. Stipe had to admire the cinematic effect, even if it meant he couldn't see her face, not that it was really necessary anyway.

"It's been such a long, long time," the woman said in a sultry, husky voice. "But it was worth the wait."

Stipe liked the sound of that.

"We're going to be so good together." She came around to the foot of the bed. "Again."

Again?

She crawled onto him and he saw her face. Shocked, he scrambled back, slamming his head sharply against the headboard. It was Shari, his ex-wife.

"What the fuck are you doing here?" he yelled.

She sat up, straddling his legs. "I got tired of waiting for you to call."

"Why would I call you?" He'd seen her around the conventions but had purposely ignored her. How many times had she remarried? Three? Four?

"To resume my role as Dr. Kelvin, of course."

He was about to throw her out, until he looked at those enormous breasts, her nipples big enough to hang a coat on, and decided it would be more polite to fuck her first. No sense turning her away completely disappointed.

"Of course." He slid back down the bed.

"I still have what it takes to play the part, don't I?" She leaned over him, letting her breasts swing in front of his face.

He buried his face in her cleavage and pressed her breasts around his head. He mumbled something against her sternum that felt, more than sounded, like "Oh, yes."

She grabbed him by the hair and pulled him away from her bosom. "So when do I start?"

"You can start right now." He searched for his erection to put inside her but was having a hard time finding it.

"I meant, when do I report to the set?"

"Let's talk about this afterward." He abandoned his search. If she wanted it, she could find it. Taking one of her massive breasts in both hands, he devoured the nipple, licking, sucking, and drooling with abandon.

"Do I have the part or don't I?"

Stipe could see she wasn't going to give up. He fell back against the mattress, defeated, still panting with excitement, his cheeks wet with his own drool.

"No, you don't. We're going with a younger cast."

Her face crinkled with rage. Stipe sighed. As soon as she left, he'd have to call Milo's office, get a double-D girl to come down right away and finish him off.

But she didn't leave. She was remembering the last time she saw Stipe, in a lawyer's office, signing their divorce papers.

To Stipe's surprise, she smiled, all traces of anger gone.

"I guess I'll just have to settle for the merchandising." She took his head in her hands and mashed his face against her breast.

He hungrily slathered all over it, unable to believe his good fortune. She was going to fuck him anyway. What a mature woman. Then, her nipple in his mouth, his face mashed against her huge breast, he realized something.

Merchandising? What merchandising?

He tried to ask, but his words were lost in her flesh. That's when he realized something else. He couldn't breathe.

Shari didn't understand what he said, but she could guess. She pinned him to the mattress with the entire weight of her body, smothering him with her breasts.

"I just remembered. You never amended your will after the divorce, darling." She grabbed the mattress to hold herself in place as he squirmed frantically underneath her, scratching at her back, kicking his legs. "If you die, I get your share of *Beyond the Beyond* merchandising."

His struggle turned into a desperate, panicked flailing, during which he accidentally inserted himself in her. She gasped.

She read somewhere that terror, rather than diminishing an erection, only made it harder. Now she had clinical proof.

He clamped his teeth on her nipple and bit it off. She screamed and was surprised at the erotic charge it gave her. His squirming was hitting all the right spots.

"Yes," she panted, "yes."

Just as she was nearing orgasm, Stipe froze, twitched, and died. She rolled off the corpse and caught her breath.

It was like being married to him all over again.

Charlie spent an hour on the phone with Milo Kinoy, who was at one of his castles in Scotland, and told him that Kimberly Woodrell owed someone $250,000, and if it came out what she spent the money on, it would ruin her and probably the network, too.

Kinoy asked if the $250,000 would keep the secret quiet, and Charlie said he was confident that it would. This wasn't really a case of blackmail, he explained, and the person Kim was indebted to relied on confidentiality to stay in business.

They made the necessary arrangements, Kinoy expressed his appreciation to Charlie, and then it was over.

Charlie went into the living room, where Doyle Klemm was sitting in one of the chrome chairs, which was probably the most painful thing that happened to the intruder that night. Kim stood at the window with her back to them both. It was too dark to see the beach. All she could see was her own reflection staring back at her.

"The money will be wired into Dr. Himmelstein's Swiss bank account within the hour," Charlie said.

"I guess that settles it." Klemm sighed, stood up, and

glanced at Kim's back. "I'm sorry it came to all this, lady. It was nothing personal."

Kim didn't say anything. Klemm turned and offered his hand to Charlie. "No hard feelings."

Charlie debated whether to shake his hand. Who knew how many people this guy had tortured, raped, or killed? If he could arrest him, he would. But then Kim's secret would come out. He had to let this guy walk.

But did he have to accept a handshake? Yes, he did. There was an unspoken professional code of conduct, even between cops and crooks, that demanded he accept the peace offering.

"You might take this experience as an omen." Charlie shook Klemm's hand. "Maybe consider a career change."

Klemm picked up his drill off the coffee table. "I appreciate the advice, but this is what I do."

"I catch you doing it again, and you won't walk away."

Klemm nodded. "Fair enough."

The intruder left through the front door. As soon as he was gone, Charlie looked at Kim.

"Milo didn't ask what the money was for, but he says don't expect your performance bonus this year."

"Milo had no choice," she said. "He's invested way too much in me and The Big Network to let two hundred and fifty thousand jeopardize everything."

She turned to face Charlie. "I guess I'll never really be the first woman to run a network, will I?"

"I don't see why not."

Kim walked slowly toward Charlie. "Do I disgust you?"

"No."

She stopped a few inches away from him and let her

robe slip off her shoulders. She was naked. "Prove it."

Charlie had to admit Dr. Himmelstein deserved every penny of his $250,000. He couldn't tell what was real and what was manufactured. And without closer examination, there was nothing about her physically that betrayed her original sex. Certainly his body was fooled. He had a stiff one before her robe hit the floor.

"You're not my type," Charlie said.

"Too masculine?"

"No." He picked up her robe and offered it to her. "Too network."

She snatched the robe from him and put it on, cinching it tight around her waist for the first time since he'd met her.

"I suppose you'll want something for your silence."

"Just a good night's sleep."

And with that, Charlie went to bed.

ACT THREE

Fourteen

*L*eigh Dickson sat at a table outside Starbucks in Sherman Oaks the next morning, sipping coffee and reading Harold Pinter's *The Dumbwaiter.* He thought he made a pretty picture for any woman on the prowl for handsome, educated, witty men.

Of course, the play was not actually about waiters, but she would appreciate the subtle irony and be undeniably intrigued by him. Because, living in L.A., she would be starving for genuine intellect, for a man with cultured tastes, shrewd wit, and shocking good looks.

Unfortunately, she was starving somewhere else today. After a good twenty minutes of posing, Leigh closed the book and decided to pose across the street at Tower Records in the classical music section.

He got up and walked down the street, slipping on a pair of sunglasses to shield his sensitive eyes from the harsh glare. Soon he would have to wear them to hide himself from the harsh glare of adoration. Or so he hoped.

He'd won the role of Mr. Snork over fifty other hope-fuls, but the only reason he was there was because his agent tricked him. Leigh thought he was auditioning for an updated version of *The Elephant Man.*

But once he got the part, his agent convinced him it was a career-making opportunity. It certainly was a mon-eymaking one. But the idea of spending the next five years wearing an elephant nose terrified him.

His terror was misplaced. He should have been wor-ried about crossing the street.

A brown Chevette tore away from the curb, tires squealing, Bev Huncke hunkered over the steering wheel screaming "Die alien scum," targeting Leigh Dickson with her starship *Endeavor* hood ornament.

She slammed into him with a satisfying, squishy smack, the car lurching as it rolled over his body with a moist, grinding crunch.

The last thing Leigh Dickson saw, cheek against the gory pavement, a cloud of exhaust in his eyes, was a blood-splattered license plate that read SHTLCRFT3.

The Chevette sped away, driven by what witnesses would later describe as a "lady with a penis on her face." The police never found anyone matching that general de-scription.

Thrack of Oberon watched Spring Dano jog down the grassy median of San Vicente Boulevard, her breasts as solid and immovable as the Statue of Liberty's.

On a sunny day, tanned, perfect babes and tanned, perfect hunks jogged up and down the median, from Bar-rington in Brentwood to Ocean Avenue in Santa Monica, hoping to get noticed. And they were, according to in-surance company statistics. Parked cars, pedestrians, and other vehicles were routinely sideswiped, crushed, and smashed by drivers craning their necks for one more peek of perfect pecs or bouncing buns.

The median was one of the great unpublicized short-cuts into the entertainment industry. If you distracted an agent, producer, or director long enough to get him involved in a major traffic accident, you were on your way to a walk-on role in a series or a weekend read of your spec script.

Spring Dano already had a series job, but old habits are hard to break. Besides, she'd become accustomed to the screech of twisted metal and the cries of mowed-down pedestrians when she jogged. Knowing her beauty could cause such turmoil and destruction gave her the motivation to keep those Nikes moving.

Already today, while lying in wait for her, Thrack witnessed two collisions and a hit-and-run. Now he was about to stage an accident of his own.

Spring Dano was jogging off the median, across San Vicente, and onto Gretna Green Drive, where Thrack was waiting for her behind an enormous juniper bush, his taser ready. He was going to zap her with a couple hundred volts, drag her into his van, and let her experience his majestic superwarp plasma pleasure warhead before he strangled her. That way, she could die happy, and he could say he did something to Dr. Kelvin that Mr. Snork only dreamed about.

The moment she passed the bush, he leaped out, taser crackling with electricity. Not a wise move. Had he studied her résumé, he would have noticed that under "other skills," right between clog collecting and aura masseuse, she had earned a black belt from the Pat Morita School of Self-Defense and Method Acting.

She grabbed his wrist, wrenched down his arm, and

jammed the taser into his superwarp plasma pleasure warhead. He was zapped backward, deep into the juniper
bush, the entire plant shaking like it was digesting him.

Spring jogged in place for a moment, staring into the
vibrating bush, but saw no sign of her attacker.

"Thanks for the workout, sleazebag," she said, then
jogged on.

Kim shook Charlie's shoulder, and before she could get
out the words "wake up," he grabbed her by the arm,
flipped her on her back on the bed, and straddled her, his
clenched fist poised to strike over her face.

"Go ahead, hit me," she said. "It couldn't make things
any worse."

"Don't *ever* startle me like that." Charlie lowered his
fist and relaxed. "What is it?"

"I'm ruined."

Charlie fell back on the bed and closed his eyes. "Kim,
as far as I'm concerned, last night never happened. Forget about it."

"I wish I could. But last night the creator and stars of
Beyond the Beyond were murdered. I just got the call from
Jackson Burley."

Charlie sat up in bed. *The Company. It had to be.*

"What am I going to do, Charlie?"

"You?" He looked down at her. "Three people are
dead."

She glared at him. "And a network, don't forget that."

Charlie couldn't get out of bed fast enough.

Conrad Stipe was lying naked on a metal table, his eyes
and his mouth wide open, his nose flattened, dried blood
on his lips and chin.

But he was in far better shape than the person being

reassembled, bit by charred bit, by a couple of coroners on another table across the room. One of them was whistling.

Detective Lou LeDoux grimaced. "How can they stand it?"

"Somebody had to put Humpty Dumpty back together again," Dr. Chapman said, examining Stipe's testicles. "Or how would they have known *exactly* how he fell?"

Asshole, Lou thought, sharing a glance with his brother-in-law Charlie, who was thinking the same thing.

Dr. Chapman snortled to himself and moved down the length of Stipe's leg with a magnifying glass. "He had sex before he died. There are traces of seminal fluid on his thighs."

Charlie glanced at his watch and wondered how much longer this would take. Alison and Burley were waiting at the studio for news.

"I have a keen eye for the cinematic moments in everyday life," Dr. Chapman said.

"Excuse me?" Charlie asked.

Dr. Chapman looked up from his examination of Stipe's toes. "Take this room, for instance. Each body tells a story. I think it would make a hell of an anthology series."

"Yeah," Lou said. "Maybe get that Cryptkeeper guy to host."

Charlie should have known by now not to mention to anyone that he worked for a studio, unless he absolutely had to. The problem with L.A., on top of everything else, was that everyone had a story to pitch.

"I'm not in development," Charlie said. "I'm in security."

"Oh." Dr. Chapman tried to cover his disappointment with a shrug. "Do you know anyone in development?"

"Afraid not."

Behind Dr. Chapman, two coroner's assistants came in lugging body bags. "More pieces," one of them said to the Whistler.

They hefted the bags onto an empty table next to the Whistler, who unzipped the bag and reached inside, pulling out a charred bone shard. He tried unsuccessfully to place it into the puzzle and tossed it back in the bag. Whistler reached in for a new piece and came out with a burnt ear, which was surprising, since the corpse already had two.

"What's the story on that one?" Lou asked Dr. Chapman.

"Opened the door to his house and it blew up." Dr. Chapman examined Stipe's fingers. "Not a good day to live on Ardwyn Street."

"Why do you say that?" Charlie asked.

Dr. Chapman poked Stipe in the belly. "He lived on the same street, opposite side of Ventura Boulevard. See, that's a story right there."

Why was everyone in L.A. a writer, director, or actor waiting to be discovered? Charlie wondered if everyone who lived in Washington, D.C., was a closet politician, or if every Detroit resident harbored dreams of designing the car of the future.

Dr. Chapman peered into Stipe's open mouth and smiled. Using a pair of tweezers, he plucked out a long, pink thing and held it in front of his eyes. "Cool."

"What is it?" Lou asked.

"A nipple." Dr. Chapman held the severed flesh up to Charlie's face. "Now you tell me there isn't a great story in this."

The brass plaque on a window table at Kenny Rogers's Roaster said RESERVED FOR EDDIE PLANET. Eddie stuck it there right before he grabbed a tray and went to the chicken line.

In his heyday, the plaque used to rest on tables of distinction at places like Pinot, La Serre, The Bistro, Jimmy's, and Ma Maison, courtesy of the management, who were always glad to have a producer of his stature grace their restaurants.

In the more recent, mediocre days, he used to slip the maître d' at La Guerre a couple Abe Lincolns to put his plaque on the power table by the men's room a few minutes before he arrived. It wasn't a window seat, but anyone with a bladder and bowels couldn't avoid running into him eventually.

But now, in the dark, waning days of his production deal, he found himself unable to get a reservation at La Guerre. So he squeezed behind a Formica table at Kenny Rogers's, his window seat facing the front entrance of La Guerre, where he could see the industry players arriving for lunch.

UBC President Don DeBono rode up in his '59 Caddy with Monroe Mooney. Two years ago, Monroe was a droopy-faced, chubby character actor. Then he hocked everything he had to overhaul his body. Dr. Himmelstein sucked the fat out of his buttocks and his gut, then injected it into his pecs, penis, and chin to give him all the attributes God forgot. Any blemishes or wrinkles were wiped away with an all-body chemical peel. Overnight he went from a day-player to series lead, if today's lunch meant anything.

Eddie's wife, Shari, tried the same overhaul, only not with Dr. Himmelstein. Now her buttocks were lopsided, her skin was pasty, and her mouth looked like a suction cup. As long as the lights were low, and the suction cup was applied to his groin, he didn't care. Of course, that was happening less and less often. His sex life, as well as his career and his luncheon reservations, seemed to ride on the ratings.

He glanced to see who was sitting at the four prime window seats. Superagent Clive Odett shared martinis with Sean Connery. Aaron Spelling and Tori were fighting over the bread sticks. Brad Pitt and director Fred Schepsi were hunched seriously over their salads. Writer-producer Stephen J. Cannell was arm wrestling with Robert Blake.

Eddie could remember twenty years ago when Cannell was begging for a *Hollywood and Vine* writing assignment. Eddie didn't think Cannell was sophisticated enough for the job. Now the guy had his name on a building.

The business was funny that way. One minute you're on top, next minute on the bottom. Eddie saw fate as a fat guy in a recliner, stuffing his maw with Cheez Doodles, aiming his remote at the TV like a gun. Every producer's career took a bullet. The trick was avoiding the fatal shots. Eddie's career just had its head blown off.

Still, he had survived worse. It was all in the spin. Never let them think you're down. Always look for the angle.

Eddie would go back to the studio and say he was at Kenny Rogers's place, developing projects, tossing around ideas. It was the truth, but people would read a lot more into it.

If only more stars had their own restaurants, he'd be set.

Eddie started to make a list of celebrity restaurateurs on his napkin, but all he could come up with was Roy Rogers Chicken. He couldn't even remember if Roy Rogers was still alive. So he widened his list to include celebrity food labels. Paul Newman sold salad dressing. That had promise. He could say, "I grabbed a salad with Paul Newman."

He was struggling to make Jimmy Dean sausage into something positive when his cell phone rang. It was the fat guy with the Cheez Doodles, clicking his remote again.

Fifteen

The walls of Jackson Burley's office served as his résumé. His writer-producer credits, photographed off the TV screen, were all framed, along with cast photos, reviews, and yellowed advertisements for his shows.

Whenever he felt insecure, all he had to do was take a gander at his wall to confirm he knew what he was doing. Burley had spent a lot of time looking at the wall the last few hours.

Burley paced in front of his cluttered desk, the heels of his $350 tennis shoes lighting up with each step.

Alison sat on the leather couch, legs drawn up under her, dark circles under her bloodshot eyes, chewing on her ponytail.

Charlie stood between the two of them, giving his report.

"I met with some of my LAPD contacts." Charlie

didn't think it would sound half as good if he said his brother-in-law was handling the case. "Chad Shaw was killed by muggers in the garage of his apartment building. Leigh Dickson was mowed down by a hit-and-run driver. And Conrad Stipe was murdered in bed. Spring Dano was attacked, but she escaped, and I have her on the lot, under twenty-four-hour guard."

"Jesus Christ," Burley said. "This is the worst blood-bath in TV since *My Gun Has*—" He abruptly caught himself when he realized who he was talking to. "I'm sorry, Charlie, I didn't mean that."

"It's okay," Charlie said. Besides, Burley was right. "The only physical evidence they have to go on is a piece of nipple removed from Conrad's mouth."

"A nipple?" Alison shivered, sickened.

"The killer seduced Stipe," Charlie said, "then smoth-ered him with her breast."

"Murder by hooter," Burley muttered. "That's a new one. I wonder if I could ever get it past the network cen-sors."

Charlie pressed on, ignoring the remark. "None of the witnesses to Leigh Dickson's death could give a usable de-scription of the hit-and-run driver. Spring Dano says everything happened so fast that she never actually saw her attacker."

Alison sighed. "I don't suppose the police have any idea who did this."

"No," Charlie said. "But I do."

They both looked at him. "I think The Company is re-sponsible."

"Why?" Alison asked.

"It's Clive Odett's style. Look what he tried with Spike Donovan in Vancouver, and what happened to Javier Grillo in Hawaii."

"There's just one problem with your theory, Charlie," Alison said. "They were all Company clients, except for Chad Shaw."

But it was Odett's style. It had to be Odett. He *wanted* it to be Odett.

Alison could see the disappointment on Charlie's face. He really wanted to go after The Company. Her guess was he still felt responsible for what happened to Javier Grillo, and he would look for any opportunity to go after them.

"You want to know who's behind this?" Burley asked rhetorically. "UBC, MBC, and DBC. They're afraid The Big Network is going to steal the entire eighteen-to-thirty-five demographic from them. They figured if they killed *Beyond the Beyond,* they could bring down the network before it's even launched."

Charlie shook his head. "I don't buy it."

"Trust me, Charlie. I know how the criminal mind works." Burley swept his arm over his credits. "I've written more cop shows than anybody in this town. The Company has no motivation. The networks have plenty. And I'm not going to give in to their terrorism. I've decided, in consultation with Kim Woodrell, to keep *Beyond the Beyond* in production. We're going to start recasting as soon as the new show runner is in place."

"Whoever is responsible for what happened will come after them next," Charlie said. "They'll all be in grave danger."

"We're counting on you to protect them," Burley said. "And we've found the perfect guy to take over *Beyond the Beyond.* He's a proven show runner, and we know from experience he won't be intimidated by these killers."

"I'd like to meet him," Charlie said, "as soon as possible."

Burley opened his door and stuck his head out. "Come on in," he said to someone outside, then stepped aside to let him in.

Charlie's worst fear was that the producer would be represented by The Company. But Charlie didn't get much sleep after last night's escapade at Kim's place and could be forgiven for not imagining an even more horrifying possibility.

Eddie Planet strode into the room like he was coming on stage to accept an Emmy. "Hey, Charlie, my man. How's it hanging?"

Charlie stared at him in shock.

"You look terrific." Eddie pointed at him, as if there was some doubt who he was talking to. "Have you lost a few pounds?"

Charlie slugged him.

Eddie fell against the wall, dragging down the cast photo of *Dracula, M.D.*, an Edgar award, and three positive reviews for *The Missionary Mercenary* as he slid to the floor.

Alison bolted up off the couch, shocked. Burley moved a safe distance away.

It was the second time in two days that Charlie had punched someone in anger, and it felt great. In fact, he wanted to do it again.

Charlie took a step toward Eddie, who immediately scrambled on his hands and knees behind Burley's desk. Alison quickly threw herself in front of the desk, blocking Charlie's path.

She yelled, "Enough!"

He glared past her at Eddie, peeking up from the other side of the desk, holding his bloody nose, and had to laugh. "You expect me to protect *him?*"

"Why not?" Alison was genuinely confused.

He glanced incredulously at Jackson Burley, who took another step back, holding up his hands in surrender.

Charlie shook his head, disgusted, and walked out of the office.

Clive Odett was stuck in traffic on the Ventura Freeway when news reached him on his mobile fax, cellular phone, in-dash TVs and radios, that two Company clients were dead and that Eddie Planet was the new executive producer of *Beyond the Beyond*.

How could a show runner get hired without The Company being consulted first? Odett gripped the steering wheel, not that he'd had any reason to use it in the last twenty minutes. Something wasn't right. He was losing control of the situation. That had never happened before. He couldn't let it continue.

"I want to know who's muscling in on our client list," Odett barked at Zita over his cell phone. "I want every one of our agents on this. I have to know which agency benefits from pulling our clients out of play."

"What makes you think it's another agency?"

"It has to be. No one else has the guts."

He hung up and stared at the ribbon of idling cars between him and the Coldwater Canyon exit. This was what they called a freeway in Los Angeles. Using that logic, a parking lot should be called a race track.

In twenty minutes, he hadn't moved half a mile, more or less mirroring his progress, or more precisely, *lack* of progress, acquiring control of *Beyond the Beyond* and The Big Network the last few days. The traffic offended him.

He stomped on the gas. The Hummer surged forward, slammed into a Honda Accord and climbed over it, crushing it like a Japanese beer can. And he just kept going. The trapped cars on the Ventura Freeway became Clive Odett's private pavement, the Hummer effortlessly flattening all makes and models on his way to the exit.

Eddie held an ice pack to his nose and did something he'd never done before. He left his golf cart behind at the Tower and *walked* to his bungalow.

He needed to think, to analyze all the angles.

Eddie knew this was his big chance, maybe even his *last* chance, to get his career back on track. He wasn't going to blow it again. His broken nose was a painful reminder of the mistakes made the last time he had a real shot at a comeback.

Charlie Willis still wrongly blamed Eddie for all the murders committed by the mob to keep *Frankencop* on the air, just because Eddie happened to produce the show. Couldn't he see that Eddie was a victim, too? The mob made him clear every creative decision through them first; they even forced a star on him, a guy who couldn't act unless he knew what his "dick motivation" was first.

Because of the mob, he wasn't allowed to work his TV magic and lost the chance to turn *Frankencop* into his biggest hit since *Saddlesore* twenty years ago. What did Charlie Willis lose? A TV career he never had to begin with. Fuck him.

Eddie had bigger concerns.

Obviously, Guy Goddard and his lunatic Beyonders killed Stipe, but why did he have to kill Chad Shaw and Leigh Dickson, too?

Because Goddard's a fucking lunatic, that's why. And Eddie Planet certainly couldn't be blamed for the actions of an insane person, not that anyone knew he and God-dard met. And even if someone *did* know, what did Eddie do wrong? Nothing. He shot the shit with him. Schmoozed. Commiserated. It's not like he told Goddard to go out and kill somebody.

No one could prove anything, because Eddie Planet didn't *do* anything.

The only thing Eddie Planet had to worry about now was what to do with all the money he was going to make off the show fate had just given him.

Eddie was halfway to his bungalow when he remembered he had new digs now. He'd taken over Conrad Stipe's old office and inherited his double-D secretary. Her name was Brougham, which her mother thought was very classy, since it seemed like every elegant car that passed their trailer park was a Brougham-this or Brougham-that.

She took the news of Stipe's death well. She started scraping his name off the door with a letter opener. Brougham was still doing that when Eddie came in.

"There's someone waiting in your office," she said.

"Who?" Eddie asked.

Brougham shrugged, which wasn't easy, considering the considerable weight of her bust. "She's some writer Mr. Stipe hired. She was in the office when I got back from lunch."

Eddie tossed his ice pack on Brougham's desk and strode into his office, stunned to see a woman in a sleeveless T-shirt sitting at the desk, hunched over a copy of the *Beyond the Beyond* pilot script. She had rings in her nose, lip, ear, and eyebrow, and a Confederation insignia tattooed on her shoulder.

Eddie suddenly realized there was one angle he forgot to consider. The Beyonders. Stipe probably hired her to curry favor with the fans, which reminded Eddie that he'd have to do something to mollify Guy Goddard, short of giving the nutball his part back.

"Sit down." Melvah Blenis scribbled something in the margin of the script. "I want to finish this thought."

Eddie walked up to the desk, snatched the script from her, and dropped it in the garbage without even looking at it. "Get out of my office before I drag you out by your nose ring."

"That's an Orgoglian mating clip, which you'd know if you weren't completely illiterate." Melvah bent over, lifted a stack of magazines off the floor, and dumped them on the desk. "Before you embarrass yourself any further, read these."

Eddie glanced at the magazines, Xeroxed copies of *Beyondzine* with badly drawn caricatures of the *Beyond the Beyond* cast for covers. He'd seen a few fanzines before, but the only ones he paid any attention to featured Dr. Kelvin in a variety of explicit positions. He liked those.

"Conrad Stipe may have created the show, but he was completely out of touch with the universe. A lot has changed in twenty years, and he didn't stay on top of it," Melvah said. "The mistakes start on the first page of his script. Stipe thought the Zidruts were still at war with the Nerglids, even though the Zidrut homeworld was consumed by Flerbian fungus in a classic story published way back in *Beyondzine* number 112."

Eddie knew now he was dealing with a hard-core Beyonder, which meant her grasp on reality was about as firm as a Hollywood promise. He turned to the outer office. "Brougham, call security."

"Belay that order," Melvah snapped, getting both

Eddie and his secretary's attention. "If you're going to make calls, start by getting me an office. I've got to start rewriting this piece of shit."

She handed Eddie her studio drive-on pass. It was called in by Clive Odett's office.

"I'm Melvah Blenis, your new producer," she said. "You got a problem with that, take it up with The Company."

She was represented by Clive Odett? How could that possibly be? He needed time to sort this out. He didn't want to risk angering Clive Odett or Guy Goddard at this point.

"Why would I have a problem with that? I'm glad to have someone as knowledgeable as you on board." Eddie gathered up the magazines and handed the pile to her. "I want you to take these and show them to the other writers right away. Brief them on every detail of the universe. We don't want to make any more mistakes."

The other writers were stuck in a trailer clear across the lot. It would take her half an hour just to walk there and would keep her far away from him until he figured out all the angles.

"What about the first episode?" Melvah asked.

"Send me a memo." Eddie wouldn't read it, but he'd sell it for a buck a page. Before she could argue, he pushed her out the door and slammed it shut.

Sixteen

*E*ver since his electrifying encounter with Dr. Kelvin, Thrack of Oberon's superwarp plasma pleasure warhead was in a constant state of launch readiness.

When Melvah returned to the starship *Endeavor*'s Van Nuys landing site and saw Thrack waiting for her in the shuttle port, his silver space pants bulging, she thought he was just very glad to see her. She opened the back door of her Econoline van, climbed in, and sprawled out on the brown shag carpet. He eagerly jumped in after her.

After thirty minutes of intense, deep-space exploration, she emerged from the van sweaty, weak-legged, and satisfied. He was exhausted, spent, and most of all, amazed because, as anyone could see, his superwarp plasma pleasure warhead was still on the launch pad.

"It's your lucky day." He reached for her, but she squirmed away.

"I have to brief the captain," Melvah said and wobbled toward the ship.

She opened the screen door to the bridge and entered to find Captain Pierce in his command chair, drinking a glass of orange Tang. Bev Huncke sat at Ops, Artie Saputo on his knees in front of her, his head pinned between her legs as she stapled a big rubber Zorgog ear to his skull.

The captain swiveled in his chair toward Melvah as she strode in. "Report," he demanded.

"The alien impersonating you has been destroyed, sir."

He sat up straight and nodded, pleased. "Then the way is clear for me to resume my command."

"Not quite, sir. The conspiracy is larger than we thought."

"What do you mean?"

"Pinnacle Pictures controls the show. They won't let you take command. They're already replacing Stipe and the cast with more of their own."

"They're insidious." Pierce gazed at the main viewscreen, pondering the grave situation.

That's when Thrack came in behind Melvah, slamming the screen door. Captain Pierce whirled around, irritated by the interruption, and saw Thrack's groin saluting him.

"Damn it, I ordered you to do something about that," Pierce snapped, disgusted.

"I tried, sir," Thrack whined. "It just won't go away."

"I can vouch for that," Melvah replied. "It defied my best efforts."

Bev Huncke released Artie's head and set her bloody stapler on the console. "Maybe I should try, sir." She hadn't had sex in six years, and even then it was with an unconscious bicyclist hit by a car on Mulholland. Her car, to be exact.

Pierce glanced at Melvah. "Opinion?"

Melvah shrugged. "If you believe it will work, Captain."

"I can't think with that in my face," the captain said, then nodded at Bev. "Permission granted."

Bev rose, with some effort, from her chair and waddled outside. Thrack took a deep breath and followed after her.

"If that doesn't work," Artie said, "I can rig a small explosive."

Artie stood up and looked at his reflection in Mr. Snork's view screen. He liked what he saw. The horsey ear was a definite improvement.

For a moment he thought about plucking out his other eye and getting another Zorgog one, then it occurred to him he would be blind.

Captain Pierce massaged his temples. "The infernal aliens. There must be a way to stop them."

Melvah crouched beside the captain's chair and lowered her voice. "If I may make a suggestion, sir."

He leaned toward her. "Yes?"

"We need a powerful agent who can convince the studio to give you the role."

Captain Pierce narrowed his eyes and sat back in his seat. "You're suggesting we find an alien who speaks their language to negotiate their surrender."

"And I know just the man, Clive Odett." Melvah was doing her part for Zita, who held up her end of the bargain by getting her on the show.

"Very well. Prepare an away team," the captain said. "Then bring this agent to me."

Shari was in her bathrobe the next morning, leaning over the toaster, waiting for her Pop-Tart to pop up, marveling at all the good luck that had come her way.

All it had cost her was a nipple, a small price to pay for untold millions in merchandising royalties. And if she had known Eddie would get her ex-husband's show in the deal, it would have been a seriously premeditated murder.

Even without the handsome financial rewards, she didn't have any regrets. Stipe deserved to die for killing her career.

He cast her in the pilot off a *Man from U.N.C.L.E.* guest shot and an incredible blow job in his office. She was eager to be a series star, but in telling her about the part, he left out the bit about the computer breasts. By the time she found out, she was already signed. But he had her convinced she would be such a big star when the series was over that it wouldn't matter.

"Sally Field was Gidget, a teenage surfer slut, and they made *her* the Flying Nun," Stipe had said. "You think giving people an excuse to stare at your fabulous knockers for an hour will be a liability?"

She wasn't entirely convinced, but while they were shooting the series, they were both so stoned that she didn't worry about typecasting or anything else. There was always some heroin for the heroine when Stipe was around. She gladly wore the lowest-cut uniforms they could get away with and jumped at the chance to do a nudie spread in *Playboy*. In fact, she jumped at everything, even Stipe.

It was only after the series bombed, and she found herself married to Stipe, that the nightmare sank in. The only people in America who watched the fucking show were casting agents.

One day she came home to find that Stipe was gone, along with their bank account, credit cards, and even her jewelry.

She ended up dancing at an airport strip joint, where she discovered she had a following among horny men with bad skin and started her own fan club.

The fan club grew into a small *Beyond the Beyond* mail-order business that, combined with the stripping, kept her comfortable. It was at the club that she met Eddie, who said he was there casting for *Saddlesore*, the hit Western he was producing. Shari said she wasn't aware TV was doing topless Westerns. Eddie said he wasn't looking for bodies, he was looking for charisma.

So Shari gave him some charisma in the backseat of his Lincoln Continental, which she parlayed into a bit part on *Saddlesore* and a quickie wedding in Vegas.

But Eddie's career went up and down, mostly down, and she'd resigned herself to it when the new *Beyond the Beyond* came around.

Now she couldn't believe all the good luck that was coming her way. It was even rubbing off on Eddie. She hadn't counted on Eddie getting her ex-husband's show.

She was so lost in her thoughts she didn't hear Eddie creeping up behind her, his broken nose swollen, the pop-tart in his monogrammed pajamas ready for her toaster. He yelled, "Gotcha," grabbed her breasts, and rubbed himself against her.

She yelped in pain and jammed her elbow into his doughy stomach. He staggered back into the refrigerator, activating the drink dispenser, which shot a stream of cold water right into his ass.

Eddie squealed, then glared furiously at her. "What's the matter with you?"

She thought: *My ex-husband chewed my tit off, you stupid fuck.* She said: "I'm so sorry, honey."

She rushed up to him, covering his face with kisses. "My boobs are tender, it's that time of month."

His wife was the only woman he knew whose time of the month lasted four weeks. "Can't you reschedule? We're celebrating."

"Of course we are, poochy." She pulled down his pajamas and took his schmeckle in her hand, pumping it back to life. "You're the executive producer of *Beyond the Beyond.*"

"That's right, baby. Single card, top of the show."

"You're the big man." She felt him pulse in her hand. "Everyone has to answer to you."

"I'm the show runner," he panted. Twenty-two episodes, on the air, was truly the best aphrodisiac.

"And I'm the star," she said.

"The star?"

She stopped her pumping. "Of *Beyond the Beyond.*"

He looked at her blankly, his schmeckle throbbing in her fist. She chastised him with painful squeeze.

"Reprising Dr. Kelvin," she said. "It's *my* character, Eddie."

"You can't."

"Why not?" She let go of him. "You're the show runner, aren't you?"

"Yes, but someone else already has the part."

"Fire her," she demanded.

"You'll always be the original, *classic* Dr. Kelvin," he said pleadingly. "But Spring Dano is the right demographic for the show."

She couldn't believe this. For twenty-five years people saw her *only* as Dr. Kelvin. She couldn't get any other part.

You'd make a great Dr. Quinn, but the show is a Western, and everyone thinks of your breasts as twenty-fifth-century computers. . . .

You can't play Amelia Earhart. It'll pull audiences out of the story. They'll be thinking the whole time, "What the fuck does she care about a plane trip? She's been to Mars. . . ."

Sure, you'd make a wonderful cop. In outer space. This show takes place on the mean streets of urban America. . . .

And now that there was finally another opportunity to play Dr. Kelvin, her one and only role, suddenly she wasn't right for it.

You'll always be Dr. Kelvin, but you aren't the right demographic for the show.

It wasn't fair.

Eddie, seeing the rage on her face and the prospect of a thorough hand job evaporating, knew he had to make good fast.

"Don't worry, baby, Eddie's gonna take care of you." Eddie gave her a smile, his pajama pants bunched around his feet. "You can be the voice of the ship's computer."

She shoved him against the refrigerator, which shot another stream of ice water at his ass. He yelped and jumped away from the offensive appliance.

"The computer is going to be a major character," Eddie said. "Sexy, spunky, and opinionated."

She plucked her Pop-Tart out of the toaster and walked out of the kitchen. Their marriage had just ended. If he couldn't even get her a part on his own show, what good was he? She decided to divorce him before the first merchandising dollar came in. She'd kill him, but if two husbands turned up dead in one week, it was sure to draw some attention.

"What about me?" he whined. "I've got some husbandly needs here."

"Stick it in your computer," she replied. "I hear it's very sexy."

Eddie's first act as executive producer was to issue a memo that all the trash from the *Beyond the Beyond* writing and production offices was to be collected and brought to him for "security purposes." He had Brougham pack up all of Stipe's notes, memos, and rough drafts, which he was having shrink-wrapped for sale at the big BeyondCon convention next week. Now that Stipe was dead, even a Post-it note reminding him to have a boil lanced was worth fifty bucks.

His second act as executive producer was to take Stipe's *Beyond the Beyond* premiere script with him to the executive bathroom for a thorough read. In his opinion the episode, "The Terror Trout of Talos-10," wasn't bad, your typical fish-people-kidnapping-women-for-breeding-experiments story. What it needed was a few more battles, a sexy computer voice, and a recurring character for Jackson Burley to play.

Eddie was still sitting on the toilet, the script open on his lap, when the bathroom fax chirped and spit out William Katt's résumé. The *Beyond the Beyond* cast wasn't even buried, and already agents were hitting Eddie up with potential replacements.

The bathroom phone rang. Eddie snatched it up.

"If that's Billy Katt's agent," Eddie said, "tell him we found someone younger looking who has more female appeal. Tell him we cast Ernest Borgnine."

"It's Clive Odett calling for you," his secretary said.

Eddie shit when he heard the news. Literally. But it was a good thing, since he'd been sitting on the toilet constipated for the last hour.

"Put him on hold. I'm in a meeting."

Eddie hung up the phone, giggled, and stamped his feet. Only a few days ago, Clive Odett dismissed him as the car detail guy. Now he was calling to sign him.

God, Eddie loved the TV business.

Now he knew, without a doubt, that all his stars were in alignment. He could feel, in the very marrow of his bones, that this show was going to be his second coming. Watch your back, Aaron Spelling. Eddie Planet is coming at you.

Eddie picked up the phone. "Clive, it's so good to hear from you. It's been too long." They'd never actually met, except for the car-detailing thing, but Clive Odett wouldn't know that. Agents in Odett's league thought they knew everybody, and when they genuinely did know you, then you had it made.

"Yes, it has, Eddie," Clive replied. "I wonder if you're free for lunch today."

"Let me check." Eddie flipped loudly through his script. His current agent, Stumpy Leftcowitz, had offices coast to coast. Unfortunately, they were all Kinko's copy centers. Stumpy was the one guy in America who took Kinko's "We're your branch office!" ads at their word. Stumpy's biggest client was the decapitated head of a celebrity dog, which was attached to a malfunctioning robot in the hilarious UBC sitcom *Boo Boo's New Dilemma*.

"I guess I can move some players around, open up a space for you on the board."

"I'm so very glad to hear it," Clive said, his voice flicking out of the phone like a serpent's tongue. "I have a meeting with Alf's people at Celebrity Galaxy. We'll meet afterward." Click.

Eddie slammed down the receiver and stood up, so preoccupied with the surprising turn of events he didn't even notice that he wiped himself with William Katt's résumé instead of the toilet paper.

Seventeen

Gharlane was inside his storage unit, scrutinizing an old issue of *Big Hooters* with a jeweler's loupe, when Charlie Willis scooted by in his golf cart on routine patrol of the facility. After so many months away from home, it felt good to do something routine for a change.

"How's it going?" Charlie asked. Gharlane sat on a stool in the center of his unit, directly under the single bulb that hung from the ceiling. The unit was crammed full of boxes bulging with decades' worth of men's magazines.

"I'm getting closer to discovering the truth." Gharlane dragged his loupe slowly over the centerfold, his body curled over the magazine so far, the bumps of his vertebrae poked through his Grateful Dead T-shirt.

"The truth?" Charlie asked.

Gharlane raised his head. "Last night I saw a movie

with Julia Roberts that had a love scene. They showed her breasts, but not her face. Well, those were definitely *not* her breasts. Wrong shape entirely. They belonged to a body double, and I'm tracking those breasts down."

"Why?"

Gharlane stared at him and scratched his bony knee, which stuck out through the hole in his faded jeans. "I thought you were a police officer once."

"I was."

"Then you should be outraged. The producers perpetrated a fraud on the American public," Gharlane said. "A lot of people paid seven bucks to see Julia Roberts, not a body double. I think the public has a right to know just whose breasts they were looking at."

"I never thought of it that way," Charlie said, an idea occurring to him. He'd have to talk to Lou about it. "You gonna be around the next couple days? I may need a favor."

Gharlane nodded. "Sure."

Charlie had to get to the studio, but first he had to finish his security check. He steered the cart down the row of storage units, checking to make sure all the corrugated, sliding doors were secured with padlocks and that nothing was amiss.

Alison Sweeney sat in her jelly-bean-blue Miata outside Canoga Stor-All, a map book open on her lap, checking it against the address she'd written on a slip of paper. No mistake about it. This was the place.

Maybe she wrote the address down wrong. There was an easy way to check. She got out, walked up to the front office, and went inside. There was no one beside the counter.

"Hello?"

No one replied. Just a few feet away, and to one side, was a half-open door. She leaned over the counter to peer inside, but all she saw was part of a TV set, the edge of a recliner, and the leg of a coffee table. She might have seen more, but that's when a snarling dog hidden on the other side of the counter leaped up, snapping at her ponytail.

She screamed, staggering back into a man's arms. Reflexively, she jammed her elbow into his stomach and stomped on his foot. He yelped and released her, freeing her to spin around and poke her fingers into his eyes, just like she was taught in her self-defense class.

He lost his footing and slammed against the wall, sliding down in a heap on the floor, one hand over his watering eyes, the other on his sore belly.

"Wow," she said.

Alison was proud of herself. It was the first time she'd ever put her self-defense skills into practice, and she'd easily felled a man. But pride quickly turned to panic, because now she recognized her attacker.

"Charlie?"

He nodded and struggled to his feet, still gripping his stomach. "Hell of an elbow you've got there, Alison."

"I'm sorry." She helped him to his feet. "I didn't mean to do that."

Charlie grimaced and staggered to the counter, mainly so he could lean on it without being too obvious.

"I really did *do* that, didn't I?" she asked. "You didn't fake all that just to make me feel good."

Charlie wiped the tears out of his stinging eyes and tried to bring her into focus. "I'm not that eager to please, and I'm certainly no match for a woman of your physical prowess."

A few years ago, back when he was a Beverly Hills

cop, he was shot in the gut by the crazed old TV star Esther Radcliffe, who was late for a sale at Neiman Marcus. The bullet they dug out of him made a nice paperweight. The wound hadn't bothered him in months, but then again, nobody had elbowed him in the stomach lately. Now the pain was back, along with a few painful memories.

"I took a couple of self-defense classes at Pepperdine." Alison rolled up her sleeves another notch or two. "Now I've got the killer instinct."

Charlie looked down at McGarrett, his tail thumping proudly on the floor. Apparently, he had the killer instinct too. Everyone was pretty happy with themselves around here, except for him.

"So, are we still working together?" she asked.

"Is that why you came down here?"

"After you walked out yesterday, I wasn't sure you were coming back."

Truth was, neither was Charlie.

Someone once told him the key to the movie industry was getting the audience to suspend their disbelief long enough to get sucked into the story. But Charlie learned it was also the key to *working* in the industry. He was able to suspend his disbelief, to fool himself into believing that the people he was working for deserved his help. Until now. Until Eddie Planet.

After Esther Radcliffe shot him, Pinnacle bought Charlie's silence by making him the star of *My Gun Has Bullets*. The show was pitted against Eddie Planet's *Frankencop*, which was financed entirely by the mob, who tried to make it a success by actually killing the competition. Charlie survived but was never able to pin anything on Eddie.

"Eddie Planet is a liar, a con man, and a coward," Charlie said. "He'll do anything to get a show on the air and keep it there. *Anything.*"

"So will most of the producers on the Pinnacle lot."

Charlie smiled at her. "Except none of them nearly got me killed."

"Give them time." She smiled back.

He had been giving the situation a lot of thought during his patrol of the storage units. Could he protect Eddie Planet? What made Eddie different from everyone else he was asked to look out for? Was Eddie any worse than Nick?

The only difference between them was that Eddie was a threat Charlie already knew, just as Nick would now be. If Charlie continued as a studio troubleshooter, there would be a lot more Eddies and Nicks in his future. Shortly before Alison elbowed him in the gut, Charlie had made up his mind.

"Regardless of what I think of Eddie Planet, the fact is that someone is killing people involved with *Beyond the Beyond,*" he said. "I can't walk away from that."

She sighed, relieved. "You're going to stay."

"I never left."

"So what's the plan now?"

"Put the new cast and crew under constant guard, but it's a short-term strategy. I have to find out who is behind this. What I haven't figured out is how."

Alison gave it some thought, pursing her lips and wrinkling her brow. She looked so adorable he had the sudden urge to kiss her, but he held it back.

"It's a shame there isn't some way to make them come to you," she said, "besides waiting for them to try and kill another actor."

Charlie looked at her. She just showed him the way.

"What?" She looked back at him.

The solution was so obvious it was invisible.

Before he knew it, he was giving her the kiss he was resisting only seconds before. The instant their lips met, she melded against him, returning the kiss, her hands sliding up his back and drawing him to her.

The screen door banged, startling them both. They pulled back from each other, and Charlie saw Lou LeDoux standing at the door. Lou was showing up for his shift.

"Should I come back later?" Lou asked.

Charlie and Alison let go of each other, both feeling a bit awkward.

"No," Charlie said. "I'm glad you're here. I need you to do me a favor, but give me a second."

"Only a second?" Lou said. "No wonder your wife ran off with the gardener."

Lou disappeared into the apartment. Charlie looked at Alison, whose face was flushed. He wasn't sure whether it was embarrassment or passion, but finding out which would have to wait.

"Can you find Eddie Planet for me?" he asked. "It's urgent that I see him right away."

"You know how to find the killers, don't you?"

"No," he replied. "I know how they'll find *me.*"

Before tourists entered the Pinnacle Studios tour, they were funneled down a money-sucking gauntlet of neon storefronts known collectively as Pinnacle City, "the Capital of the State of Hollywood."

Pinnacle City was downtown urban America as envisioned by the Brady Bunch, where the Happy Homeless danced with rap-singing members of the Goodtime Gang, and the Smile Police gave out chocolate tickets to all the nice girls and boys. The kids usually had the tasty tickets jammed in their mouths before their parents realized they cost ten dollars a pop.

Shopping and dining in Pinnacle City was a multi-media entertainment experience designed to drive children into a state of frenzy and bludgeon their parents senseless, willing to spend anything to shut their kids up and have some peace.

All their senses assaulted, most people cracked, gladly forking over $3.50 for a watered-downed Coke, fifty dollars for a Pinnacle T-shirt, or seventy-five dollars for a stuffed Muck Thing toy.

By the time the shell-shocked tourists staggered, ears ringing and eyes watering, to the front gates to pay thirty dollars a head for the studio tour, they'd already been soaked for twice that much on the walk from the parking lot.

Of course, the Los Angeles Planning Commission saw this as a model of urban planning and were adopting it into their long-term strategy for reinvigorating the city.

This was one of Thrack's favorite places.

He could come here, in full Confederation uniform, and not feel out of place. Tourists even asked to have their pictures taken with him.

But mostly he liked it because of the Celebrity Galaxy, the sci-fi restaurant. Each booth was a space capsule, and the food was served on flying saucers. It was the fancy restaurant he took lucky space gals to for special occasions.

Thrack sat outside with Melvah behind the restaurant on a bench shaped like a rocket, watching the two space-suited astrovalets parking cars for people who came to Celebrity Galaxy for lunch. There were quite a few, even though the food was lousy.

Celebrity Galaxy was another vanity tax shelter for overpaid Hollywood movie stars, this one jointly owned by actors who made it big in sci-fi. Kurt Russell, Sigourney Weaver, James Cameron, and Alf all had money in the restaurant.

People didn't come for the food, they came to see the underwear Sigourney wore in *Alien*, Kurt's eye patch from *Escape from N.Y.*, and other framed, jarred, and stuffed props from movies.

Melvah impaled an empty Styrofoam cup on Thrack's hard-on so people would think he had a drink in his lap. No sense drawing any unwanted attention. Thrack noted with pride that it was a Big Gulp cup.

A few hours earlier, Zita had called Melvah at the office and let her know Odett was taking a meeting with Eddie Planet and that it would be a good opportunity to nab the superagent.

Melvah agreed. She also thought it would be a good idea to kill Eddie Planet as soon as possible, but Zita argued against it, saying it would be easier to sign him.

Melvah tried to talk to her about taking over the show herself, but Zita had a meeting with Tom Arnold that couldn't wait. Melvah would bring it up again tonight. She wanted to see the issue resolved before BeyondCon this weekend.

Thrack nudged Melvah with his elbow and motioned to his cup. "Want a drink?"

He snortled hysterically. Melvah couldn't help but smile, even though she was watching the two astrovalets. One of them drove off in a Mercedes, leaving the other behind.

Melvah saw Clive Odett's Hummer turn into the parking lot. The eager astrovalet stepped forward to greet him. She jammed a taser in his back, jolting him with a couple hundred volts, and dragged him back to the bench. Thrack got up to greet Odett instead.

Unfortunately, Thrack forgot to take the cup off his crotch before he stood up. That would have been a serious problem if not for the fact that Clive Odett was oblivious to anyone who wasn't someone. Odett was too busy talking on his cell phone to notice the cup, or even Thrack.

Thrack opened the driver's side door and was awed by what he saw. The Hummer was the greatest piece of machinery Thrack had ever seen. In-dash TVs. Fax machine. Phone. Leather seats. There was even a satellite dish on the roof. Thrack didn't just want to have it, he wanted to *live* in it.

Clive Odett started to climb out of the Hummer, flipping the phone shut with one hand and holding out the keys with the other.

In Los Angeles, rich people lived in private neighborhoods, safe behind gates, burly guards, security cameras, and laser-light sensors, but they gladly handed over their cars to anyone standing outside a restaurant. It was, in Thrack's mind, one of the things that made this city great.

"Don't try to park it in a compact spot." Odett smiled. "I hate picking Toyotas out of the tire treads."

Thrack touched him with the taser. There was a loud snap, the shock kicking Odett right into the passenger seat, leaving him wide-eyed and twitching, his hair standing on end. Thrack jumped into the driver's seat, slammed the door shut, and stomped on the gas pedal.

Thrack was halfway across the parking lot, trying to tune the SciFi Channel on the dashboard TV, when he saw the reflection of a Ford Crown Victoria chasing after him in the rearview mirror.

Charlie Willis wasn't prepared for this. He came here hoping to intercept Eddie before his lunch, and instead he arrived to see Clive Odett carjacked by a guy in a silver space suit with a Styrofoam cup stuck on his crotch. Before Charlie knew it, he was chasing the Hummer.

Did he really intend to rescue Clive Odett? It didn't matter. A carjacking was a carjacking, and his instincts were taking over.

The Hummer picked up speed. The carjacker didn't bother to weave around the parked cars but simply slammed through them, creating an obstacle course for his pursuer.

Charlie was reaching for the cell phone to call the police when the Hummer sideswiped a station wagon, sending it spinning across his path. He wrenched the wheel with both hands, narrowly avoiding the wagon but forcing him to charge through the open, compact parking space between two minivans.

Sparks flew on both sides of the sedan as Charlie sped between the minivans, shearing their paint off to the metal.

Thrack caught the sparks out of the corner of his eye, reminding him to jolt Odett one more time for good measure. *Snap!* Odett bounced off the dashboard and crumpled on the floor. Thrack saw a tour bus turning into the parking lot, blocking the exit to the street and the on-ramp down to the Hollywood Freeway.

No problem. It was the long way anyhow.

Thrack turned sharply, smashing into a light post, and headed straight for the cyclone fence separating the lot from the steep freeway embankment.

The light post broke, flew over the Hummer, and landed right in front of Charlie, who swerved to avoid it, sending him head-on toward the tour bus. Charlie swerved again, fishtailing, the bus clipping the back of his car, tearing off the bumper.

The Hummer flattened the fence and headed straight down the embankment, which sloped to the five lanes of northbound traffic at a sharp, 60 percent grade. Charlie didn't know how steep the embankment was when he, without even thinking, followed the Hummer.

Unlike the Hummer, Charlie's Ford Crown Victoria wasn't a 190-horsepower V8, with four-wheel drive and a 130-inch wheel base. While the Hummer hugged the embankment down to the freeway and barged into traffic, the Crown Victoria rolled end-over-end down the slope, landing in the slow lane like a discarded soda can.

Charlie was upside down and strapped into his seat, covered with broken glass, the inflated steering-wheel airbag all but obscuring his view of the Hummer disappearing onto the westbound Ventura Freeway. That's when the first car crashed into him.

Thrack was oblivious to the wreckage behind him. Just as he was getting on the Ventura Freeway, *The Powers of Matthew Starr* came in on the SciFi Channel.

Eighteen

*E*ddie Planet never made it to lunch. Some accident at Pinnacle City shut the whole place down. He hoped Clive Odett was sitting there, waiting for him. That way, word would get around that Eddie Planet was so hot he stood up Clive Odett.

Just to make sure the word got around, as soon as he got back to his office he told Brougham to tell every secretary on the lot what he'd done.

Missing lunch gave him a few extra minutes to punch up his casting suggestions for *Beyond the Beyond* before heading to Kim Woodrell's office with Jackson Burley.

Kim was, as usual, dressed in black, wearing a loose blouse, trim jacket, and a short skirt that made every meeting a gynecological exam.

Eddie was sure she did it to disarm men, to make them feel uneasy, but staring at a woman's crotch was something he felt comfortable doing.

Burley, on the other hand, didn't know what to do with his eyes and kept them glued to the wall behind her while she perused the list of casting suggestions.

She set the paper down and looked at Burley. "What do you think of this?"

Burley cleared his throat. "I think the addition of the interstellar bounty hunter character is a compelling, dynamic step in the modernization of the franchise."

"That's because it's the character Eddie threw in for you," she said. "And I'm throwing it out."

Burley's face reddened as if he'd been slapped.

She looked at Eddie and leaned forward, so Eddie could stare at her breasts through the open collar of her shirt. "You really think Ricky Schroder is the actor to replace Chad Shaw?"

"It's *Rick* Schroder now," Eddie corrected. "And he has a very commanding presence. I think he's the next David Hasselhoff."

"I don't want the next David Hasselhoff." Kim crumpled up the paper into a ball and threw it on the floor. "I want the next Johnny Depp. The next Woody Harrelson. This show is supposed to be *hip.*"

"I see what you're getting at, and I have just the man." Eddie paused a moment for dramatic effect. "Jaleel White."

"Urkel?" Kim asked incredulously.

"We'll show a side of him no one has ever seen before," Eddie said. "The man. The leader. The rugged action hero of the nineties."

"We're talking about the same person, right? The kid from *Family Matters.*"

"He's got a huge following," Eddie added. "He could be the next Will Smith."

"Will Smith didn't play a mousy-mouthed nerd for

ten years," she said impatiently. "Is this the best you can do?"

"I say, let's stop searching in the dark for the next teen idol," Burley said. "Let's bank on proven appeal. I can get Kent McCord on the stage and in uniform in two hours."

She sat back in her chair and regarded them both. "Hey, let's go for broke. What about Lee Horsley?"

"Now we're on to something," Burley said, shooting Eddie a smile.

But Eddie wasn't smiling. He was on the verge of crying. That idiot Jackson Burley was going to get them both thrown off the show.

Kim stood up. "I'm wondering if we have the right creative team on this show."

Eddie figured he had five seconds to save his professional life. "There is one actor who has proven appeal and has the potential to be the next break-out star."

"Who?" she asked.

Good question. Eddie didn't have the slightest idea. He glanced at her, then at Burley, drawing the moment out as if he was toying with them, instead of frantically searching his mind for a name. Hundreds of faces flew across his psyche like numbers on a roulette wheel.

He was about to speak, to say the first name that occurred to him, when the door to Kim's office flew open and Charlie Willis marched in, a gash on his forehead, dried blood all over his shirt, and tiny bits of broken glass in his hair.

"Charlie Willis," Eddie blurted out.

And, as if on cue, Charlie said, "I want to be the next Captain Pierce."

"You're joking," Kim said. She wasn't half as stunned as Eddie.

"I've never been more serious," Charlie replied. "If I

am the star of *Beyond the Beyond,* the killers will make me their next target."

Kim stared at Charlie. "It looks like they already have."

It had taken firefighters twenty minutes to pry him out of the car with the Jaws of Life, but besides forty-two stitches in various parts of his body and a world-class headache, he came out just fine.

"Charlie Willis is absolutely the wrong choice, which makes him the right choice." Eddie had no idea what he was saying, but he meant it passionately. "Cutting edge, risky, unpredictable."

"*My Gun Has Bullets* was a notorious bomb," she replied.

"Only because he murdered someone," added Burley, who created the show and still believed it could have been a hit, albeit with Kent McCord. "It was a solid franchise with drawing power."

"You're a lousy actor, Charlie," she said. "No one wants to see you back on television."

"It won't get that far," he said. "This is an undercover assignment. I have no intention of actually staying with the show, assuming I survive the attempt on my life."

"Just announcing you've got the part will destroy the show before it even gets on the air," she said. "The press remembers you as a joke."

"No, they remember him as the guy who kicked the mob out of prime time," said Eddie, hoping to score a few points with Charlie and Kim at the same time. "Right now, the press isn't interested in the show, they're interested in the murders. If we cast anyone *but* Charlie Willis, it will stay that way. Charlie will be news. He's the one person who will focus attention back on *the show.*"

And more important to Eddie, it would make Charlie, and not him, the target of Guy Goddard's wrath. "I also think Charlie has George Clooney potential."

Kim looked at Charlie. "Can you guarantee that the killers will take a shot at you *before* we start shooting? What if we have to go on the air with you? It will kill the show and the network."

"That's a risk we have to take," Charlie said. "Because if you cast another actor as Captain Pierce, you could be sentencing him to death."

Eddie had to admire Charlie. That was a line that begged for a pulse-pounding music cue and a freeze-frame. The guy was a rotten actor, and a dullard, but he had a knack for the melodramatic.

She met Charlie's gaze while waving off the others. "I want to talk to him alone. You two, wait outside."

Eddie Planet and Jackson Burley hurried out, knowing there was nothing more they could do anyway. As soon as the door was closed, Kim got in Charlie's face.

"So this is it, Charlie. The payoff. It sure didn't take you long."

"What are you talking about?"

"Don't give me any more of your nauseating do-gooder bullshit. This is blackmail. You want a network series, thirty-five-thousand an episode, or you'll reveal my secret."

Charlie took a deep breath before speaking, he wanted to remain calm. "I'm not interested in the money or the show. I just don't want anyone else to die."

She applauded. "Very good. You projected the sincerity, but you have to work on capturing the emotion."

"As long as I'm the star, I won't have to find the killers. They'll find me. Whoever they are, they don't want *Beyond the Beyond* to get on the air. I'll catch them or they'll kill me. Either way it goes, I won't be in the show when it premieres."

Kim looked at him. "I don't believe you. No one is that selfless."

Charlie shrugged. "Fine. I'm blackmailing you. Do I get the show or don't I?"

He saw the answer in the hatred and frustration in her eyes.

For the second time in his life, Charlie Willis was going to be a TV star.

It took twenty-six rolls of heavy-duty duct tape to secure Clive Odett to the toilet in the starship *Endeavor*'s high-security brig, which looked to the untrained eye like a typical quarter bath decorated with *Beyond the Beyond* wallpaper.

Thrack and Bev stripped him, sat him on the open seat, and taped him into place, his arms bound to his sides, his legs stuck tight against the porcelain. This way, neither of them would have to clean up after him or risk him escaping during a trip to the can.

But their ingenuity didn't end there. They took ten soft-drink straws, stolen from McDonald's, Scotch-taped together to make one giant straw, stuck one end in the toilet tank and the other to his face. That way, he always had something to drink. Finally, they tied a string around the flusher and ran it up to Odett's ear. All he had to do was lower his head, and he could flush his own toilet.

All that was left was feeding him. Otherwise, he was a totally self-cleaning prisoner.

Clive Odett didn't appreciate their thoughtfulness. The moment he opened his eyes and saw his reflection in the vanity mirror, he started squirming so much that

Thrack had to whack him with the plunger a few times to calm him down.

Subdued and bleeding, Odett stared furiously at his captors, a woman with an elephant nose and a guy with a roll of duct tape stuck on the bulge in his pants.

"Don't fuck with the force field," Thrack said. "Have some water and relax."

Odett slurped some water from the straw and spit it at Thrack. The ensign was about to calm Odett down some more when Captain Pierce showed up.

"That's enough," Pierce said. "He has to be alert if he's going to talk to these aliens."

The sight of himself taped to a toilet was shocking enough for Clive Odett. But the sight of Guy Goddard, in his faded *Beyond the Beyond* uniform, made what was already a surreal experience all the more horrific.

"You expect me to *represent* you?" Odett said.

"Not me," the captain said, "the Confederation of Aligned Galaxies. You have to let the aliens know that this insidious conspiracy will never succeed."

"What aliens?" Odett asked.

"The ones attempting to replace the crew of the *Endeavor* with evil doubles," he said. "They must be stopped at all costs."

Odett suddenly realized who killed his clients. It wasn't another agency. It was this bunch, a has-been actor and his deranged groupies. Now they expected him to negotiate a deal to get Guy Goddard back on the show.

"You didn't have to go to all this trouble," Odett said. "It would be my privilege to help an actor of your stature in the industry. Whatever you want is within your grasp with The Company behind you. Let's go down to my office, go over the deal points, and work out a negotiating strategy."

"Yes, you definitely speak their language." Captain Pierce smiled. "We'll talk again, Mr. Odett."

Captain Pierce walked out. Thrack and Bev followed after him, closing the door behind them.

Odett stared at his reflection in the mirror. Right now, Zita was probably slitting throats all over town looking for him. The blood of a thousand agents would flow down Wilshire Boulevard and all for nothing. Zita would never figure out where he was. This kind of insanity wouldn't occur to anyone.

He was on his own. The master negotiator would have to talk his way out of this. Then he'd come back and kill each and every one of them.

Nineteen

Beyond in Planet's Orbit; Charlie Willis to Star

In a stunning development, cop-turned-actor Charlie Willis will limn Captain Pierce in the Big Network's *Beyond the Beyond* revival, stepping in for Chad Shaw, who was killed in a mugging earlier this week.

This will mark the return of Willis to the small screen he bloodied only a few short years ago as star of the infamous *My Gun Has Bullets* series, which claimed one life and the career of TV's grand dame, Esther Radcliffe.

"He's thrilled to be back in series television," says Eddie Planet, *Beyond the Beyond*'s new executive producer, taking over the reins in the wake of creator Conrad Stipe's brutal murder.

Willis disappeared from the public eye after the *My Gun Has Bullets* scandal, and industry wags are said to be shocked he'd peg his return on another violence-plagued production.

"Charlie Willis embraces risk," says Planet, defending his controversial casting decision. "He embodies the strength, courage, and determination that has made Captain Pierce a hero to generations of fans. Any other actor would just be playing the part. Charlie Willis *is* the part."

Terry Bloss will segue from the defunct *Peter Pan* into the role of Mr. Snork, replacing Leigh Dickson, who was killed by a hit-and-run driver. Spring Dano remains as Dr. Kelvin.

Planet promises the addition of Willis to the cast will give "a gritty, Tarantino edge" to the deep-space adventures.

Eddie Planet was reading *Daily Variety* and enjoying his new heated toilet seat for the first time, when he got a phone call from another galaxy.

"Planet here," Eddie said.

"This is Captain Rick Pierce of the Confederation starship *Endeavor*," said the familiar voice. "According to a deep-space transmission I've intercepted, you have replaced Conrad Stipe in the Confederation high command."

"If you're saying I'm the new executive producer of *Beyond the Beyond*, that's true." Eddie had to be careful what he said. He didn't want to piss the lunatic off, but he also didn't want to say anything that could be incriminating if the police were tapping Goddard's phone. "What can I do for you?"

"Give me back my ship!" Captain Pierce yelled.

"You know I'd like to, but network has given the job to somebody else. Charlie Willis is our new captain."

"Will the network listen to Clive Odett?"

Odett was representing Guy Goddard? Eddie didn't believe it any more than he believed Goddard really commanded a starship.

"They might, but the Charlie Willis deal is locked."

"We'll see about that." Captain Pierce hung up.

Eddie set the receiver back in its cradle, pleased with his performance. If anyone was listening, nothing he said could come back to haunt him. And he made it clear to Goddard that the network was the villain, not Eddie.

Of course, he'd also made Charlie Willis a target. But isn't that what Charlie wanted? Besides, Charlie could take care of himself.

Just to be on the safe side, though, Eddie decided not to leave the safety of the studio. He'd live in his office, where he had everything a man could want.

Eddie wrote a note to himself on the *Daily Variety* to have his brass plaque placed on the studio's best table as soon as possible.

Thrack of Oberon stood with his hands on his hips facing Artie and Bev, who took turns trying to toss plastic rings on his superwarp plasma pleasure warhead.

After both Melvah and Bev failed to diminish his turgescence, he had tried to whip the beast into shape himself but succeeded only in spraining both his wrists.

He began to wonder if his erection would ever go away. It was painful and uncomfortable, but it could make him a real babe magnet at the BeyondCon. He was pondering that possibility when the landing party returned from Thrifty Mart with potato chips, beer, Cheez Whiz, and some plastic rings.

Now his plight became a pleasant way to pass the time in the backyard until their next mission.

He looked down to see that Bev succeeded in landing three rings on his bulge. He was impressed with her aim and his size.

"Congratulations," Thrack said. "You win. Anyone up for some baseball?"

Before the others could answer, Captain Pierce stormed out of the house, a rolled-up *Daily Variety* gripped in his hand. "Red alert!"

His crew quickly lined up in a row, side by side, for his inspection.

The captain couldn't help but look at Thrack's most prominent feature, which now sported three plastic rings. "It's bad enough it's still there, do you have to decorate it?"

He turned his back on Thrack, who quickly slid the rings off. The captain stepped up to Artie and slapped his chest with the *Variety*. "The aliens have found another impersonator for me. Destroy him."

"I've developed a powerful new weapon," Artie said. "I'm dying to give it a test."

"Make it so," the captain said.

McGarrett lay beside Charlie Willis's recliner, barking in his sleep and passing gas.

It was Charlie's fault. For lunch, he roasted a couple of hot dogs on the Grill-Master out back, piled them high with relish, onions, and mustard, and gave one of them to McGarrett. Then he let the dog wash it down with a light beer.

Charlie figured the dog had only a couple of good years left, so he ought to have the things he enjoyed, even if it meant some foul air. He lifted his T-shirt up over his nose and thought about what had happened yesterday at Pinnacle City.

The hot dog and a couple of painkillers didn't make things any clearer.

Could he be certain it was Clive Odett's Hummer that he saw? After all, he didn't actually *see* Odett in the car. Charlie called Lou, who checked with Odett's office. According to Odett's personal assistant, the superagent wasn't at Pinnacle City yesterday, he was away on a religious retreat. Since no one reported him missing, there was nothing the police could do.

Maybe the carjacking incident had nothing to do with Clive Odett or the *Beyond the Beyond* killings. Or maybe it did. It was all a confusing muddle.

But now he didn't have to figure it out. The bad guys, whoever they were, would step right up and introduce themselves.

His portable phone rang. He snatched it up and said hello.

"One minute you're managing a storage unit and the next thing you know, you're a TV star," Alison Sweeney said. "See what a kiss from me can do?"

It suddenly hit him that in the chaos of the last twenty-four hours he forgot to call her. He felt terrible.

"I'm sorry you had to read about it," he said, pacing in front of the window. "I should have called you."

"It's okay. I know how busy you stars can be."

"I have no intention of sticking with the show. I'm setting myself up as the target so the next time the killers strike, no one else will get hurt."

"Except you."

"Don't knock it, it was your idea," he joked, trying to lighten things up. He failed.

"Don't you dare make me responsible for this," she snapped. "It's a stupid plan. And if you *had* called me, I would have done everything I could to make sure it didn't happen."

She hung up.

Charlie tossed the phone on the recliner. She had a point. Maybe that was the real reason he hadn't called her.

He glanced out the window and saw a guy standing on the sidewalk in an orange polyester uniform, a tank strapped to his back, holding some kind of hose in his gloved hands. At first, Charlie thought it was the exterminator. But he didn't call one, and something wasn't right about this guy.

So Charlie stepped closer to the window and squinted at him. The guy turned toward the building, and that's when Charlie saw his hairy, pointed ear and dead, yellow eye. And that's also when he noticed the thing the guy was holding looked a lot like . . .

. . . *a flamethrower.*

Charlie dove to the floor the same instant the stream of fire smashed through the front window and splashed against the recliner, setting it aflame and melting the phone.

McGarrett dashed out the open back door, head and tail hung low, fur smoking, passing gas the whole way.

Charlie tipped over the coffee table and, using it as a shield, peered out the window to get a better look at the crazy son of a bitch who was trying to kill him.

The assassin, disguised like some kind of hell horse, marched toward the window, spraying the room with fire, washing everything down with flames.

The hell horse spotted Charlie and blasted the coffee table, turning it into fireball. Charlie scrambled back, everything around him on fire, the hair on his arms singed off.

He crawled out the back door, the flames licking at him. Safely outside, he slumped against his Grill-Master, gasping for breath, finding it all very hard to believe. Thirty seconds ago he was just sitting in his recliner, listening to his dog fart. It never occurred to him that someone might come after him with a flamethrower.

He had to think fast. The entire apartment was engulfed in flames, and in two seconds the hell horse was going to come back here after him.

Charlie looked around. There was no place to hide. All the storage units were locked.

There was also no place to run. The fences around the property were ringed with razor wire. If he tried to climb them, he'd snag himself for sure.

He was trapped.

Then he realized what he was leaning against. His eyes fell on the Grill-Master's propane tank, and he smiled.

When Artie first saw Canoga Stor-All, he was certain he had the wrong address. *Again.* But Bev Huncke, a former postal worker who now worked at the Department of Motor Vehicles, gave him the address and even got him a picture of his target.

He was pretty certain the guy he saw running out the back door, his ass on fire, was Charlie Willis. Even if it wasn't, Artie was having way too much fun to give a shit. His homemade flamethrower was better than anything Chief Engineer Glerp ever came up with. Artie couldn't wait to try this sucker out on a gas station somewhere. But first he had to toast Charlie Willis.

And that was going to be easy, because the stupid jerk was just standing there in the open, beside a trash dumpster.

Artie smiled. "Eat hot death."

He squeezed the trigger, shooting a stream of fire at Charlie Willis.

An instant before Artie exploded, he saw the hissing propane tank a few feet away from him and wondered what it was doing there.

Charlie dived behind the dumpster, landing hard on the asphalt, the ground rocked by two strong blasts. Flaming chunks of flesh, metal, and mortar rained down all around him.

He was still lying there, his face against the ground, when a yellow, plastic eyeball rolled under the dumpster and came to a stop against his cheek.

ACT FOUR

Twenty

*M*aybe you ought to let the paramedics take another look at you," said Harvey, the police artist.

"I'm fine." Charlie sat in the back of his golf cart, holding an ice pack to his forehead.

Harvey sat in front of Charlie on a tiny folding chair, a sketch pad open on his lap, staring skeptically at what he was drawing.

Charlie glanced at the sketch. "The ear was more pointed, and the eye looked like this." Charlie reached into his pocket and pulled out a scorched, plastic eye with a yellow marble rolling around inside it.

Harvey abruptly closed the sketch book. He had enough. "Is this some kind of joke?"

"Do you see me laughing?" Charlie said.

Firemen were still hosing down the blackened remains of his apartment, and a dozen coroners were picking up chunks of the killer off the pavement. As of now, he was homeless, jobless, and pointless. There was nothing funny about it at all.

"I'll work on it," Harvey said. "When I'm done, we can beam the picture into space and wait for word from Mars."

The artist walked away.

Charlie dropped the ice pack, resigned to the fact the police weren't going to do a damn thing. So Charlie considered the bright side. He and McGarrett survived. Most of his belongings were in one of the storage units, all of which came out of the blast relatively unscathed, except for a few gore-splashed and fire-scorched metal doors.

"What the hell happened here?" Lou LeDoux staggered up to Charlie in a shocked daze.

Charlie watched the coroners, who were dragging sacks of scorched body parts alongside them as they moved slowly and methodically over the pavement. "This is what happens when someone tries to kill you with a flamethrower and you fight back with a propane tank."

"No shit," Lou whistled.

"Isn't that why you're here?"

"I came to see Gharlane. He wasn't hurt, was he?"

"He wasn't here."

"What about his magazine collection?" Lou looked gravely at Charlie. "It wasn't damaged, was it?"

"No."

"That's a relief. Because I did that favor you asked for. I've been huddling with the lab boys and a team of anatomists at UCLA. They studied the nipple Stipe bit off, the bruises on his face, the amount of mass necessary to smother him, and did some calculations."

Lou reached into his blue-checked jacket and pulled

a snapshot from the pocket of his orange shirt. "They came up with this."

It was a photo of a clay model of a woman's breasts.

"The murder weapon," Lou declared proudly. "Think Gharlane can ID 'em?"

It was a ridiculous idea, but everything that was happening was so crazy anyway that it seemed to beg for craziness in response. Besides, nothing else Charlie tried seemed to be working.

"It can't hurt to try," Charlie said.

"Easy for you to say," Lou replied. "You don't have to explain it to my captain."

It would have been the perfect sexual experience, if only Zita hadn't gotten her hair caught in Melvah's Orgoglian mating clip.

Writhing passionately atop Melvah, Zita tossed back her head and accidentally tore the ring out of Melvah's nostril. Melvah screamed, blood spurting all over her face.

While Melvah went to the bathroom to stop the bleeding, Zita spent the next fifteen minutes trying to untangle the bloody ring from her hair.

It was a real mood killer.

Both were hoping that a little sex would soften the inevitable confrontation, that it would be a pleasurable reminder of what they could do for one another when they worked together. Neither one of them wanted to upset their alliance, but each had clear, separate goals that were already beginning to clash.

Instead, the sex had gone wrong. They were both weary, bloody, and frustrated. Not a good combination for rational discussion and compromise.

Melvah marched out of the bathroom naked, a wet

rag pressed against her nose, and stood in front of Zita who, in frustration, had started sawing off her blood-matted hair with a steak knife.

"Eddie Planet cast Charlie Willis as Captain Pierce," Melvah said. "For that he must die."

"I already told you, he's a potential client. He lives."

"I'm supposed to become the producer of *Beyond the Beyond,*" she said furiously, tossing the bloody towel aside and revealing her torn nose. "That was the deal, remember?"

"You *are* a producer," Zita said. "But if you are going to make it in this business, you're going to have to grow up."

"What is *that* supposed to mean?" Melvah grabbed Zita by the jaw and jerked her head up. People were always telling her that, and afterward most of them either walked with a limp or ate through straws.

"You're in the real world now, Melvah. If we kill Eddie Planet, another show runner will be hired to replace him."

"*I'll* replace him."

There were many things Zita liked about Melvah. Her strong sense of self. Her devotion to her art. Her ability to kill with ease. But Melvah had no clue how the television business worked. She had to learn that *Beyond the Beyond,* more than anything else, was a *business.*

"No, you won't." Zita took Melvah's wrist and wrenched her jaw free from her grasp. "The Company has power, but not enough to accomplish that. Neither the studio nor the network is going to give the series to someone it has never heard of, no matter how many people we blackmail, torture, and kill. There's too much money at stake. You're going to wait and be satisfied with being the power behind the throne, for a while any way."

Melvah face flushed with fury. "Eddie Planet doesn't know a thing about the universe. He's illiterate."

Still holding Melvah's wrist, Zita gently began stroking it with the sharp edge of the knife, just enough so Melvah could feel it but not enough to cut her.

"I know how you feel, Melvah," Zita said softly. "Eventually, you will get the show, the same way I finally got The Company. The only reason Clive Odett is still alive is because he may have a few secrets I don't know about. But I'm being patient and methodical, just like you have to be."

Melvah's eyelids fluttered, the stinging caress arousing her, tempering her disappointment. "All right."

"I knew you'd understand." Zita ran the knife over the back of Melvah's hand and along each finger.

"Charlie Willis has to go."

"Of course he does," Zita said. "He's cost us several clients, and thanks to him, the police are asking questions about Clive's disappearance. But more important, we want Dustin Woods for the part."

Melvah yanked her hand away, causing Zita to slice her. But Melvah was oblivious to the pain, to the blood dripping from her hand onto the floor. Seeing her standing there like that, naked and bleeding, skin flushed with rage, excited Zita so much it momentarily took her breath away.

"There is only *one* Captain Pierce," Melvah balled her hands into fists, causing the blood to stream out of her wound, "and it's Guy Goddard."

Zita knew she had to handle this delicately. This would be, perhaps, the hardest reality of all for Melvah to grasp. However, the fact that Melvah used the actor's name was a good sign, one that Zita took as encouragement.

Zita dropped to her knees in front of Melvah and picked up the bloody towel and wrapped it around Melvah's hand, pressing firmly to stop the bleeding.

"One day, *Beyond the Beyond* will be yours, but Guy Goddard will never, ever, be Captain Pierce again," Zita said. "I know how much you admire him, but he appeals to a very narrow, very old, demographic. If *Beyond the Beyond* is going succeed, if the *universe* is going to prosper, you have to draw in young viewers, and he won't."

"He *is* Captain Pierce," Melvah whispered, her voice quivering.

"And Captain Pierce would sacrifice himself to save the universe. Wouldn't he?"

Melvah nodded, a tear rolling down her cheek. Zita pressed her face against Melvah's stomach and gently licked her navel ring.

Melvah ran her fingers through what was left of Zita's hair and cried. She saw the future clearly. She would save *Beyond the Beyond* and keep the universe alive, but it would cost Guy Goddard his life. He would kill anyone who tried to be Captain Pierce, so Zita would have to kill him.

But Zita was right. It was the universe that mattered. And Melvah Blenis was its protector now, so she had to make sacrifices.

Right now, with Zita's tongue moving from her navel ring to one just a bit lower, the sacrifice didn't seem so hard to make.

Charlie's new home had one bedroom, one bath, power steering, and a view of Soundstage 9.

The decor of the Winnebago, Charlie's dressing room on the Pinnacle Studios lot, was modern American passenger jet, coach class. The cloth upholstery on everything resembled a plaid shag carpet. The matching curtains were closed over the windshield, and the driver's seat was turned to face away from the dashboard, so the seat was now considered "a deluxe armchair."

Charlie sat in the passenger seat–cum–deluxe armchair, feet up on his built-in dinette set, reading the pilot script for *Beyond the Beyond* and not understanding a word of it.

He was wearing Pinnacle logo sweats and a *Muck Thing* T-shirt, an ensemble he bought for $45 at the studio store. The rest of his clothes, taken from the wardrobe department, were hanging in the tiny closet that separated the bedroom from the kitchen.

The refrigerator was filled with soft drinks and sandwiches lifted from the *Beyond the Beyond* snack table, which was in the adjacent soundstage. The remains of his Domino's Pizza dinner were on the stove.

The only things he brought back to his new home from his storage unit at Canoga Stor-All were his gun and, for some crazy reason, his badge. Sitting on his built-in nightstand, right beside his built-in bed, was a melted, misshapen lump of lucite with Esther Radcliffe's bullet in it.

He didn't know how important that paperweight was to him until he thought he'd lost it. He spent three hours sifting through the ashes of his apartment before he found it. Somehow, the fact that it was melted by the fire only made it more valuable to him—it now immortalized *two* near-death experiences.

He was concentrating on his script, trying to make sense out of the Captain's line, *"If that quantum singularity is a tachyon particle disbursement field, then it's possible the Nerglids exist in an alternate dimension in the space-time con-*

tinuum!" A timid knock at the door interrupted him. Charlie parted the curtain and peered cautiously out the window. Alison stood outside. He opened the door and motioned her in.

"Isn't it a little late to be at the studio?" Charlie asked.

"I just came back. I had an errand to run." She dropped a leash on the table. "I went by the vet and picked up McGarrett for you."

The vet, Dr. Gaston Grospiron, was an old friend of Charlie's and had offered to board McGarrett for free until Charlie found a place to live. It wasn't the first time Dr. Grospiron had come to McGarrett's aid. Several years ago, he wrote a very moving letter to the court on McGarrett's behalf. He explained that McGarrett was docile and kind and raped Boyd Hartnell to death only because the studio exec was covered in excrement and had a head of golden retriever hair implanted in his scalp.

Under ordinary circumstances, the vet promised, McGarrett was no threat to society.

"That was very nice of you," Charlie said, "but he'll be more comfortable with the vet. There's barely room for me in here."

"I know. That's why I got him a place of his own."

Charlie looked confused, so Alison held out her hand to him. "Come with me."

She led him outside into the warm, still Los Angeles night. They walked around the soundstage toward the backlot, the acres and acres of fake storefronts and building facades where countless movies and TV shows were shot.

"Where are we going?"

"Not far."

That was a shame, because Charlie liked the feel of her hand in his and wanted it to last.

They walked down Madison Avenue, casting long shadows on the dark, plaster facades. It was so realistic that for a moment Charlie fantasized that they were the last living couple on earth after some horrible plague.

The street ended and became a frontier town in the old West. Now Charlie and Alison were time travelers, hurled through some quantum singularity or tachyon disbursement field and emerging in the past.

She led him between the sheriff's office and the frontier store to a lush, green patch, roughly a quarter acre, surrounded by a tall cyclone fence. A waterfall cascaded into a tiny river that ran past a tall oak tree, a bright red fire hydrant, and a Tudor doghouse with a redwood deck, sliding glass doors, and an air conditioner. Charlie looked closer and saw McGarrett inside the doghouse, sleeping peacefully on a sheepskin rug.

"This used to Boo Boo's home," she said, referring to the late, beloved celebrity dog. "Pinnacle has kept it up as a sightseeing attraction on the studio tour. I figured, why let it go to waste?"

"The dog is living better than me," Charlie said. "Think he'll trade?"

She laughed, and he realized how much he had missed the sound of it these last few days. They walked back to his motor home in silence, hand in hand. But it was a comfortable silence, both enjoying the simple, intimate pleasure of being together.

When they reached his Winnebago, he turned to her to invite her for a drink and saw the tears running down her cheeks.

"What is it?"

She didn't know if she was crying because she was relieved that Charlie was safe, or because she'd almost lost him. Either way, it surprised and unsettled her.

"Don't just stand there, Charlie." Alison sniffled and wiped away her tears. "Kiss me, you idiot."

They tumbled into the motor home, locked in an embrace, hands all over each other.

Alison fell back into the driver's seat. Charlie supported himself on the armrests and mashed his lips against hers. She opened her mouth, taking him in hungrily, while her hands found the waistband of his sweats and yanked them down.

Charlie tore open her blouse, the buttons popping off in all directions, and buried his face in her breasts, pulling and sucking on each nipple until she gasped.

Her hand found his erection and squeezed it, feeling him throb with each of his moans. Charlie dropped to his knees, and she lifted herself up, allowing him to pull off her jeans and panties. He propped her legs on his shoulders and devoured her.

She ran her hands through his hair as he licked her, his tongue searching for her clit, trapping it between his lips.

Alison moaned, the pleasure so intense it bordered on pain. She arched her back, bringing herself up to meet his hands, his lips, his tongue. As her breathing quickened, he strummed her clit with his tongue and slid two fingers inside her as fast, and as deep, as he could, bringing her to the edge of orgasm.

Then he stopped and stood up. She launched herself at him, knocking him back against the table, which would have tipped over if it wasn't nailed to the floor.

She put her arms around his neck and lifted herself up, wrapped her legs around his waist, and took him inside her, riding him slowly at first, then faster as her hunger and his need took over.

His fingers dug into her buttocks and forced himself into her even deeper, beyond her point of endurance into a shuddering, quaking orgasm.

She bucked against him, tossing her head from side to side, grimacing as the pleasure rocked her. It was more than Charlie could stand. He came in a sharp, powerful jolt, thrusting as deep as he could, his legs shaking.

When it was over, they remained entangled in each other, their bodies slick with sweat.

"Is that the best you can do?" she asked, a mischievous smile on her face.

"That was just foreplay. Hold on tight."

She buried her face in his neck and he carried her to the bedroom, where they both soon discovered there were some advantages to having a bed that was nailed to the floor.

Charlie Willis wasn't the only one whose new home had four wheels.

Thrack of Oberon moved himself into the Hummer, now dubbed *Shuttle Craft Four,* which was parked in the driveway next to the starship *Endeavor.*

He was lying on the backseat, eating Cheez Doodles and surfing the net, his laptop plugged into the car's built-in modem. Thrack was flaming a couple of fuckhead writers from the new *Beyond the Beyond* because they thought the *Endeavor* security guards wore red uniforms, when everybody knows they're *blue.*

He just finished threatening their unborn children and was about to elaborate on his plans to defile their wives with his superwarp plasma pleasure warhead, when Melvah opened the door and slid in beside him.

The first thing he noticed was the gash on her nostril.

"A girl with sharp fingernails like yours shouldn't pick her nose," he said, holding up his index finger. "I designated this finger as my nose finger, so I keep the nail real short and smooth."

She grabbed the finger in her fist and wrenched it back until he yelped. "Artie blew himself up and Charlie Willis got away. That means it's up to us to kill him. You're not going to sit around picking your nose while Charlie Willis is still alive."

"You're the same rank as me," he whimpered. "You can't give me orders."

She wrenched his finger back until he yelped again. "Charlie Willis was the guy who chased you after you snatched Clive Odett. What if you led him to us? What do you think the captain is going to do if he finds out?"

Melvah let go of his finger, and he yanked his hand away from her. He thought again about the captain and his hatchet.

"Fine. You find him, I'll kill him," Thrack said, then stuck his sore finger in his nose just to show her he still had his self-respect.

Twenty-one

*T*he great starship Endeavor
glided through the glittering cosmos, an arrow in search of a tar-
get it would never find.

Captain Pierce sat in his command console, leaning for-
ward, his sharp, hawklike eyes riveted to the front viewscreen.
Where others saw an endless pattern of stars, he saw the future,
he saw discovery, he saw humanity.

Yeoman Cathy McNally, cheerful and eager to please, thrust
a CompuClipboard in front of him. "The duty logs, sir. They need
your signature."

He marked the CompuClipboard with a space pen. "Thank
you, Yeoman."

The captain turned his attention back to the screen, so he
didn't see the yearning in her eyes, the lovesick poutiness of her
lips. She was in love with him, like so many women under his
command. The yeoman returned to her station, already impatient

for another task that would allow her to speak to him again, if only for a moment.

Mr. Snork scratched his nose and approached the command chair. "We've seen a lot of God's miracles on our voyages through space together, but I think she tops the list."

Dr. Kelvin's computer breasts heaved in deep computation. "Scientifically speaking, there's nothing miraculous about the yeoman. Her chemical composition is actually ninety-four percent water—"

"Enough, Doctor," Mr. Snork snapped. "There are some things science just can't explain."

Suddenly, the ship was rocked by a tremendous turbulence and, on-screen, a strange, undulating cloud appeared out of the blackness.

"And this may be one of them now." The captain turned to Dr. Kelvin. "Analysis?"

"It's some sort of quantum singularity," she said. "I'm detecting huge fluctuations in guadro-gamma emissions. If it continues to grow, it could tear space itself apart."

"Then we better stunt its growth," the captain said. "Arm all weapons."

The turbolift doors hissed open, and an officer with six beady yellow eyes and two big horsey ears strode onto the bridge. "I don't think so, Captain."

"Everybody down!" the captain yelled, pushing Dr. Kelvin to the floor and whipping a gun out from its hiding place under the seat, aiming the weapon right at the alien's head.

"Freeze, you son of a bitch," the captain said. "You so much as twitch, and I'll send you straight to hell."

Alison dropped her script, pushed past the startled director and camera crew, and rushed onto the set. Spring Dano, Terry Bloss, and a handful of extras were lying flat on the ground, while Fred Grayson, aka Security Chief Zorgog, cowered in Charlie's gunsight, his flipper hands raised. The first rehearsal of the show, and already there was trouble.

"Charlie, what are you doing?" she asked.

"Call security," Charlie said, looking very heroic in his polyester Confederation uniform. "This is an assassin."

"No, he's not," Alison said.

"The guy with the flamethrower was wearing the same bizarre disguise."

"Charlie, that's Fred Grayson. He's one of the series regulars. He plays Security Chief Zorgog. That's the way his character looks."

"Fred?" Charlie squinted at the man. He'd met him only once before, informally, at a table reading of the script in Eddie's office. "Is that you?"

"Yes," Fred said, his shaking flipper hands still raised. He remembered what happened to the last poor guy Charlie Willis pointed a gun at on a set. "Please don't shoot me. I have a wife and kids."

"I'm sorry." Charlie lowered the gun. "I'm terribly, terribly sorry, I didn't recognize you with all that makeup on."

Fred backed off the set in a hurry. Charlie suddenly became aware of all the terrified actors looking up at him from the floor.

"You can all get up now. My mistake. There's no danger. You can relax."

The actors started to get up. Ashamed, Charlie jammed the gun in his pants and helped Spring Dano to her feet.

"I'm so sorry, Ms. Dano." Charlie smiled politely. "I hope you'll forgive me."

She kissed him on the cheek. "I'm glad you're watching out for us."

Alison grabbed him by the arm and jerked him away from Spring.

"Haven't you ever seen the show?" she asked him.

"Not all the way through," Charlie admitted. "It was hard enough for me just to get through the script, especially after last night."

Alison blushed, surprised at her embarrassment, because last night was not something she regretted. It was something she hoped to repeat as soon as possible, and as soon as she had some sleep. They'd spent the entire night making love, unable to sleep, their desire for each other seemingly insatiable.

Charlie glanced back at Grayson, still in his Security Chief Zorgog outfit, yelling into his cell phone, pacing nervously. "He seems upset. Maybe I should apologize again."

She pulled him in the opposite direction. "Don't worry about Fred, I'll take care of it. That's my job."

"I know I made a fool of myself," Charlie said, "but the killer was in the same getup as him. What are the odds of that?"

"It's not that unusual."

"You've seen people, out there in the real world, who look like him?"

She nodded. "I can find at least fifty people dressed exactly the same way right now."

"Where?" Charlie asked.

Charlie Willis stood in the lobby of the Pinnacle City Marriott in his Confederation uniform, but it was Alison Sweeney, in jeans, a Donna Karan jacket, and one of his shirts, who was out of place.

The whole ride over in the golf cart from the studio, which adjoined the hotel, Charlie was concerned about going out in public dressed like a spaceman.

"Don't worry," Alison said. "No one will notice."

Charlie thought she was being sarcastic until he walked into the hotel. People in homemade and mail-order Confederation uniforms were everywhere, and they were easily the most conservatively dressed of the hundreds of Beyonders attending BeyondCon. There were aliens, monsters, and astronauts of all sorts, as well as plenty of Snorks, Kelvins, Glerps, and, as promised, Zorgogs.

"What is this?" Charlie asked.

"It's BeyondCon," Alison said, "a celebration of *Beyond the Beyond.*"

Charlie moved cautiously through the crowd, passing a six-breasted nymph of Zontar on the arm of a Snorkian ambassador. For the first time, he found himself wondering if The Company was the only threat he should be worried about.

"They're all crazy," he said.

"Why do you say that?" she asked.

"Look at how they're dressed."

"They're dressed just like you."

"I'm an actor playing a role."

"Today, so are they. You're looking at stockbrokers and schoolteachers, dentists and insurance salesman. There are probably even a few cops here."

Somehow, the idea of one of these people carrying a loaded weapon didn't give him much comfort. She saw the expression on his face and knew what he was thinking.

"These people are intelligent, well educated, and firmly in the middle class. They are the reason the show is coming back," she said. "Most of them grew up watching *Beyond the Beyond.* This is just their way of feeling closer to the show. Not all of them are Beyonders, you'll find a broad cross section of sci-fi fans here."

"They've modeled their lives after a TV show," he said. "To me, that qualifies as mental illness."

"I see," she said contemplatively. "What would you think about a guy who spent his childhood watching cop shows and then became a cop because that was the one person he saw in his life who was able to make things right?"

Charlie decided, then and there, never to talk again while making love. It was too risky. From now on, it was strictly grunts and moans and *Oh, God*s.

"There's a difference." Charlie wasn't sure exactly what it was, but intuitively knew there was one. He wasn't like these people at all, except for today, that is.

He followed her into the Grand Ballroom, which was crammed full of dealers selling all kinds of science-fiction merchandise. Suspended over the crowd of Confederation officers, Snorks, *SeaQuest* crewmembers, Cardassians, Ewoks, and Narns, was a huge replica of the starship *Endeavor*.

Across the ballroom, and unseen by Charlie, Thrack of Oberon was in his polyester Confederation dress uniform, moving slowly down the crowded aisle, poking into as many space gals as he could with his superwarp plasma pleasure warhead.

He was about to bump into the rear end of a shapely *Logan's Run* babe when Melvah grabbed him. "Look who's here," she hissed.

Thrack scanned the crowd and found a familiar face. "Wow, Richard Hatch still has the same cool hairstyle he had in *Battlestar Galactica.*"

"Not him." She pulled Thrack behind a *Beyond the Beyond* black-light poster display and pointed to the far end of the ballroom. "It's Charlie Willis."

Thrack couldn't believe it. The shitbag scumlicker

was even wearing a captain's uniform. "I'll cut his head off and use it as a bowling ball."

"I don't care what you do," she said, "as long as he doesn't survive. Now get out of here before he sees you."

"Relax, I blend in, like a shadow in the night," Thrack said. "I could sneak up behind him and he'd never see it coming."

"But he'd feel it." She grabbed the hard-on that was pressed against her ass. "Do him outside."

"Do me first." He winked and nodded toward her hand.

"Sure," Melvah said.

She yanked his hard-on onto the tabletop and smashed her fist down on it. Thrack dropped to the floor, squealing in agony.

"You're done," Melvah said, walking away, without even noticing that she'd managed to cure him.

Charlie and Alison left the ballroom and entered the adjoining conference hall, where hundreds of *Beyond the Beyond* fans gathered in front of the stage.

The original Mr. Snork, Kent Steed, sat on-stage in his faded uniform against a backdrop painted to look like the *Endeavor* bridge. His ragged rubber elephant nose dangled limply on his puffy face, and he clutched a copy of his book, *Call Me Mister Snork,* on his lap. Sitting beside him was a fat man wearing an elephant nose and a nametag that read "Warren of Eddore" who moderated the discussion.

"I believe I was wearing a red shirt when we landed on Altair-Seven," Steed said.

"What about when you landed on Naren-Three?" asked someone in the audience.

Steed stared into the audience for a long moment. "I don't remember."

"How can you not remember?" the same someone asked, astonished.

Warren of Eddore, sensing a problem, sputtered to life. "He doesn't remember because, as you will recall, in the previous episode his brain was invaded by neural fleas. We must assume the effects lingered for several episodes."

"Exactly," Kent Steed mumbled, scratching the three nicotine patches under his sleeve and yearning for a quick sip from his hip flask.

There were nods and mumbles of agreement in the audience.

"Does anyone else have a question for our honored guest?" the Warren of Eddore asked. Sixty hands, three flippers, and at least two pincers shot up. "Yes, the arthropod in the back with the orange hair."

"In 'The Lofficier Maneuver,' the serial number of the starship *Endeavor* was changed to NCE-174A," the lobster man asked. "Should it have been, NCE-174*F*?"

Kent Steed and the moderator shared an uneasy glance. Steed cleared his throat.

"That's really a question for the captain," Steed said, "and sadly, he's not here."

"Yes, he is," the green-skinned lady beside Charlie cried out, already lifting his arm into the air. "This is the new guy. I saw his picture in the paper."

All eyes, real and plastic, were on Charlie.

"What do I do?" Charlie whispered to Alison through a gritted-teeth smile.

"The star of *Beyond the Beyond* would run right up there," she smiled back. "And you are the star, aren't you?"

This was worse than facing a killer. But with several hundred people staring at him, it was too late to back out.

Reluctantly, he climbed up on the stage and offered his hand to Kent Steed.

"It's a pleasure to meet you," Charlie said.

Steed shook his hand and whispered, "Can you get me a guest shot?"

Charlie pretended not to hear him and faced the audience. "I'm Charlie Willis, and I'm very excited about portraying Captain Pierce. I hope you'll enjoy the new show. Thank you."

There was some light applause. He started to walk away when the lobster yelled out. "You didn't answer the question."

Charlie stopped. "I don't know the answer, I'm sorry."

"How can you be Captain Pierce if you don't know the answer?" someone else yelled.

"That was the old show," Charlie said. "I'm in the new show. Ask me a question about the new show and I will be glad to answer it."

More hands, flippers, and pincers shot up. Charlie looked into the crowd, his eyes settling on a young man in a slacks, a button-down shirt, and a sport jacket. A safe bet. Charlie, relieved, pointed to him.

"Yes, sir?" Charlie said.

"In the last episode of *Beyond the Beyond*, Captain Pierce discovered that his mother might have been half Nebulan," the young man said. "Will we discover, in the new series, that Captain Pierce is no longer entirely human?"

Charlie had no idea. He looked at Alison, who obviously didn't know either. Everyone was staring at him, including Kent Steed and Warren of Eddore.

"Welcome to *Beyond* fandom," Kent Steed muttered.

Taking a deep breath, Charlie was about to apologize for not knowing the answer to this question, either, when

233

a deep voice boomed out, echoing through the ballroom.

"The darkest reaches of space. The farthest boundaries of adventure. One starship journeys into the unknown, exploring the mysteries that lie . . . beyond the beyond.

A euphoric cheer rose up from the audience, and Guy Goddard emerged from behind the backdrop in his Confederation uniform. He held up his hand and the applause instantly stopped, the audience transfixed.

"What makes us human isn't in our genes, it's in our hearts and in our souls," he intoned, shaking his fist for emphasis, pausing meaningfully between each word. "What makes us human is the quest . . . the quest for knowledge, for truth, for peace. It doesn't matter whether I have Nebulan blood in my veins. To be human is to embody humanity, no matter where you come from or how you look."

The audience broke into thunderous applause that rumbled through the Pinnacle City Marriott like an aftershock, making it all but impossible for anybody but Charlie Willis to hear Guy Goddard say to him:

"I'm Captain Pierce of the Confederation starship *Endeavor.* Who the fuck are you?"

Twenty-two

*A*ll it took was one penetrating look from Captain Pierce, and the impostor slithered off the stage like a Vidian shit slug. The officers in the ballroom saw through the impostor then, the truth revealed by a single gaze power packed with all the strength and courage that made Captain Pierce a legend throughout the cosmos.

The evil doubles were so sure of their success they thought they could pass themselves off as the real thing in front of hundreds of Confederation officers. It was laughable, really. Who did think they were dealing with? Were they hoping that Captain Rick Pierce, veteran of the bloody Umgluck wars, would just sit this fight out?

Wake up and smell the meteor shower, boys. These space boots were made for stomping, and they're gonna stomp all over you. Captain Pierce wasn't some candy-assed bureaucrat who tackled the universe from the safety of a starship bridge. No, sir.

When the Glube king wanted to destroy the *Endeavor* with a death beam, what did he do? Tore his shirt off, flexed his pecs, and tied the alien bastard's antennae in a bow around his throat. When the six-breasted nymph of Zontar wanted to enslave the *Endeavor* crew, what did he do? Fucked her so good she led her own army into a lava pit to save him. When the Dorcons reduced his crew to cubes and took over his ship, what did he do? Hit the self-destruct button. One second away from obliterating his own ship, the gutless villains surrendered. The biggest asteroids in the universe were between his legs.

He was a legend in the Confederation because he wasn't afraid to look the enemy in the face and punch it. Diplomacy by fist, that was the Captain Pierce approach. Once they regained consciousness, then he could teach them to respect freedom, liberty, and basic humanity.

After holding the BeyondCon audience spellbound, reciting the Confederation Oath of Allegiance, Captain Pierce slipped out of the Pinnacle City Marriott through a fire escape, jamming the door closed behind him with a wedge of wood he brought along just for that purpose. He didn't want any overzealous Confederation officers following him and jeopardizing his mission.

Killing the alien impostors wasn't working, so it was time to find their king and make him eat his crown, then drag him back to the ship for some straight talk with Clive Odett in his own twisted language.

It would be no problem infiltrating the alien stronghold. The idiots sold tickets. Captain Pierce marched down the Main Street of Pinnacle City, USA, to the studio tour gate. He didn't mind paying. If thirty bucks was all it cost to save the universe, it was mighty cheap.

"That went well," Charlie said as he steered the golf cart away from the hotel and along the Pinnacle City promenade.

"It would have, if you hadn't walked off the stage," Alison replied, glancing at all the colorful neon storefronts.

"They didn't want to see me. To them, *he's* Captain Pierce. I'm just a jerk in a stupid outfit."

"Maybe if you'd stayed up there they would have had the chance to get to know you. You were up and off so fast they probably don't even remember what you look like."

"You seem to be forgetting something," Charlie said. "I'm not staying with the show."

She gave him a coy smile. "Maybe you'll change your mind."

The promenade spilled out onto a large plaza between the Pinnacle City eighteenplex and a parking structure where, on the second floor, Thrack sat in his idling Hummer, watching the golf cart crawl across the cement like a bug waiting to get stomped.

The wait was over. Thrack floored it.

Charlie steered the cart off the plaza onto the access road that led to the studio. "This is just an undercover assignment."

"But what if you like it?"

"I don't. And I *won't.*"

A familiar rumble drew Charlie's attention. He glanced over his shoulder and saw a banged-up Hummer charging across the plaza toward them.

"Hold on." Charlie slammed his foot on gas pedal, but the cart barely accelerated. "Can't this thing go any faster?"

"The studio carts go twelve miles an hour, tops. What's the hurry?"

The V8 turbo-diesel growl of the Hummer answered her question. She jerked around in her seat and saw six thousand pounds of metal closing in on them so fast she could make out the tread pattern on its four monster tires.

"Charlie," she said, her eyes wide with fear, "we can't outrun it."

And there was no way to evade the Hummer on the wide-open access road. In just a few seconds, they would be run over. Which left only one option.

Charlie shoved Alison down. "Get flat on the floor, *now.*"

She scrunched down under the dashboard, her face against the metal floor, and for the first time since she was a child, she prayed.

Thrack hunched over the wheel, feeling the roar of the engine as he bore down on the golf cart. He saw himself as the lion chasing after the stupid deer in those great wild animal specials on TV. The deer could weave and dodge all it wanted, in the end it was dead meat.

But then Charlie Willis did something the deer never did. He turned around and came at the lion, running right for its slavering jaws.

Charlie headed straight at the oncoming Hummer, carefully steering toward the center grille, away from the monster wheels. He was counting on the Hummer being seven feet wide and about two feet high. If he was wrong, he'd never live to find out.

At the last possible second, he let go of the wheel,

grabbed the steering column for support, and leaned his body straight out the side of the cart.

The two vehicles collided, the Hummer shearing off the windshield, the rooftop, the steering wheel, and the seatbacks of the cart as it mowed over them. Alison screamed, and so did Charlie, his hair grazed by the monster tires as the cart passed underneath the Hummer.

Thrack wailed with delight as the cart ripped apart in front of him, but he couldn't help wondering why he was missing out on all the gore. That was half the fun of running someone over.

The instant the ravaged cart cleared the rear of the Hummer, Charlie sat up and discovered he had no wheel to steer the speeding cart with. It didn't matter, he couldn't afford to stop now anyway.

The golf cart veered out of control toward the Pinnacle eighteenplex, while behind them, the Hummer continued to barrel down the access road, leaving a wake of twisted fiberglass and shredded vinyl.

Thrack was about to turn off the access road and charge down the incline toward the freeway when he glanced in the rearview mirror and saw the decapitated cart weaving across the plaza, and Charlie Willis in the driver's seat. Thrack wrenched the wheel, spinning the Hummer around and steering it back toward the plaza.

Charlie took his foot off the gas pedal, stopping the cart in front of the theater. Alison sat up slowly, still dazed, her jacket torn off her back by the undercarriage of the Hummer.

"Stay here," Charlie said. "It's me he wants."

Before Alison could argue, Charlie ran across the open plaza toward the parking structure lobby.

Alison watched in horror as the Hummer roared up

the access road and headed for Charlie. He was an obvious target, easy to spot among the tourists in his bright red Confederation uniform.

Terrified tourists scrambled out of the Hummer's path as it tore across the plaza, reaching the structure just as Charlie dashed into the elevator, the doors closing behind him.

Thrack slammed on the brakes, skidded to a stop, and glanced up to see the elevator rising in a glass shaft, Charlie inside.

Bastard! Thrack shifted into reverse, tires screeching, then jammed the Hummer into drive, blowing through the parking structure entrance toward the upper floors.

Charlie leaned against the glass, panting for breath, his chest aching, watching the Hummer speed up the structure after him. He had no idea what to do next.

Thrack raced up the structure, floor by floor, people diving out of his way. At each new level, Thrack glanced out the passenger window to make sure Charlie was still in the ascending elevator. He was.

A Mercedes 500S backed out in front of Thrack, and he plowed into it without stopping, tearing off $7,000 worth of German trunk space.

The elevator stopped at the sixth floor, an empty rooftop parking lot. Charlie stepped out and could hear the Hummer smashing through cars below. He figured he had a minute at best.

Charlie stepped around the elevator and looked over the edge of the low cement wall. The plaza was six floors down. He could forget about jumping.

He glanced across the lot and saw the stairwell. That was a possibility. No way the Hummer could get him in there. He was about to make a run for it when the Hummer practically flew up from the floor below.

Charlie glanced back at the elevator. The doors were closed. It was gone.

He had nowhere to go. So there was only one thing he could do.

Charlie turned back and faced the Hummer.

And gave the driver the finger.

Enraged, Thrack stomped on the gas pedal. "You're mine, *asshole!*"

Charlie stood his ground, staring at the Hummer as it charged toward him. When the Hummer was close enough that he could see Thrack, and the delirious fury in his eyes, Charlie dove to one side and hit the cement rolling.

Thrack slammed on the brakes and twisted the wheel. But it was too late. There wasn't enough pavement left. The Hummer spun sideways and burst through the cement wall into thin air. The last moment of Thrack's life was spent searching in vain for a switch to activate a parachute.

Alison was standing in front of the theater, her cell phone pressed against her ear, on hold with the 911 operator, when the Hummer plunged off the sixth floor of the parking structure, flipped over, and slammed upside down into the plaza.

Because Los Angeles has a strict antismoking ordinance, the first thing visiting Walla Walla native Jan Curran did when she emerged from Celebrity Galaxy was light a cigarette, the same cigarette that dropped from her lips when, mouth wide in shock, she saw the Hummer fly off the parking structure.

The Marlboro hit the pavement and rolled a few inches, where it met a tiny, creeping finger of gasoline and ignited it, the flame sizzling across the cement like a burning fuse.

Charlie Willis struggled to his feet and leaned over the edge of the parking structure, just as the Hummer exploded, spitting out a fireball that sent him staggering back, singed by the flames six floors up.

"You really think I have star quality?" Bev paced nervously in front of Clive Odett, stealing glances at herself in the mirror.

"I haven't seen such natural beauty since I discovered Winona Ryder working in a Pacoima 7-Eleven," said Clive Odett, trying to exude sincerity and passion, which wasn't easy when every turn of his head flushed the toilet he was taped to. Why couldn't she just sit still?

He'd been left alone with Bev for the last few hours, which was fine with him. He immediately pegged her as the captor most vulnerable to his charms. All he had to do was look at her, it was as obvious as the elephant nose on her homely face. Make her believe she could be beautiful, if only she'd let him transform her. And he couldn't transform her taped to a toilet, could he? So she'd let him go. Then he'd bash her skull in and run, once the circulation returned below his waist.

"You discovered Winona Ryder?" she asked.

"And Meryl Streep, though she lacks your powerful presence and smoldering sexuality."

Odett's stomach growled, ruining the moment. But that couldn't be helped, he hadn't eaten in at least a day.

"But you must know that already," he said. "Every time you walk down the street, don't you feel the stares? People can't help themselves. It's your undeniable magnetism."

Bev studied herself in the mirror. It was true, people *did* stare at her, everywhere she went.

"To think, if you hadn't kidnapped me, I might never

have had this miraculous opportunity to meet you," Odett said.

She always knew she was destined for more than the DMV or Postal Service could ever offer her. She was just waiting to be discovered. Who knew it would happen like this?

She gave herself a second look. Streep wasn't a bad actress, but could she *be* a Snork? Could Streep be as regal? No, she couldn't. But Bev did it every day, *effortlessly*. Maybe Odett was right. She was a natural-born actress.

For a moment, she could almost see herself accepting her Oscar, her Snorkie nose wrapped in sequins. She'd thank the Academy, the Confederation of Aligned Galaxies, and . . .

Odett's stomach growled again, intruding on her thoughts, reminding her that they'd taken care of his liquid needs but never even thought about feeding him. He'd been so nice to her she decided to make him something special to show her thanks.

"You need something to eat," she said.

"Sushi would be nice," he replied. "We can get some on the way to the agency."

But she was already out the door, much to Odett's frustration. He shook his head, inadvertently flushing the toilet again.

Bev went to the kitchen and searched the cupboards for food, but all she could find were assorted flavors of space food sticks, some pasta, catsup, a six-pack of beer, and a half-eaten bag of Cheez Doodles.

To anyone less resourceful than Bev Huncke, this would be a disaster. She saw the makings of a gourmet meal. All she had to do was boil the noodles, warm up the catsup with some mushrooms from the backyard, sprinkle some crushed Cheez Doodles over everything, and she'd have delicious spaghetti primavera parmesan for two.

She started boiling the water and dreaming about her movie career.

Twenty-three

*T*here were two commissaries on the Pinnacle Studios lot. One was the Studio Grill, a huge cafeteria where secretaries who thought of themselves as "preproduced screenwriters" came to trash their bosses over diet Chinese chicken salads; where slick-haired, junior development execs ate prepackaged sushi and pretended the crab was real; and where key grips, gaffers, best boys, and focus pullers faithfully ate brownish globs of Salisbury steak without ever asking what was in it.

The Studio Grill was open to anyone who equated microwaves with home cooking. It shared the same building, and the same kitchen, as the Terrace Room, but the similarities ended there.

The Terrace Room was a private restaurant for studio vice presidents, big-name actors, A-list directors with overall deals, and executive producers of current series.

The maître d' checked all lunch reservations with the business affairs department. Any director whose deal was not being renewed or actor who suffered a bad opening weekend at the box office was politely, but firmly, invited to pick up a tray at the Studio Grill next door.

Legendary studio chief Leroy Waterland used to eat lunch each day at the Terrace Room, sitting in a booth on a raised platform against the back wall, catered to by a personal chef and waiter. Anyone who approached his table without being invited was thrown off the lot and never allowed to return. This, of course, turned out to be his undoing. He choked to death on a pimiento because no one dared go to his table for fear he was just coughing.

That little pimiento caused a revolutionary upheaval in the entertainment industry. Upon his death, the studio was sold to the Japanese, who later sold it to a world-class pornographer. But despite the tumultuous changes in ownership and the industry, the Terrace Room, and the exclusivity that came with it, remained.

Which was why Eddie Planet was so glad to be there, his RESERVED FOR EDDIE PLANET plaque planted on the edge of his table where everyone who came in could see it. But what really made it special was seeing Kenny Rogers come in, only to get stopped by the maître d', who made a quick call and then escorted the red-faced singer to the door. Lately, Kenny's chicken had a bigger audience than his TV movies.

Eddie thought about inviting Kenny to his table, to spare him the embarrassment of being thrown out, but decided not to mess with God's master plan. It was no coincidence that Kenny Rogers showed up on Eddie's first day back in the Terrace Room. Obviously, this was a blatant message for Eddie from the big producer himself: You're at the top and you're staying there.

It made Eddie think about having his plaque *mounted* on the table. Maybe even redirect one of the ceiling track lights so it aimed a subtle beam right at the plaque. He was figuring out the best way to approach the maître d' about it when a comment broke into his thoughts.

"Look, it's Keanu Reeves." Brougham pointed across the dining room at David Geffen's table.

He swatted her hand down. "I've told you a dozen times, *do not point* and *do not stare.*"

Eddie had invited his secretary to lunch because there was no way he was going alone, and it never hurt to be seen with a gorgeous woman with huge breasts. Even so, he regretted it.

"This is not a bus tour of the stars' homes," Eddie hissed. "In here, we are all equals, so we aren't impressed by anyone else. If you point or stare, that means you're impressed, which means you're not at their level, which means you don't belong in the Terrace Room."

"If you're as famous as everyone else, why do you have to have your name on the table?"

"Because I care about the environment. Do you have any idea how many old-growth redwoods are sacrificed each day for those little cardboard 'table reserved' placards?" Eddie abruptly stood up. "Time to go."

Eddie pulled her chair out so hard she almost fell out. While strolling to the door, he winked at Jennifer Aniston, nodded at David Kelley, and gave a knowing smile to Mike Nichols.

As soon as they were outside, the valet brought Eddie's cart around. He tipped the guy a buck, and they sped off between the soundstages toward his bungalow.

"There's Guy Goddard," Brougham said.

"Where?" Eddie asked, slowing down.

"Over there," she said, looking straight ahead.

Eddie looked all around but couldn't see him. "Where is he? Where do you see him?"

"I thought you said not to point."

"In the Terrace Room," Eddie snapped. "Out here it's open season, honey. You can point, stare, and foam at the mouth. Now where is he?"

She pointed to Eddie's left, where Guy Goddard, in his faded Confederation uniform, marched into the *Beyond the Beyond* soundstage.

What the hell was he doing here?

Eddie glanced at his watch. The crew broke for lunch and wouldn't be back for another half hour. He had to get Guy off the lot, as quietly and as quickly as possible.

"Take the cart and go back to the office," Eddie said. "I've got some memos on my desk you can shrink-wrap."

She scooted off in the cart, and Eddie went inside the dark soundstage. He slipped between two flats and found himself standing at the rear of the *Endeavor* bridge. Someone was sitting in the command chair, his back to Eddie.

"Guy?" Eddie asked.

Captain Pierce flicked a switch on the armrest console. "Security, this is the captain. Intruder alert. There are aliens on board."

Captain Pierce turned around slowly in the command chair to face Eddie, who clapped enthusiastically.

"Wow, it's like time just stood still. Seeing you in that chair, hearing the voice, what can I say? It gave me shivers."

"You lied to me," the captain said. "You are one of *them.*"

"Hey, I'm your biggest fan, you know that." Eddie smiled as warmly as he could. "And I've used every bit of my power and influence to get you back on the show in a major role."

"Then you've rid the ship of evil doubles and restored my command."

"Even better." Eddie said. "You get to be the voice of the computer."

Captain Pierce shot him.

The taser hit Eddie in the chest and blasted him against the wall, the voltage shaking him so much Captain Pierce could hear the coins rattling out of his pockets.

But they weren't coins. They were car keys.

It wasn't hard finding Eddie Planet's car. The Lexus was parked right outside the soundstage, under a huge sign that read, THIS PARKING SPACE RESERVED FOR EDDIE PLANET.

Captain Pierce stuffed Eddie in the trunk and drove off the lot, pausing at the intersection outside the main gate as a fire engine, ambulance, and several police cars sped past, sirens wailing.

Melvah arrived at the starship *Endeavor* at its crash site in Van Nuys, expecting to find Captain Pierce on the bridge, where she would have to tell him that, once again, they'd failed to kill Charlie Willis.

But when she arrived, the starship was unsettlingly empty and quiet, like the episode in which everyone but the captain was transformed into shadows. He walked the corridors of the *Endeavor* alone, a single voice in the universe, before he realized there were shadows everywhere, even where the light wasn't positioned to cast them. Eventually, the captain discovered that a godlike alien entity was responsible for turning his crew into shadows and that it was all part of an experiment to see how long a man could survive utterly alone.

She'd expanded the story in fanfic, exploring the possibility that the godlike creatures were also shadows, plotting to turn all shadows everywhere into sentient beings. Things got complicated when, in the finale, Captain Pierce's shadow thought he was in command. Captain Pierce was forced to beat his own shadow to death.

It was a harrowing story and one well worth dramatizing as an episode of the new *Beyond the Beyond*. This kind of brilliant storytelling, with grounding going back twenty years in the universe, would never occur to an outsider like Eddie Planet. Which was why Melvah had to run the show, and run it *now*. If television didn't work that way, then Melvah would just have to change that, too.

Zita might understand business, but she obviously knew very little about *Beyond the Beyond* or, as Captain Pierce said in just about every episode, the *indomitable human spirit*. Frankly, Melvah was beginning to have her doubts about the future of her relationship with Zita, despite their shared interests and fantastic sex.

Perhaps it was seeing everyone she cared about dying around her for the cause. First Artie, now Thrack. At least Thrack died on a historic day, one that would enshrine his memory in fandom forever. It would have meant a lot to him.

If she did what Zita asked, then she wasn't just betraying Guy Goddard and Bev, but Artie, Thrack, and all of fandom.

Although Captain Pierce wasn't here, Melvah knew Bev certainly would be. Bev made a tremendous personal sacrifice to guard Clive Odett. Bev had missed Beyond-Con, which comes around only once a year.

Melvah wandered down the corridor to the brig to relieve Bev and break the horrible news to her. She heard the toilet whining and gurgling before she got to the door.

Clive Odett was taped to the seat, his head slumped

forward, keeping the toilet in constant flush. His mouth and eyes were open wide, spaghetti sauce around his lips, a few noodles dangling from his chin. His *indomitable human spirit* had long since relocated to hell.

Bev was sprawled on her back on the floor, covered in spaghetti, sauce, and mushrooms, a broken plate not far from her body. Melvah bent a little closer and saw a half-eaten mushroom still in Bev's mouth.

Melvah left the room, went outside, and saw a cluster of decapitated mushroom stalks amid the weeds, grass, and garbage. She didn't have to be *Miss Agatha* to solve this mystery. Bev poisoned herself and Clive Odett with pasta and wild mushrooms. How Clive Odett talked Bev into doing something as bizarre as cooking him a meal was something Melvah would never know.

The most important question now was how this unexpected tragedy affected the universe. She was mulling the possibilities when Captain Pierce drove a Lexus into the landing bay. She ran up to him as he emerged.

"What happened to your shuttle craft, sir?" she asked.

"It's parked in orbit around the alien home world. This one belongs to their leader."

Melvah stared at him. "You took Eddie Planet's car?"

"It was the easiest way to escape undetected by their sensors. I've brought him here to negotiate with Odett."

Melvah peered into the car. "Eddie Planet is with you?"

"In the trunk." Captain Pierce started toward the ship.

"Captain, wait. There's something you should know."

He turned around. "Yes?"

"Thrack died trying to kill your evil double. But the impostor survived."

"Then it's even more imperative we get Odett and Planet together and put an end to this madness."

"I'm afraid that won't be possible, sir. Bev and Odett are dead."

The Captain closed his eyes and took a deep breath. "How?"

"She made him spaghetti, with mushrooms from the yard. They were poison."

"Damn it!" His eyes flashed open, face rigid with anger and loss. "I don't know how many times I've told the crew *never* eat anything that isn't canned, vacuum-sealed, or frozen. One tiny mistake like that can be fatal. Let's hope Ensign Huncke's tragic end will be a lesson to cadets throughout the galaxy."

Suddenly Melvah saw how this could all work out for the benefit of the Confederation, and most of all, for her. They all would get what they wanted, and Artie, Bev, and Thrack would not have given their lives for nothing.

Captain Pierce picked up a shovel. "Come along, Ensign. Let's bury our dead."

"You have to kill Eddie Planet," she said. "Right now."

"That won't change anything. The alien bastards will just replace him with one of their own. Maybe we can turn him against them and destroy the alien conspiracy from the inside."

"We already have, Captain. I've infiltrated the alien hierarchy. If you kill him, *I* will replace him."

The Captain smiled. "Very well. You take his place. I'll handle the rest."

She ran off. The captain hefted the shovel and went to the car.

Eddie Planet was squeezed between the spare tire and the jack, barely able to breathe. What little air there was reeked of his own piss and excrement—the electric shock opened every sphincter in his body. If he survived this ordeal, the next time he was constipated he was going to stick his finger in an electric socket.

But as miserable, uncomfortable, and scared as he was, he was glad Lexus's renowned quiet ride didn't extend to the trunk. He heard the entire conversation between Melvah and Guy Goddard.

From what little he heard, Eddie was able to jump to some pretty sound conclusions about his captors, their activities the last few weeks, and their current mental states.

So just as the trunk popped open, and before Goddard could smash his head with the shovel, Eddie yelled, "Dr. Kelvin is my wife!"

Captain Pierce paused, the shovel suspended over his head. "What did you say?"

"I'm married to a Confederation officer," Eddie said quickly. "You kill me, and Dr. Kelvin will bring you up on charges with the high counsel. You'll be court-martialed, stripped of your command, and banished to the bottomless ice quarries on . . ."

Eddie's mind was a blank. He grabbed the first thing that popped into his head. ". . . on the frigid slopes of Brougham. But even that won't be as cold as the hatred in my wife's heart for you, a man she trusted with her life."

"I don't believe you," the captain said, wincing from the horrible stench.

"Fine, don't believe me. Ask her yourself. Her address is on the registration slip in the glove box."

The captain shot Eddie with the taser again and closed the trunk before the fresh stink could hit him.

Twenty-four

*T*he Pinnacle City promenade was cordoned off with yellow police tape to keep people away from the crime scene, but it didn't do much good. The best view of the action was from any living room in Southern California.

Fourteen news helicopters circled over the plaza, creating gale-force winds and so much noise that people on the ground could hardly hear their own thoughts. Which, in Charlie's case, wasn't such a bad thing. The more he thought about his situation, the bleaker it looked.

Alison was somewhere on the other side of the police tape, no doubt trying to put a positive spin on events for the press. By now, the reporters probably knew he was the guy who trashed the parking lot here a couple of days ago. And they probably knew, or soon would, that yesterday he blew somebody up. She'd have to find a rational explanation for it all that made him look like a hero instead of a homicidal maniac.

Charlie didn't envy her the task. Then it occurred to him, as he sat on a bench, watching police officers pick through the wreckage, that pretty soon he'd have to do the same thing.

He wanted to believe that Clive Odett was responsible, but why would he send out killers dressed like aliens?

And if Charlie really saw Odett being carjacked, who was behind it, and where was the superagent now?

So who else benefited from the deaths?

Jackson Burley believed the other networks were so scared of The Big Network taking off that they would resort to murder to stop *Beyond the Beyond* from succeeding.

Charlie would buy that theory if *Beyond the Beyond* was already on the air and getting big numbers. But it wasn't. The fact was, most shows fail, and he doubted the networks would start killing people until they knew if the series, and with it the upstart network, was a real threat.

So whom did that leave?

Eddie Planet came immediately to mind. Charlie was trying to rethink everything from Eddie Planet's greedy perspective when Lou LeDoux ambled up and took a seat beside him on the bench.

"I'm beginning to feel like a cop in one of those bad private eye shows," Lou said. "You know, the stupid schmuck who's always running down license plates for the hero and yelling at him for turning the city into a war zone. The cop who never gets the credit for making the bust."

"Gharlane ID'd the breast," Charlie said, "and you're afraid I'm going to take all the credit."

"I didn't say that. But since you brought it up, I want

you to think about the trouble you'd be in with the police if it wasn't for me running interference, at great personal risk to my own career, I might add."

"I have, and I appreciate it. The bust is all yours."

"What about the movie rights?"

"Lou, it's all yours. Domestic, foreign, and home video."

"Gharlane really knows his tits. He matched the workup to a woman in a ten-year-old strip-joint calender."

"Who is it?"

"Shari Covina," Lou said dramatically.

Charlie shook his head. "Should that mean something to me?"

"It would if you ever watched *Beyond the Beyond*. She was the original Dr. Kelvin, the lady with the computer breasts. She was also Stipe's ex-wife."

Shari Covina Stipe Planet didn't go to BeyondCon, a decision she figured cost her a couple grand at least. But she couldn't afford to be seen in her Dr. Kelvin uniform, which would have revealed her bruised breast.

So she put her time at home to good use. She spent the day watching informercials and taking copious notes.

The most popular format, from what she could see, was the fake talk show, with an unctuous host or has-been actor interviewing the huckster in front of a studio audience about his or her wonderful product or moneymaking scheme. All were designed to fool the brain-dead viewers into thinking they were watching a real talk show, not that there was a whole lot of difference anymore.

Shari took special note of a ballsy infomercial that copied Larry King's set and even had a Larry King lookalike, suspenders and all, interviewing the huckster.

The other format that worked pretty well was the

huckster showing off the cars, the women, and the homes he bought with all the loot he made off his product or scheme. The implication being, if you sold ceramic angels or signed up for "900 Ways to Become a 900 Number Millionaire," you too could be getting laid in your Malibu estate. That format wouldn't fit her needs, but she studied it anyway for salesmanship pointers.

Shari saw infomercials as the future of her *Beyond the Beyond* merchandising empire. Coming up with the program would be easy. She'd hire a fat black lady and make it look like Shari, Kent Steed, and Guy Goddard were being interviewed by Oprah. They'd talk about how elegant *Beyond the Beyond* dinnerware is, how stylish their logo sunglasses are, and what a great decorator touch a cast statuette adds to any room. Maybe she'd even throw in a 900 number fans could call and test their *Beyond* trivia skills at six bucks a minute.

She was watching John Davidson on a Hawaii beach, quizzing some real estate huckster about his miracle scheme for "turning toxic waste dumps into quick cash!" when there was a knock at Shari's door.

She muted the TV, went to the door, and peered through the peephole, stunned to see Guy Goddard standing on her front porch in his Captain Pierce outfit. It was easily ten years since she last saw him, and probably at least that long since he'd changed his clothes.

Shari opened the door. "Guy Goddard, I'll be damned. I was just thinking about you."

"Sorry to trouble you, Doctor," Captain Pierce said, "but the fate of the universe hangs in the balance."

That's when she noticed Eddie's Lexus idling in the driveway, but Eddie was nowhere to be seen.

"There's a vast, alien conspiracy to replace the *Endeavor* crew with evil doubles," the captain said. "I've got their leader in the trunk. He says he's your husband."

"Uh-huh," She didn't want to say anything more substantial than a grunt until she figured out what was going on.

Shari had heard the stories about Goddard, of course. That he was some kind of recluse, that on the few occasions he appeared in public, he did so only "in character." She figured it was a gimmick, and she played along with it for laughs when she last saw him, at a mall opening in El Cerrito.

Now, as he led her to the car, she gave some serious thought to the probability that Guy Goddard was insane. And if he was, how best to use this situation to her benefit.

Obviously, the conspiracy he was talking about was the revival of *Beyond the Beyond* with a new cast, and the alien leader he'd captured must be Eddie.

"What happens to him if he's not my husband?" she asked. She wanted to know all her options.

"I'll steer the ship into a black hole and shove him out an airlock."

So Guy Goddard would kill him. That raised some interesting possibilities.

The captain unlocked the trunk, releasing a foul stench that almost made Shari vomit. She saw Eddie stuffed inside, soaked in sweat, piss, and shit, wincing against the harsh sunlight.

"Thank God you're home," Eddie said. "Tell him it's me."

Shari covered her nose and mouth and gave it some thought.

Don't worry, baby, Eddie's going to take care of you. You can be the voice of the ship's computer.

"Sweetie pie?" Eddie urged, his voice shaky. "What

are you waiting for? For God's sake, tell him who I am."

"I've never seen this man before in my life," she said.

Eddie bolted up in the trunk. "Shari, he's going to kill—"

The captain slammed the trunk closed on Eddie's head, abruptly silencing the executive producer.

"That's what I thought," Captain Pierce said to Shari.

She nodded and backed away from the car. The captain took a couple steps toward her.

"There is one thing that troubles me, Doctor."

"What is that, sir?"

He held up a slip of paper. "Why was your address on his vehicle registration?"

Shari felt her heart pounding in her chest. *You're Dr. Kelvin. What would she say?*

"Captain, if he can replicate the crew of the *Endeavor,* how hard could it be to counterfeit a registration slip?"

"Why would he do that?" the captain asked.

Oh shit, I don't know.

"For just this eventuality. Don't underestimate the intelligence of your adversary, captain. You don't want to make the same mistake here that you made with the gelatin worms of Kunzel-Four."

He stared at her, and for a moment Shari was worried. Guy Goddard wasn't just insane, he was homicidal. If he thought she was part of whatever paranoid conspiracy he blamed Eddie for, then she was dead, too.

"I've missed your wisdom and sound counsel, Doctor," the captain said at last, smiling. "It's good to know that your computers are still in top shape."

Shari gave him the traditional Snorkie salute and the parting words, "Be prosperous and multiply, Captain."

He crumpled the registration, dropped it on the ground, and got into the car.

She watched him drive off, then hurried back in the house, closing the door behind her and turning the dead bolt.

Shari couldn't believe her incredible lucky streak. Who could have predicted that Guy Goddard would emerge from oblivion and save her the cost of a messy divorce? Now she would get everything that belonged to Eddie, free and clear. And she didn't have to do a thing for it.

With her dual inheritances, she was set for life. She was considering a quick trip to Las Vegas to see if her luck would hold, when there was a knock at the door.

Peering through the peephole, she saw her second Confederation captain of the day.

Her first instinct was to walk away, then her common sense got the better of her. Someone who'd go to the trouble of dressing up like that and finding out where she lived was a die-hard fan. Odds were his pockets were full of wadded-up cash he was eager to spend on personalized memorabilia.

As rich as she was going to be, she was short on cash right now.

So she put on her best smile and opened the door, noticing for the first time that the fan had a friend, a fashion nightmare in a checked jacket, yellow shirt, and gray slacks. At least they both had clear skin.

"What can I do for you?" she asked.

"Shari Covina?" Lou asked.

"Yes," she replied, looking at Charlie. "But you can call me Doctor if you like."

"I'm Charlie Willis, a security consultant for Pinnacle Pictures."

"Interesting uniform," she said. "Does your jurisdiction extend into the galaxy as well?"

"I'm Sergeant Lou LeDoux, LAPD." Lou flashed his badge with one hand and held out a piece of paper with the other. "We have a warrant to see your boobs."

She slammed the door, but Charlie already had his space boot in the way. He pushed the door open and saw her bolt down the entry hall.

Charlie chased after her, taking her down in a flying tackle before she reached the kitchen. She landed face-down on the hardwood floor and immediately began kicking, squirming, and screaming. He straddled her waist, pulled her arms behind her back, and reached for his cuffs but couldn't find them.

"Looking for these?" Lou leaned down and slipped the handcuffs around her wrists, effectively subduing her.

Although it had been years since Charlie was either a real or fictional police officer, old habits were hard to break. Charlie got up, embarrassed, and lifted Shari to her feet.

That's when Charlie saw the wedding photograph on the wall.

The bride in white with the plunging neckline was Shari. The groom in the powder blue tuxedo and lecherous grin was Eddie Planet.

Twenty-five

*M*elvah Blenis did what she was born to do. She ruled the universe. She created planets, moved stars, and determined the fates of entire civilizations. With a few taps on the computer keyboard, she could move through time or dim a distant sun. She could give life, take it away, or evolve it into an entirely new being.

She was omniscient, omnipotent, and omnivorous. She was an executive producer.

At least for the moment.

When Brougham returned, after searching the entire lot for Eddie, Melvah was already at Eddie Planet's desk, rewriting his inept pilot script.

She told Brougham that Eddie had left her in charge and to inform the set that a revised draft would be published tomorrow morning. Then Melvah got to work, pitting Captain Pierce and the *Endeavor* against the shadows.

The scenes just flew out, the story tumbling out of her faster than her fingers could type it. Every word and action was a surprise, written without thought. Her subconscious mind was doing all the work. The story was emerging perfectly plotted, every line of dialogue exactly right. It was as if she'd been waiting to tell this story, to do this job, her entire life. She didn't dare stop, didn't dare rest, for fear of ruining the flow.

The phone rang. Melvah ignored it and let Brougham answer the call. Melvah's priorities were in another galaxy. But while her subconscious mind was writing, her conscious mind heard Brougham say:

"How do you spell *Zita?*"

"I'll take it," Melvah yelled, snatching up the phone before Brougham could argue. "Hello, Zita."

"Melvah?"

"I'm back," she said in a singsong voice, swiveling in the chair so her back was to Brougham.

"What happened to Eddie?" Zita said.

"I don't know, you'll have to ask Guy Goddard," Melvah replied. "The good news is, I'm in charge. The universe has been saved."

Zita tried to keep her voice level and firm. "Melvah, we talked about this."

"This is the first time in sci-fi history that fanfic has become the foundation fic from which the future fanfic will be written. You realize we're witnessing the birth of an entirely new form of literature? It transcends fanfic as we know it."

"You can't be executive producer of *Beyond the Beyond.* The business doesn't work that way. Didn't you listen to a word I said?"

"*I* did, but Captain Pierce wasn't there, was he? He's acting on his own."

"It's the last acting he will ever do."

Melvah felt her entire body tense. "This is what we've been fighting for, Zita. We both have what we want now."

"I told you how it would be," Zita said coldly.

"So what? The universe is what matters."

"The Company *is* the universe. And Guy Goddard is going to learn that." Zita hung up.

Melvah set the receiver down and turned back to the computer. Her fingers were poised over the keys, but her hands were trembling. The words wouldn't come.

Melvah had made a horrible mistake, Zita made that very clear. The Confederation, countless worlds and galaxies not yet explored, were still at risk.

The universe was on the precipice of an evolutionary change, one that wouldn't come without one last painful sacrifice.

Melvah got up and left, nearly colliding with Alison Sweeney as she ran out the door.

Alison watched her go, then turned to Brougham.

"What was she doing in Eddie's office?"

"She said Mr. Planet left her in charge," Brougham replied.

"Where's Eddie? I need to see him right away."

Kimberly Woodrell, Jackson Burley, and Milo Kinoy were very concerned about how news about more deaths involving Charlie Willis would impact the show. They wanted to meet with Eddie as soon as possible and discuss counter-publicity strategy.

"I don't know," Brougham said. "Last time I saw him, he was on the set with Guy Goddard."

What was Eddie doing with Guy Goddard? If it was for publicity, no one told her about it. "Did he have an appointment with Eddie?"

"No. We saw him on our way back from the Terrace

Room. That was hours ago, and Mr. Planet still hasn't come back. His car isn't in his spot. I've tried reaching him on his cell phone, but there's no answer."

"Who gave Guy Goddard a drive-on pass?" Alison asked.

Brougham typed a command on her computer and looked at the screen. "Nobody."

It wasn't the first time that someone got into the studio without a pass, yet she couldn't help feeling that something was very wrong.

The success of a TV series can be measured by the goodies handed out to the crew.

If a series survives until Christmas, the studio gives everyone a T-shirt or a baseball cap with the show's logo on it. If the series manages to survive the season, sweatshirts, tote bags, or script binders are passed out. After the first thirteen episodes of the second season, the crew is rewarded with a show jacket, either in satin or leather. And so it goes.

After a couple of seasons on the air, it's possible to arrive at work totally decked out in show clothes and merchandise.

Victor Ratliff never worked on a television series, but most of his celebrity clients did. Although the attorney had the money to adorn himself with designer names, he preferred *TV Guide* chic.

He showed up at the precinct in a *Murder One* satin jacket over Armani slacks and shirt, a *DreamWorks SKG* cap on his head, his notes in a *Dr. Quinn: Medicine Woman* leather binder.

"My client has nothing to say to you," Ratliff said, sitting beside Shari Planet at the interrogation room table. Charlie and Lou sat across from them.

"She doesn't have to," Lou said. "Her tits say it all."

Charlie wasn't surprised that Shari hired Ratliff. When Charlie was in a similar position, he called Ratliff, too. The attorney had a remarkable record of getting celebrities off, which wasn't particularly hard in L.A.

"I'll have that warrant overturned faster than a hamburger patty at McDonald's," Ratliff said. "It was a blatant violation of my client's Fifth Amendment rights."

Charlie studied her, trying to put the pieces of the plot together. She was Eddie Planet's wife. It figured. Everything always came back to Eddie.

Eddie Planet probably had her kill Stipe so he could get the show.

It sounded good, and Charlie wanted to believe it was true, but it raised a nagging question: Even if that *was* the reason they killed Stipe, what did they have to gain by murdering the new cast?

Nothing.

So Clive Odett did it.

That didn't work, either. Odett may have had a motive to kill Chad Shaw, but Leigh Dickson and Spring Dano were his clients and, as far as Charlie knew, they weren't making any moves to switch agencies.

No, there was something missing here. And Shari knew what it was, Charlie was certain of it.

Shari stared back defiantly at Charlie.

"We got her cold," Lou said. "I can see her bruised boob from here."

"Whatever bruising is evident on my client is a direct result of your excessive use of force when you two barged into her home without a warrant."

While Lou and Ratliff parried, Charlie and Shari watched each other, engaged in a silent battle. He was trying to put the plot together before she found a way out.

"Let's drop the bullshit, okay? We're gonna match the nipple in Stipe's mouth to her," Lou said. "Then we're gonna match his teeth to her wounds. It's as good as a confession. All that's up for discussion now is how long she's going to spend in prison."

Charlie saw something change in Shari's eyes. Actually, he felt it more than saw it. In that instant, he knew she found her escape and that he'd lost.

"It was an accident," Shari said.

"Excuse me?" Lou said.

"Shari, don't say another word," Ratliff snapped.

She shot him a harsh glance. "The detective is right, why make it worse for myself? Conrad and I were having an affair. The revival of the show rekindled our old feelings for each other. We always had a very physical relationship. Once we started again, we couldn't stop. We drove each other wild."

Lou snickered. "You're telling me that you were coming so hard, you didn't notice you were smothering him?"

Charlie stifled a groan. Lou pretty much summed up her entire defense for her. And knowing Victor Ratliff, Charlie figured it would be a successful one at that.

"He liked to bury his face in my breasts," she said. "It was a turn-on for him."

"You weren't aware he was struggling?" Lou asked.

She smiled coyly. "Of course I was. I *liked* it when he squirmed, and so did he."

"You didn't notice something was wrong when he chewed your nipple off?"

She shrugged. "I like it rough."

"You can't get rougher than murder," Lou shot back.

Ratliff cleared his throat. "This is a clear case of involuntarily manslaughter. You'll only compound this tragedy by sending this poor, aggrieved woman to prison.

At least that's what I will tell the jury, and they'll agree. I think it's to the advantage of the taxpayers and my client if we work out an agreement that will keep this out of court."

Shari was going to get away with murder. No jury would believe she'd intentionally killed a man with her breasts, even though Charlie was certain she did. At worst, she'd get a year in jail, a couple of years probation, a book deal, and an instant TV movie sale. The sordid scandal would only enhance her career.

Her career.

The back of Charlie's neck tingled. If Stipe's death wasn't an accident, Shari Planet needed a motive, and Charlie just discovered it.

It was a miracle Eddie hadn't been smothered yet himself.

"You must be one lousy actress," Charlie said.

"What do *you* know about acting?" Shari hissed.

Charlie shrugged. "For one thing, I'm in *Beyond the Beyond* and you're not. You're so bad, you couldn't get either Stipe or Eddie to cast you. And you were *fucking* them."

"I'm a terrific actress." Shari's faced flushed with fury. "I've got the Nebula and Hugo awards to prove it."

"Then you must be a rotten lay," Charlie said. "I guess Spring Dano is better at both."

"I am Dr. Kelvin, no one else will *ever* be." Shari pounded the table with her fist. "The network and the studio think the audience wants a new, young cast. But they're wrong. The fans want us. You'll see."

The fans. All those people dressed up in the same ridiculous costumes as the astronaut who carjacked Odett and the Zorgog who tried to kill Charlie.

And then it hit him, everything coming together all at once.

The assassins weren't in disguise.

Charlie stood up abruptly.

"What's wrong?" Lou asked.

Charlie went back over everything that had happened since he returned from Hawaii, looking at it from an entirely different perspective. Suddenly, he saw the one important clue he overlooked.

"We need to talk—now." Charlie left the room and waited for Lou in the hallway.

Lou came out, closing the door behind him. "I think we've got her right where we want her."

"Forget about her for a minute," Charlie said. "The night Conrad Stipe was killed, someone else was murdered on the same street. His house blew up."

"Yeah, so?"

"Can you get me the address?"

"What difference does it make? I'm in middle of an interrogation here."

"Humor me."

While Lou went into the squad room, Charlie paced in the hall. Lou came back in two minutes, holding a file.

"The stiff's name was Dermot Elroy," Lou read from the file. "He lived at One ninety South Ardwyn."

"What was Stipe's address?"

Lou reached into his pocket for his notebook and flipped it open. He looked up, shocked. "Holy shit. One ninety North Ardwyn."

"Someone *else* wanted Stipe dead, only the killer got the address mixed up and murdered the wrong man." Charlie punched the wall. "Damn it, why didn't I see it before?"

Odett wasn't behind the carnage. And the botched attempt on Stipe showed that Shari Planet wasn't the only other killer out there. There was a *third* force at work.

Lou glanced nervously at the door to the interrogation room. "Does that mean she didn't do it?"

"No," Charlie said. "She did it."

Lou sighed with relief. "Then what are you so pissed off about?"

"I assumed the murders and the attempts on my life were all connected," Charlie said. "They are, but not by the same killer. They're connected by *the show.*"

Twenty-six

*T*he police car dropped Charlie Willis off in front of the Pinnacle Studios main gate, but when he tried to go in, a guard stopped him.

"Do you have a pass?"

"I'm Charlie Willis, I work here. I'm the star of *Beyond the Beyond.*"

The guard shared a look with his counterpart in the security shack. "You got some ID?"

Charlie suddenly remembered how he was dressed. No wallet, no identification. Just his Confederation insignia.

"My ID is in my trailer, along with my clothes. This isn't how I really dress. I'm in costume."

"Uh-huh."

"Look, why don't you just escort me to my trailer and I can show you my ID when we get there."

"I don't think so."

Charlie thought about it from their point of view. A

guy dressed like a spaceman is dropped off by the police in front of the studio. What did he expect the guards to think?

"Do me a favor, call extension 7404, and ask Alison Sweeney to look out her window at the front gate. She'll vouch for me."

The guard looked at his partner, who shrugged and dialed the phone.

Alison Sweeney was at her desk, watching six TVs at the same time, the sound muted. Each station was broadcasting reports on the melee at Pinnacle City.

Her phone rang. It was the front gate, saying there was a crazy person dressed like Captain Pierce who wanted her to look out the window. She did.

Charlie Willis waved at her.

"I'll be right down," she said.

The guards apologized to Charlie, but he told them to forget it, they were doing their jobs. Even so, Alison was still upset as they walked back to the building.

"They stopped you, but they didn't even notice when Guy Goddard walked through without a pass."

Charlie stopped. "Guy Goddard was here? When?"

"While someone was trying to run us over. Eddie was talking to him on the set."

"Where's Eddie now? I need to see him."

Alison shook her head. "I don't know. His car is gone, and he's not answering his cell phone. The execs here and at the network are in a panic. To be honest with you, after what happened to us, I'm worried about him."

If what Charlie suspected was true, she had reason to be.

"What can you tell me about Guy Goddard?"

"He hasn't worked in years, probably because he refuses to be seen in public wearing anything but his Confederation uniform. The only role he'll play is Captain Pierce, not that he will ever be offered it again."

Charlie remembered his brief encounter with Goddard a few hours ago.

I'm Captain Pierce of the Confederation starship Endeavor. *Who the fuck are you?*

Guy Goddard had to be pissed off that he was rejected for the revival, not once, but *twice,* just like Shari. Charlie couldn't help wondering if Guy Goddard was willing to kill over it, too.

Clive Odett and Eddie Planet had nothing to gain from the *Beyond the Beyond* killings. But Guy Goddard and Shari Planet did, regaining their roles if they were lucky, getting revenge if nothing else. Maybe they were in it together and maybe not.

"Where have you been?" asked Alison.

"With the police. Shari Planet killed Conrad Stipe."

Charlie filled her in on the details, along with his suspicion that someone else wanted Stipe dead but got the wrong address.

"Oh, my God," Alison said. "Is Eddie Planet involved?"

"I don't know. Can you can find out where Guy Goddard lives?"

"Sure. I can call the Screen Actors Guild, find out where they're sending his residuals. Why?"

"Good. You call, I'll drive." Charlie took her by the arm and led her toward her car. "If my hunch is right, Eddie could be in deep shit."

Eddie Planet spent a good part of his life avoiding physical labor. He hired other people for that. His monthly payroll included a gardener, a pool man, a maid, and a detail service that came to wash his car.

He didn't own a single tool. If something needed to be installed, planted, maintained, inserted, adjusted, or applied, someone was hired to complete the task, freeing him to create. He never so much as changed a lightbulb.

Which is why it was absurd to ask him to dig his own grave, much less one with room for three.

Captain Pierce wasn't wild about the idea either, especially since it was taking Eddie so damn long to do it. But it had been many years since Captain Pierce exerted himself, too. One of the many perks of authority was having plenty of underlings to assign the strenuous work to. Unfortunately, all of his loyal crew members were either dead or unaccounted for.

And despite a strict diet of space food sticks and Tang, the strange atmosphere on this bizarre planet had taken its toll on his once-lean physique. There was a time when he could wrestle a globulan mebocite, make love to three women, and engage in a laser battle with an entire army of Dorcons and not break a sweat. But after twenty minutes of digging, he was so exhausted he had to drag Eddie Planet out of the trunk to do the work.

While Eddie Planet dug, Captain Pierce stood in the shade of the back porch, holding a Confederation handkerchief to his nose with one hand and a .357 Magnum on Eddie with the other.

After two hours, the grave was barely three feet deep. And the longer Eddie worked, the worse he smelled. Sweat, shit, and piss were caked on him like a second layer of clothes. Captain Pierce wanted to kill him just to stop the odor. But there was a worse stink in the house to deal with first.

"Enough!" the captain yelled.

Eddie dropped the shovel and dropped to his knees, hands folded in front of him.

"I made a terrible mistake, and I'm ready to make amends. Let me live, and I'll not only make you the Captain but co–exec producer too!"

He wasn't sure why he was bothering to beg. Between the electric shocks and the hard work, he was probably going to die from a massive heart attack at any moment.

"Get up," the captain barked. "I'm not done with you yet."

"I can't dig anymore," Eddie whined, getting to his feet. "I've got blisters all over my hands."

"You're finished digging." The captain motioned Eddie toward the house with the gun. "It's time to bring the bodies out."

"Bodies?"

"They're in the brig." Captain Pierce jammed the gun into Eddie's back. "Move."

Eddie opened the screen door and stepped into the house.

After being kidnapped, shoved in the trunk of his car, electrocuted a couple times, and forced to dig his own grave, he thought he was past being shocked by anything. Certainly by anything as mundane as decor. He was wrong.

"I love what you've done with the place," Eddie said carefully. "Very homey."

He knew Guy Goddard was insane, but he didn't know just how far gone the man really was until he saw the bridge of the starship *Endeavor* crudely re-created in the man's living room.

"The damage isn't as bad as it looks," the captain said. "This starship is as spaceworthy as the day it left Jupiter's orbit. Chief Engineer Glerp has seen to that. All it needs are a few nitrozine power cells."

He pushed Eddie toward the hallway. The stench of rot was so strong it overwhelmed Eddie's own foul smell. The sound of gurgling water and buzzing flies echoed off the walls as they approached the bathroom. Eddie paused outside the door, not wanting to look inside.

"I really shouldn't lift anything heavy without a brace," Eddie said. "I've got a herniated disk in my lower back."

Captain Pierce lifted his foot and gave Eddie a sharp kick in the ass, sending Eddie tumbling into the bathroom. Eddie landed in Clive Odett's lap, looked up and saw the dead agent's frozen face hanging over him, flies swarming in his eyes, nose, and mouth.

Eddie screamed and scrambled back, right on top of Bev Huncke's mushy, putrid corpse. He screamed again and jerked away, slamming his head against the porcelain sink. That's when he saw Zita standing against the wall behind the door, a butcher knife gleaming in her hands.

She put a finger to her lips. *Shush.*

"Stop whining and get to work," demanded Captain Pierce, standing in the hall, unable to see Zita behind the door.

Eddie understood it then. Whoever she was, she wasn't here to hurt him. She was here to *help.*

Zita motioned for him to take away the dead woman. Eddie bent over Bev, noticing for the first time that she had a rubber elephant nose on her face. Grabbing her by the ankles, he slowly backed out of the room, dragging her out.

Captain Pierce stepped aside to let Eddie drag the corpse past him, then followed Eddie down the hall, keeping his gun trained on him.

They were nearly in the living room when Eddie looked up and saw Zita creeping up behind Captain Pierce, her knife raised high, ready to plunge it into his back.

What Eddie didn't see was Melvah beside him, on the other side of the archway, holding a baseball bat. She shoved Captain Pierce down and swung the bat at Zita's face, connecting with a loud, wet smack.

Zita's head snapped back between her shoulder blades, and she collapsed, dead before she hit the floor.

Captain Pierce glanced down at the caved-in face of his attacker, the knife still gripped in her dead hand, and gave Melvah an appreciate smile.

"Good work, Ensign."

Melvah nodded and tossed aside her bat. She couldn't bear to look at what she'd done.

Neither could Eddie. His last hope was gone.

Captain Pierce aimed his gun at Eddie. "Looks like you're going to have to dig that grave a little deeper."

Twenty-seven

While Eddie used Zita's knife to cut the duct tape that held Clive Odett's corpse to the toilet, he considered his situation.

This was the fourth act, the hero was in deep shit, and the bad guys were in control. Melvah paced in the hall, the gun held at her side. Captain Pierce was "on the bridge," contemplating his next move. But like all villains, they were so sure of themselves they'd gotten sloppy.

They gave him a knife.

All Eddie had to do was spin around and throw the knife at Melvah's neck, impaling her dead to the wall. He'd catch the gun before it hit the floor, creep silently down the hall, and as Captain Pierce swiveled around in his command chair, he'd fire a bullet right into his twisted brain. In less than two minutes, they'd be dead and he'd be free.

The end of another thrilling episode. Stay tuned for scenes from next week's show.

Unfortunately, Eddie had the imagination, but he didn't have the skill.

If this was a TV show, he had everything he needed to prevail over his captors. But in real life, even if he were able to spin around without slipping on the linoleum, Melvah would shoot him before the knife was out of his hand. And even if she didn't, he had no idea how to throw a knife anyway. He'd probably slice off his fingers and miss her by a foot.

The last piece of tape tore, and Clive Odett fell forward onto the floor, a duct-taped mummy ready for burial.

It was now or never. Lunge at her with the knife. Die like a hero.

But Eddie wasn't a hero. A hero's legs wouldn't be stiff after an hour on his knees. A hero wouldn't need to set the knife down and grab the sink to pull himself up.

Melvah looked at Eddie. "What are you waiting for? Get him out of here."

Maybe he couldn't fight his way out of this, but there was another way. He was a *producer,* and it was time to behave like one. Deal, baby, deal.

Charlie Willis pulled Alison's blue Miata over to the curb across the street from Guy Goddard's deteriorating ranch-style house. There was an old Buick parked out front with the words *"Shuttle Craft One"* spray-painted on it, a balled-up rag shoved into the tank passing for a gas cap. A sparkling new black Lexus, with the vanity plate EXECPROD, was parked in the carport beside the house.

"That's Eddie's car," Alison said, stating the obvious.

"Call the police." Charlie pulled himself out of the convertible. "I'll be right back."

"What are you going to do?"

"Take a look around. Nothing to worry about."

While Alison made the call, Charlie sprinted across the street, crept up to the side of Guy Goddard's house, and peeked through the bathroom window.

Eddie put his hands under Odett's arms and dragged him out of the bathroom. Melvah stepped aside to let Eddie past but kept her gun on him.

"Guy Goddard's a complete wacko. He really believes he's Captain Pierce and this house is the starship *Endeavor*," Eddie said. "But I think you know he's a washed-up actor and this is a dump in Van Nuys."

"I don't give a shit what you think." She followed him down the hall.

"You know he's never going to play Captain Pierce again," Eddie whispered. "Killing me isn't going to change that. But you never really cared about Goddard, did you? You have a different agenda."

"Shut up," she hissed.

Charlie ducked under the bathroom window. He had to do something to save Eddie. But what? There were at least two bad guys in the house, and one of them had a gun. Which was one more gun than Charlie had.

Keeping low, Charlie crept quickly and quietly toward the backyard. He peered around the edge of the house and saw the open grave, a shovel sticking up in the dirt.

Charlie figured Eddie had about two minutes left to live.

Eddie opened the screen door with his butt and backed outside, Odett's head clunking on the two steps leading to the yard as he pulled him out.

"There is a way you can get what *you* want."

"I've already got what I want," Melvah said. "I'm running *Beyond the Beyond.*"

Eddie dragged Odett to the grave and pushed him on top of Zita and Bev. Now he was the only one left to kill and throw in the pit. Deal, Eddie, deal.

"No, you're not. You're just sitting at my desk," Eddie said. "You kill me and they'll bring in another show runner to take my place. And he'll boot you off the lot, just like I did. You can kill every producer in Hollywood, and you'll still never get the show. But like I said, there is a way."

And if he couldn't convince her, Melvah would shoot him and bury the bodies. But she'd have to do it with her bare hands. The shovel was gone.

"I'm listening," she said.

"Let me go, and your problems are solved." Eddie tried to keep his voice from cracking.

"I don't see how."

"You were born to write this show. You know everything about the universe and, let's face it, I don't know shit about *Beyond the Beyond.* But I've got something you don't, *network approval.* I'm a certified show runner. As long as I'm executive producer, in name only, you can write every script, make every decision, while I keep the network off your back and collect my paycheck. Hell, you'd be doing me a favor."

"What about them?" She motioned to the grave with her gun. He saw some hope.

"Water under the bridge." Eddie waved his hand, brushing the whole ugly incident away. "They weren't friends of mine anyway."

Alison counted to ten, like Charlie told her, and then lit the match, touching the flame to the rag that was shoved into the gas tank of *Shuttle Craft One*. Then she ran for cover behind her Miata.

Melvah pointed the gun at Eddie's head. "I don't think so."

"Why not?" Eddie whimpered, falling to his knees.

"You have no respect for human life."

"*I* don't? *I* haven't killed anybody."

"Your actions have. Bev and I served fandom together for years. Zita and I were lovers. If I don't kill you, they died for nothing."

Melvah cocked the trigger, Eddie closed his eyes, and there was an earth-shaking explosion.

But it wasn't a gunshot Eddie heard, it was a '71 Buick Riviera blowing up.

Melvah whirled toward the sound, and Charlie burst out of hiding beside the house, swinging the shovel, whacking her across the back. She tumbled into the grave, the gun flying out of her hand and into the weeds.

Eddie rose to his feet and stared at Charlie. What an entrance. "Infuckingcredible."

Charlie peered into the grave. Melvah was as still as the corpses. He'd never seen the woman with the elephant nose before, but he recognized Odett.

Alison rushed into the backyard, a relieved smile breaking out on her face the instant she saw them.

Eddie held out his arms for a big cinematic hug. She ran to past him and embraced Charlie.

Eddie's feelings weren't hurt. She'd hug him in the TV movie version—*and* he'd take out Melvah in the bathroom with the knife. He looked beyond her at the black smoke curling into the sky behind the house. Approaching sirens wailed in the distance. What a shot. But it still needed line, a button to end on.

"The nightmare is finally over," Eddie said into the nonexistent camera. Cue the music, bring up the credits.

"Not quite," Charlie said. "Where's Goddard?"

Eddie motioned to the house. Charlie had no sense of drama. "He's on the bridge."

"What does that mean?"

"You'll see."

Charlie started toward the house.

Alison grabbed his arm. "Please don't. The police are on the way. Let them handle it."

Charlie shook his head. "I have to finish this."

The moment Captain Pierce felt the blast, he knew the *Endeavor* was under attack by the aliens. He strapped himself into the command chair and turned to Dr. Kelvin.

"Report," the captain snapped.

"We're surrounded by three unidentified alien vessels," she said. *"They've got the ship locked in a grapnel beam."*

"We're trapped," Mr. Snork said.

"There's always options, Mr. Snork." The captain opened a channel to engineering deck. "Mr. Glerp, redirect all power to propulsion and prepare for ultralight speed."

"I can't, sir," Glerp replied. "The grapnel beam has neutralized our nitrozine power cells. We're powerless."

"As long as we have our humanity, we'll never be powerless." Captain Pierce clicked off the communicator. "Dr. Kelvin, if we convert our deflector shields into reflector shields, I think we can—"

"You're all alone, Goddard," a voice said.

The captain looked up. A humanoid alien stood in front of the main viewscreen, wearing a Confederation captain's uniform. And he was right, the crew had disappeared! The bridge was empty, except for him and the alien.

Somehow, Captain Pierce always knew it would come to this. A face-to-face confrontation with evil, the fate of the universe hanging in the balance.

"It's just you and me," Charlie said.

"I may be just one man, but standing behind me are the millions of creatures on the hundreds of worlds that make up the Confederation of Aligned Galaxies. That's what this insignia on my chest stands for, buster. I'll die on their behalf before I'll surrender to your tyranny."

"Is that why you killed Chad Shaw and Leigh Dickson?"

"You can steal our faces, copy our ships, but there's one thing you can never replicate, our *indomitable human spirit.*"

Charlie understood it all now. So simple, so crazy, so very sad. Outside, he could hear the police cars and fire engines coming around the corner. Any moment now, the officers would come in.

"It's over now, Goddard," Charlie said. "The police are here. Let's go."

"You've got a lot to learn about the human race. Initiating self-destruct sequence." Captain Pierce pressed the button on a garage door remote. *"Now."*

Captain Pierce unhitched his seat belt and stood up, defiant, the remote control in his hand. "Anyone tries to board or leave this ship, and the magnetic containment field around the fusion core will fail. An instant later, the ship will explode, taking your vessels along with it."

Charlie sighed. "We aren't in outer space, and this isn't a starship."

"And I suppose this isn't a galaxy-class fusion core reactor." The captain lifted the top off the helm console, revealing a compartment packed full of dynamite, surrounded by blinking Christmas lights.

Charlie also saw a bag of nails, a sack of ball bearings, three Neil Diamond CDs, a couple bottles of lighter fluid, a box of Grape Nuts, and the innards of a garage door opener.

"I haven't seen many fusion core reactors like this," Charlie said.

"I had the chief engineer rig this one up especially for me. Anyone opens a door now, or if I press this remote, the ship explodes."

"What do you hope to gain by blowing up the ship?"

"It's not what I gain, it's what you lose. I won't let the flagship of the Confederation fall into alien hands."

"And I can't let you kill any more people." Charlie reached into the console, unscrewed a Christmas light, and tossed it across the room. "I've disarmed it."

The captain glared at Charlie in shock. "You said you'd never seen a reactor like this."

"I lied." Charlie shifted his gaze past the captain and yelled, "Come on in, boys."

Captain Pierce turned to look, and Charlie leaped into the main viewscreen. As Charlie crashed through the plate-glass window, Captain Pierce screamed in fury and pressed his remote.

The house exploded like a popcorn kernel, the walls bursting out and lifting the entire structure into the air.

The blast sent Charlie cartwheeling through the air. He smacked against the sheet-metal roof of the carport and toppled into the weeds, where he was impaled on a rusted umbrella stand.

The first thing he was aware of was agony, and that made him happy. It meant he was still alive. When he opened his eyes and blinked away the blood, he saw the bloody umbrella stand poking through his stomach. And beyond that, all he saw was flames.

And then he saw something else, a naked figure rising out of the ground, skin smoking, hair ablaze.

The fire had seared the clothes off Melvah's body and burned away most of her skin, but she didn't care. She wanted only one thing. She lifted the shovel above her blazing head and marched toward Charlie, impaled and helpless in the flaming weeds.

"You don't want to do that," Charlie croaked.

"Fuck you," she rasped and swung at his head.

In the same instant, he reached into the weeds, whipped up the red-hot Magnum, and emptied it into her, sending her skittering backward in a windstorm of bullets that dropped her right back into her grave.

And then the pain went away, and so did everything else.

Epilogue

Alamogordo Scripts Divorce

Mandy Alamogordo filed for divorce from her husband of twenty-five years, screenwriter Nick Alamogordo, citing "irreconcilable differences."

She will keep custody of their three children, their Marin County estate, and their Newport Beach vacation home. Sources say she will also receive a one-time payment of $25 million, in addition to an undisclosed monthly alimony and child support payment.

Nick Alamogordo, currently scripting *Cop Another Feel,* was unavailable for comment.

Selleck Conquers *Planet,* Shari Beds Herself

Tom Selleck has been signed to play producer Eddie Planet in *One Man's Justice: The Ordeal of Eddie*

Planet, the UBC docudrama based on the notorious *Beyond the Beyond* murders.

Selleck joins William Shatner as Guy Goddard, Jennifer Jason Leigh as Melvah, Tea Leoni as Zita, and Treat Williams as superagent Clive Odett in the two-hour MOW, which goes into production next month in Vancouver under director Anson Costo.

Meanwhile, HBO has confirmed that actress Shari Planet will play herself in *Bed of Blood,* a "tragic, erotic love story" based on her best-selling book.

Bed of Blood will chronicle her doomed affair with *Beyond the Beyond* creator Conrad Stipe (Sam Sheppard), his accidental death during lovemaking, and Shari's inspirational recovery from nipple reconstruction surgery. Harry Dean Stanton will have a cameo role as Eddie Planet.

Beyond Goes Beyond,
Saddlesore Rides Again

As expected, The Big Network has ordered forty-four more episodes of *Beyond the Beyond,* guaranteeing that the sci-fi smash will remain on the network for at least two more seasons.

The renewal of *Beyond the Beyond,* which virtually created the upstart network, was tied to a full-season commitment to executive producer Eddie Planet for another series, a revival of his classic western *Saddlesore.*

"Eddie will apply to *Saddlesore* the same winning formula that made *Beyond the Beyond* a hit," promised Big president Kimberly Woodrell. "If anyone understands the 90s sensibility, it's Eddie Planet."

Planet says *Saddlesore* will feature a "hot, dynamic, young cast and an edgy, Tarantino-esque feel" and credited The Company for negotiating "a very creative deal that benefits all concerned."

The entire *Beyond the Beyond* cast will return, though Jaleel White (Capt. Pierce), Terry Bloss (Mr. Snork), and Spring Dano (Dr. Kelvin) are all considering feature film roles for the spring production hiatus.

President Makes Example of The Company

The President of the United States wants to make an example of the unusual business practices at The Company, which he called "unlike any work environment I have ever imagined."

"Corporate America needs to examine what's going on here," the President said. "We can all learn a lesson from this."

Specifically, the President cited the agency's "innovative incentive program" that rewards employees with vacation days for each day of community service. Volunteerism among employees is made possible by flexible work hours that allow agents to toil "whenever they feel they can be most productive."

During a tour of The Company's new San Fernando Valley offices, the President visited the agency's on-site day-care center and full-service gymnasium, and enjoyed one of the daily catered lunches.

"I'm proud, and surprised, that what we're doing here has impressed the President," said Company topper Alison Sweeney. "But what we're doing is really very simple. We're treating our coworkers like *people*, not just employees. What's the point in going to work each day if it can't be fun and, at the same time, enhance the community we live in?"

It wasn't easy getting the shot of rock singer Sissy Marshak grieving over her miscarriage. It was like planning an assassination.

Buddy Schlitz bribed a nurse to find out what room Sissy was in. UCLA Medical Center, south side, sixth floor. There was no way he was gonna get in the hospital, or even in the parking lot. So what he did was, he found a dentist's office on the corner of Gayley and Wilshire that had an unobstructed view of her window.

He pretended he had a killer cavity, got an appointment, and when they left him in the chair to develop his X rays, he barricaded the door, set up his camera with a supertelephoto lens, and got a great roll of film of Sissy sobbing in Milton Nero's arms.

Yeah, Milton Nero, the married actor. Who would've guessed he was the father?

That particular picture was worth $200,000 for Buddy Schlitz. There were lots of other big paydays in his career. The morgue photo of River Phoenix. An emaciated Dean Martin in the backseat of a limo. Christopher Reeve in his hospital bed. Marlon Brando weeping after his kid offed herself.

Classic images, all of them.

And now he was getting ready to click another one. Rumor was that Taylor Largo, the best-looking guy on television, the debonair secret agent in *Diplomatic Immunity,* had the big C and was getting chemo during the season hiatus.

A shot of the glamour boy, looking bald, pasty, and haggard, would be worth major green. So Buddy asked around, found out that Largo had rented a house deep in Topanga Canyon, far from any roads or prying eyes, to recuperate. It wasn't hard finding the house. Real estate agents had looser lips than a Hollywood Boulevard hooker. Buddy got some maps, did some figuring, and went on a four-mile hike.

He found a tall tree, climbed up top, and trained his lens on Largo's house, about two hundred yards away across a deep ravine. All he had to do was wait for Largo to walk by a window, or take a sit-down in his hot tub, and Buddy had another classic.

Buddy had been up in the tree about ten minutes when he was startled by the sound of a chain saw roaring to life.

Buddy looked down and saw a man at the base of the tree, the chain saw chewing into the bark and spitting out sawdust.

"Stop!" Buddy yelled in terror.

The man switched off the chain saw. "Be glad to, Buddy. Just toss your camera into the ravine."

"Fuck you." No way the guy was going to cut the tree down with him in it.

The man yanked the cord on the chain saw and started cutting into the tree again. Buddy held on tight. The tree groaned and swayed. Buddy screamed and threw his camera into the ravine.

The camera hit a rock and smashed to pieces. The man shut down the chain saw. "Very good, Buddy. Now take off all your clothes and throw them out of the tree."

on," Buddy said. "That was a two-thousand-
a. Isn't that enough?"

neard me, strip."

Buddy peeled off his clothes and tossed them down.
clutched the tree like pale, hairless monkey. "Satisfied?"

The man took an Instamatic camera out of his pocket
and took a half dozen pictures. "Now I am. Have a nice
walk back to the road."

The man left, leaving Buddy in the tree. He'd walked
only a short distance when his cell phone rang. The man
answered it.

"I saw the whole thing through my binoculars," Taylor Largo said. "He showed up, just like you said he
would."

"The key was making it a challenge for him," the
man said. "Now you just concentrate on getting better."

"Thank you," the actor said. "My privacy means a lot
to me, especially now."

"You don't have to thank me," Charlie Willis replied.
"I'm just doing my job."